Bodies in the Park

by

Richard Albion

Dedication

The Mistress of all, she knows who she is and Frances, editor extraordinaire, patiently make me a better writer. Thank you.

Chapter One

We had lunch in Sausalito. Sophie Chandler, my partner, and I basked in the balmy sunshine while we looked across the bay toward San Francisco, our city. I'm a native, and Sophie's an import from Philadelphia.

Sophie paid the tab while I pulled my SUV around to the entrance. As we exited the parking lot, a text announced itself. Driving, I ignored it. We had nothing going on that couldn't wait until we returned to the office. Making our way back across the Golden Gate Bridge, my phone went off. The call could go to message, then it rang again.

Sophie answered, "Continental Investigations, how may we assist you?"

"Sophie? Where the fuck is Mas? I need to speak to him ASAP."

It was Lieutenant Kenzo Otake of the San Francisco Police Department, and he sounded harassed, very unlike him.

"Hold on, Kenzo, you're on speaker. Mas is driving."

"Okay, Mas, I need to see you ASAP. I need your and Sophie's input on a problem. Can we meet now?"

This urgency was entirely out of character for the calm, even-keeled Kenzo. It had to be trouble.

"Sure, we're returning to the office. Give us thirty minutes. If you get there before us, Marie is there.

What's this about?"

"Not until I see you." He clicked off the call.

I concentrated on driving and said to Sophie. "This has to be serious. I've never heard him like this."

"Well, whatever it is, we owe him."

I laughed. "You got that right, and we are in whatever 'it' is."

We were silent for the remainder of the drive, each lost in our thoughts regarding our past with Kenzo. We did owe him, he had helped us more than once, and it could have cost him his career. What I said to Sophie was true—we were in.

As we walked into the office, Marie nodded toward the inner office. Kenzo had beaten us here. He was sitting, slumped in the chair, and looked miles away.

He jumped as I said, "Good to see you, Kenzo."

"Maybe not so much when I explain why I need your assistance."

That wasn't a good opening.

Sophie said. "I assume this is off the books and confidential?"

He nodded his agreement, saying, "Yeah, way off the books and so confidential that I will deny everything I am about to tell you. At least until the shit hits the fan, you can't keep secrets in this town."

Kenzo was right about that. San Francisco was a small city, and nothing ever stayed hidden, not for long anyway. This interaction was getting interesting, and my curiosity roused.

"Okay, I need you all to promise that nothing I tell you leaves this office, that includes Marie. Do I have your word?"

Marie yelled in from the outer office, "Yes."

That brought a smile to his lips, and he seemed to relax a little.

"I am sure you've heard about the body found in Golden Gate Park a few weeks ago.

We nodded our agreement. The body of a woman had been discovered in Golden Gate Park. She was crucified, tied naked to a 'T' shaped cross. The cause of death had not been disclosed. I was sure many details were missing from the media reports. It made the headlines that you would expect, and nothing since.

"Well, there were a lot of details not in the media. We got lucky if you can call it that. A park ranger found the body; he's a veteran and called us. Secured the area and kept people away."

Kenzo paused, and I used the pause to ask. "What do you need from us? This case is a straight homicide-right?"

He looked at me, shook his head, and continued. "Let me finish, then you'll get why I need you guys. The victim was made to look like a man. She had a false beard and mustache of professional quality. The killer fitted her with a fake dick. We have kept those and other details out of the media, at least for now. I've given you the short version. I think this is just the beginning. I'll give you more information when you have the big picture.

We got another body, male, this time. He had multiple, mostly healed puncture wounds. Cause of death, we think blunt force trauma to the head, to be confirmed by the ME. He was nailed to a wooden stake and displayed by the same method in Golden Gate Park. The same park ranger found him. He's not a suspect, just a little freaked out." He paused again; this time, I remained silent, waiting and expecting more. "The second victim was three weeks after the first. That was three weeks ago tomorrow."

Sophia asked, "You haven't explained why you need us."

"Right, the only connection we can find between the two victims is that they both have KinkInc accounts, absolutely nothing else in common. She was straight but into BDSM. He was gay and in the kink community. I am still working on that. They were both restrained with what the ME believes are BDSM-style metal shackles, not handcuff-style. You both are in the Kink community, and I need your access. I think the killer is targeting kink people."

I asked, "What do you mean, you know we are both in the Kink community?"

"Fuck Mas, I'm a detective, and you're not as careful or subtle as you think you are, neither is Sophie."

Sophie blushed and laughingly said, "Got us."

"No judgment, just observation. We all deserve to be happy and get it where we can. Will you help?"

Together, we said, "Of course."

"We will need everything you have and get. Sophie will get into their social media and electronic stuff. I'll take care of everything else with Marie. We will do everything we can to assist off the books."

Kenzo looked more relieved than he wanted to. The case must bring pressure from high, and he knew it would eventually hit the media in a storm. Something like this would not, could not stay hidden in San Francisco.

"Look, guys, I can't pay you for this, not on the

city dime or mine."

I looked over to Sophie, and she nodded. I said, "No charge on this one. We all agree we owe you, and besides, we like you."

That made him smile before saying, "I'm hoping the perpetrator is done, but I doubt it. If another victim appears on the previous schedule, it'll be tomorrow. Then I know we're in deep shit for sure-no pressure."

I had a lot of questions, and so would Sophie. If we were to help Kenzo, we would need everything he had, and I was sure he would be forthcoming. We also had our back door into the San Francisco Police Department, which has been open since the first case Sophie and I worked together, known to the media as the 'Bodies in the Bay' case.

Sophie asked, "When can you get the case files to us? The sooner we start, the sooner we get this guy, and it will probably be a guy percentage-wise, as most serials are."

"Agreed, but I am taking nothing for granted on this one. It may not be kink-related, but I think it is. I will need all your resources."

"Hey Kenzo, if it is or isn't kink related, we are in, right Sophie?"

"Sure thing, Mas.

"Thank you. I will get the files over to you, everything we have, but it didn't come from me."

I told him, "Put it in a package, and Marie will pick it up from Wanatabe's café or the Dojo."

"Okay, that's doable. I'll let Marie know which. I gotta run, Thanks for this."

Kenzo left, and we called Marie into the inner office for a team meeting to get this going. Marie, the office manager and partner who tried to keep Sophie and me in check, was worth every penny we paid her. She was family. Marie began with the billing status.

"We are in good shape, nothing that can't be put off or closed out quickly. The billing is almost current, and I can complete processing the rest today. You do your thing, and I will take care of everything else. I'm ready if you need me to do anything for you,"

Sophie said, "Good, but until we get the info from Kenzo, there isn't much we can do, right?"

I nodded. "Right, but I want to visit the sites where the victims were left. I don't expect to find anything the police missed. I want to get a feel for the places the victims were left. Before I get into the facts of the case, hey, Marie, can you pull up a detailed map of Golden Gate Park, roads, buildings, etc."

"That's an easy one."

"Sophie could access the case reports from the PD before Kenzo gets his packet to us. Giving us a head start."

"Exactly what I was thinking. The reports will be ready when you get back."

With that decided, we all had our tasks. Picking up my SUV, I took off for Golden Gate Park, map in hand. Ready to inspect the crime scenes, which should have been released by now. I didn't expect to find anything new; I wanted to try and get a feel for each site, access to getaway routes, anything significant in the location itself, and anything to assist us in catching the killer. The last thing this city needed was another serial killer.

The park is a pleasure when it's not overloaded with tourists. This early afternoon, it was busy but not crowded. The crime scenes had not yet become an attraction in themselves. The first location was easily found, off Fulton Street at Arguello Blvd, right onto Conservatory Drive West, then to the Ghiradelli Card Shelter.

The remnants of crime scene tape were still attached to trees and stakes, the only evidence that anything untoward had happened there. It was an interesting place to drop a body, not in a busy thoroughfare, but not so isolated that people wouldn't be around. We needed the police reports. Sophie would have them by the time I got back.

The site was now quiet and peaceful, with a few birds chirping and the distant buzz of the traffic on Fulton Street. The site itself was a small hole set in concrete, not something Golden Gate Parks maintenance was responsible for. There was no reason for it to be where it was other than to hold the cross and body. That meant premeditation and careful planning.

The site had been trampled and inspected, so there was nothing to learn physically. Onto the other location, retracing my steps to Conservatory Drive West, I hung a left and then another left onto John F Kennedy Drive. I followed the drive through the park, a pleasant drive. We were lucky to have such a beautiful area in the city.

I took a right up 47th Ave to the Archery field. The police had removed entirely the crime scene tape from this site. There was nothing to tell of the gruesome event of three weeks ago. The area was open, bordered by a narrow road. There was a high risk of being seen here, even at night. The park is open to all twenty-four hours and patrolled.

I inspected the scene, and the same hole set in concrete was in evidence, another deliberate and carefully planned operation. I wondered if there was any significance in choosing the archery field. It was more open than the first one—something to think about. Having seen both locations, I had enough to ponder until I had the PD reports.

The drive back to the office was slow, but I was okay with it. It gave me time to think. By the killer using the same concrete base method of display, both killings had to be connected. Simple, easy, and discreet. The hole had been plugged and hidden until needed. No one would see the concrete. It wouldn't raise any suspicions. If they did, it was a harmless piece of concrete.

As expected, the two reports were waiting for me on my desk. I preferred a hard copy. I made notes on the document as I thought of them. Old-fashioned, and just the way I was used to working. Sophie was surprisingly away from her desk.

I asked Marie. "Any idea where Sophie is?"

"God, Mas, I swear you are losing it. Does target practice with Big Boots ring any bells?" I groaned. Maybe I was losing it. "And she stopped by the Dojo to pick up the official reports from Kenzo."

Being the one to set up the self-defense class at the Dojo and her firearms training, I lost track of which day was what, but I liked that Kenzo had come through as promised.

Digging into the reports is a clinical look at the events and the facts so far discovered. The first victim was a woman, Frankie (Francis) Faraday, Caucasian, age twenty-nine, single, successful small clothing business owner. I recognized the name Tightly Bound, a corset shop supplying the kink and fetish community in San Francisco and beyond. Coincidence didn't. I don't believe in them.

Frankie was reported missing by her business partner when she didn't arrive at work on Friday. Her partner wasn't a suspect: she had a water-tight alibi and no motive the police could discover. We would look into that anyway.

Frankie's partner, Anna, waited several hours before reporting her missing. She'd tried calling, texting, and emailing and called all their friends in common. Anna even had one of the staff go to her apartment, but there was no answer. That worried Anna, Frankie was always punctual. Anna called the police. There isn't a twenty-four-hour waiting period in San Francisco if someone has tried everything to contact the missing person without result.

The police interviewed Anna, nada, and visited the apartment, nada. The killer didn't take Frankie from her apartment. We needed to get access to her social media life, that would be on Sophie. Anna supplied all of Frankie's email addresses to the police and included them in the file.

Victim number two, a male, Sean Costello, Caucasian, thirty-three, gay and partnered, worked in Finance for one of San Francisco's big investment firms. Partner Adolfo is a senior stylist for an upscale salon. Adolfo was not a suspect. He alibied out, and the PD could find no motive. He was the one who called in the missing person report.

Both these reports were thin. The anomaly I found was that Sean was probably taken before Frankie and kept alive, tortured, and then killed after Frankie. That was the only timeline that made sense, how his puncture wounds had healed. I wanted that confirmation from the Medical Examiner. Adolfo confirmed Sean had no injuries or scars. Sean was a fanatic about keeping in shape. This case was getting weird.

Sophie came in and flopped down in her chair, saying,

"That was a tough session."

"How come?"

"BB had me firing a shotgun and then something called a "Desert Eagle.""

I laughed, "Why did he have you firing that cannon."

"Mas, it's not funny. I thought I was going to blow the back out of the range. Anyway, he then had me switch back to my weapon. It felt so light after that, and I shot better, and it felt good. So, what have you found in the PD reports?"

"Not much. In the reports, everything is preliminary, and we are waiting for additional details. The final autopsy report on both should be illuminating when the ME files them. If there is anything there, she will find it, and I will be looking for a confirmation of an idea. The two sites are different, and both had been scouted. The body drops were well planned, prepared, and executed, with risk of discovery, and the park's patrolled 24/7. The perp probably observed the routes and times of the patrols. Like everything government, Rangers are short-staffed. For sure, this is a well-organized, contained, and sick bastard.

"So, another serial killer is on the loose in our town. Let me start on the social media stuff. I will send you the KinkInc addresses. You are still better than me on that site -damn it.

At least she said it with a smile as she disappeared behind her monitors. Soon, the rhythmic tapping of her keyboard made my mind wander as to any motive. There had to be clues in the facts if not the physical evidence.

Serial killers always have a message about what they do. The trick is to figure it out before too many victims show up. I had to agree with Kenzo, this one wasn't done. This weekend would confirm it. Back to re-reading the dry Police reports and ready to get into the first autopsy report.

The San Francisco city ME was a dragon. She was one of the best in the country, not one you wanted to cross. Her work stood up in court and defeated many a defense attorney. However, you worked on her schedule. Her work was complete when she said it was. So, we had one autopsy report on Frankie, which was detailed as expected.

We were working on the assumption that Frankie was taken by her killer on Thursday evening. Frankie was kept alive and captive. Her time of death was between midnight and 4:00 a.m. Sunday. The body was found at 6:17 a.m. on Sunday morning, as reported by the park ranger.

There was what appeared to be one needle mark on her neck and traces of a sedative in her blood work. She wasn't sexually assaulted. The killer carefully cleaned Frankie's body and removed all traces of makeup and evidence. Her hair had been cut, not professionally. The beard and mustache were natural hair. Whoever had applied them to her had some skill, but not at a professional level. The dildo and harness are readily available to anyone online. Frankie was tied to the "T" shaped cross. The report stated this style of cross was commonly used in Roman times. It was used to increase the suffering of the crucified. In addition, the crucified's legs were often broken, and the person hung only on their torso.

This sick bastard hadn't broken her legs, just tied them so she could not use them to support herself. This person knew what he was doing. The ME was usually all business and dry as facts. Here, she recommended a psychological profile ASAP due to the way Frankie had been, in her words, processed for death—a deliberate and extended torture to inflict maximum pain.

She estimated that Frankie could have lasted a maximum of fourteen to eighteen hours, possibly less due to her small stature and the way she was tied. The cause of death was asphyxiation.

That was enough for today. I had dealt with enough death and dead bodies when I was in the PD. You never really get used to it. You deal with it however you can. This one hit a nerve, and it made me think of all the victims I had seen in my career, which was not a positive thought. I needed to have some fun to wash the negativity away.

"Hey, guys, let's get out of here. Enough for today. Start fresh tomorrow. Anyone up for a tipple?"

A chorus of "Yes" made me smile

"Marie, if Chung is in town, ask him to join us."

"He is, and I'll pass on the invite."

Chapter Two

The phone ringing hammered me into consciousness. We hadn't had too much to drink, it was just too goddamn early. Bleary-eyed, I looked at my phone, 4:57 a.m. This call had to be bad news.

It was. Sleepily, I said, "Hello, Kenzo, you got another one?"

"Yes, can you get down here? I want your eyes on this one."

"Sure, text me the location." I hung up. "Shit, another victim," I was now fully awake and wondering how many more before this ended. I turned on the coffee machine, with Sophie still asleep. I bet she would sleep through an earthquake when she was tired, not that I wanted to find out about that.

After a large cup of wake-up, I dressed, a travel mug filled, and I left for the location Kenzo had texted me. Chain of Lakes Meadow parking area. Easy to get to, down Lincoln Way to Chain of Lakes Drive, cross over MLK Jr Drive, the parking lot was on the right. It was not an area of the park I knew well. Golden Gate Park is big.

When I arrived, Kenzo huddled with several uniformed and plainclothes officers. I waited until there was a break. He waived me over and nodded to a uniform officer to let me through the tape.

"This is a bad one, burnt at the stake."

"I can smell it. Any idea if the vic is male or female?"

"We're pretty sure it's a female victim. It takes balls to leave the vics in such public places like this. He's taunting us."

"Hey Kenzo, focus. Was it the same method of display?"

"Kind of. It's the same as before, plus a stake running through it. The barrel was a recycled fifty-gallon, with concrete in the bottom to weigh it. The rest of the barrel was packed with highly combustible and intensely hot burning material. The barrel was topped with a grill, and the body was chained to the stake, with the feet resting on the grill. The intensity of the combustion had to have been phenomenal when it went up. When you get to the site, you'll see the heat burned through the barrel in several places, and the surrounding vegetation is scorched."

"Who called you guys? The park rangers?"

"No, not this time. Early morning runners saw the flames and smoke and called 911."

"Early morning runners? What time was that?"

"Three forty-ish."

"Bullshit, early morning runners! It was pitch black at that time of morning."

"Yeah, I know, I questioned that. The runners who reported the fire are ultra-runners and train in the dark and daylight. They do fifty and hundred-mile runs."

"What?"

"It's a thing. Marathons aren't challenging enough. They were pretty shaken up. The runners thought it was an accident. You know how paranoid we are about fire in California. The Fire Department showed up quickly and put it out. That's how the Fire department discovered the body. It was too badly burned, and no one's sure of the victim's gender. We'll have to wait for the ME to determine that.

Shivering in the early morning damp, I wasn't looking forward to viewing this victim. A burned corpse was the worst. The smell, the charred flesh, the contorted body...you could almost feel the pain.

We walked up the road. Our nostrils were invaded by the smell of burnt flesh and chemicals before we even arrived at the site. I looked down, scanning the ground and saw two narrow tire tracks. I pointed them out.

Kenzo nodded. "We noted them as well. It had to be the way the perp moved the barrel."

"All these dumps are well planned and executed. Have you thought about searching for more sites? The only thing in common is the concrete base for dumping the victim."

"Mas, are you nuts, searching for a twelve-inch concrete circle with a hole in the middle? That's not practical. We've asked the park rangers to keep a lookout for anything suspicious, anywhere in the park."

"Kenzo. If we can figure out why he is using the park, that would give us insight into why these specific locations."

"Maybe, maybe not."

"I am betting that the victim is female."

Kenzo looked at me and asked, "Why female? What do you know?"

"Nothing yet, just a thought. I need to follow up with Sophie and do some digging before I say anything to you. You might think I'm nuts."

He laughed, "I already think you're nuts—smart, but nuts."

"Thanks. Whoever this is has an agenda, and it's only the beginning. Let's hope the killer sticks to the three-week intervals. How's the profile coming?"

"Slowly, this additional victim will give the FBI and our profilers more to work with."

"Good. We need help. This case will be a long haul unless we get lucky, or the perpetrator makes a mistake. He's meticulous, and his choice of victim is not random. If we can determine his rationale for choosing them, that will go a long way to solving this."

"Agreed. I am beginning to wonder if he's working alone. The barrel was a big item to move solo, even with a loading trolly. Hopefully, the victim was dead when he lit it up."

"I would put money on the victim being alive when the barrel ignited. I'll be in touch as soon as I have something."

Kenzo nodded, already deep in thought about the next moves. One thing for sure: this case would be hitting the media. Journalists would be putting together one and one and making three, in this case accurately, three bodies.

I was driving home. It was still too early for Liguria Bakery to open. Home it was. More coffee, wake Sophie, then get to the bakery early. I would take her and breakfast to the drop sites for her insights. Then, I would put my idea to her for her to shoot down. Reviewing my theory as the sun rose, it seemed even more outlandish. Still, nothing ventured, nothing gained.

Sophie was still out when I entered our house. The

coffee was still hot, and I finished the pot sitting on the back deck. As the new pot brewed, I tried to reconcile the day's beauty with the gruesome sight I'd seen.

With a gentle stroking of Sophie's bare shoulder, the covers had slipped down, exposing her left breast. That started my cock hardening in the chastity device I wore in my agreement with Sophie. Kenzo was right. We were in the Kink community. Sophie is dominant, and I'm submissive, sometimes. It's complicated, but it works for us. Kink was not all of us, but it was an important part. We were still working through all the details.

She stirred as my hand strayed down toward her breast. Rolling over, she said, "Not a good idea, Mas…not if you want out of the cage anytime soon."

"I was just trying to wake you gently."

"Oh, how kind of you. The coffee smells good. Where did you go? I thought I heard the phone." The change in my expression told her all she needed to know.

"Another one." It was a statement, not a question.

"Yes, a third park location. A burning this time. Look, get dressed. We'll pick up focaccia, and then I want you to view the dump sites. I have a theory. It's out there, and it won't go away. Coffee is ready."

"Okay, Mas, sounds mysterious. Give me a few, and I'll be ready if you bring me coffee."

"Done deal." I loved this woman. She didn't question me about my idea. She would let me bring it to her. I knew she would tear into it, shred it to pieces, only to make sure the whole thing was clear in my mind. We worked well together. Sophie was ones and zeros, academic and technical. I was practical, gut-feeling, and real-life experienced. A great team.

Ready in minutes, I delivered her the coffee in a travel mug. We stopped briefly at Liguria, picked up our breakfast focaccia, and went to Golden Gate Park. We stopped at the first site and enjoyed the weather and focaccia, each with our thoughts. After we'd eaten, I showed Sophie the location of the concrete base used to support the metal cross. She looked around, taking in the scene, trying to imagine the cross and Frankie hanging on it. We only had the written reports, not the crime scene photographs yet.

"Okay, got it. It is a risky dump site and carefully prepared. The actual location of the concrete would have been partially screened from observation. Only when the cross was installed would it become more open to observers or passers-by, like the park ranger. He is careful and precise, and the locations and display must mean something to him. Let's get to the next one."

These are good observations from an analytical mind—next, the Archery butts. We were quiet on the drive over. I didn't want to disturb her thoughts. This location was more open. Sophie walked around, looking from all angles, before commenting.

"This location was a higher risk. Well prepared, and the concrete concealed until needed. He must have moved quickly to drop the body and escape. There may be two perps. Even with preparation, this task would be difficult for one person, strenuous but not impossible. He would have to be strong. Okay, last one."

"We may not be able to get close to this one. This is still an active crime scene, and Kenzo won't be there. If someone still there remembers seeing me with Kenzo, we may get access."

"When we get there, call Kenzo and have him give us access to the scene."

Why didn't I think of that? Probably because I still thought like a policeman sometimes. The new site was still being investigated, and we were lucky two officers still there recognized me, nodding and allowing us into the cordoned-off area. The air was cleaner but still had a faint stench of burnt flesh. I could see Sophie wrinkle her nose as she concentrated on the location of the burn.

"I'm done. How do you do it? The smell is still pretty awful. God knows what it must have been like when you got here."

"Yeah, it was pretty bad. Now you've seen the three sites, do you have any comments or ideas?"

Sophie thought for a moment. "We need to get this guy. He is certainly psycho. He is very well organized, particular, and meticulous in everything he does, which means he is smart, and it's going to be difficult to catch him. I don't think he will stop until he is forced to. He has an agenda, and nothing about this is random, the people chosen, how they are killed and displayed. I hope he doesn't collapse the timeline."

"Agreed on all points. Now, hear me out before you shoot me down. This case has to have a religious base or cause. I didn't get the idea until this morning with the third victim. I am betting today's victim is female. Not sure about the first victim. The second one, Sean, what does his killing and display remind you of? Don't answer that yet. Now, this one burned at the stake. Look at those two together."

Sophie looked puzzled. Her brow furled in concentration, wheels turning, but nothing clicked.

"Obviously, you didn't have a very religious

upbringing. The second victim was displayed like Saint Sebastian. Today's victim burned at the stake-Joan of Arc. Frankie, the first one, doesn't fit anything I've heard of. Then again, I didn't have an overly religious upbringing either."

"Wait, didn't Saint Sebastian get killed by arrows?"

"That's what most people think. He survived the arrows, was brought back to health, and was clubbed to death by the Emperor's guard. Sean had mostly healed puncture wounds. Blunt-force trauma to his head was the actual cause of death. That is probably why Sean was left at the archery site.

"Mas, how do you know that?"

"I read stuff. Anyway, today's victim, if it's female, Joan of Arc, burned at the stake."

"A big leap, even if it's a female, and what about Frankie, the first victim? How does she fit in your theory?"

"No idea. That's why I wanted you to see the sites and hear my theory. It has a very 'Christian' feel. Maybe there is a Saint who grew a beard, was trans, or something, I don't know."

"I'll look into that. Not saying you're mistaken. It's a bit out there."

I had tickled Sophie's curiosity, and she would dig. If there were a female Saint who grew a beard and was crucified, Sophie would find her. All I had to do was sit back and let her do her thing. If Sophie was successful, then I would take my theory to Kenzo.

Saint Sebastian is a gay icon, and Joan of Arc a trans icon. Targeting the Kink community could be a valid theory. Revenge for something? Religious nut cleansing San Francisco of sinners, well Sophie and I were sinners. Doing it one at a time didn't seem very efficient or biblical after the floods, plagues, etc. The killings had a more intimate feel, up close and hands-on as if the person was getting revenge for something. For starters, we needed more data, the crime scene photos, and the profiles from the FBI and the SFPD.

Done with the park, we meandered back home, taking our time. We stopped at our local farmers market to shop for the week's food. We were silent as we walked the market, not concentrating on what we were doing. Distracted, we made it home and put away the groceries, as we did, Sophia said.

"I will run into the office for a few minutes. We don't have anything planned for tonight, do we?"

"Not this weekend. Why?"

Sophie smiled deviously, "Oh, I thought we might have some fun."

That caused me to be concerned, and my cock started to harden in its cage, the adrenaline rush of not knowing what she had planned, only that it would be for both of us. Sophie was great at keeping me off balance in our Dominant and submissive roles. She had pushed my boundaries, and I had never regretted trusting her. I loved her in all her roles—two sides of the same coin.

She pulled out a key from around her neck, the key to my chastity cage. Twirling it, she said, "Maybe, maybe not." Continuing with a laugh, "We will have to see what happens later."

Whatever it was, it would take our minds off the gruesome events happening in our city. I had an idea.

I asked Sophie, "May I surprise you, tonight

instead?"

Smiling Sophie responded, "Well that is very forward of you Mas." She paused before saying, "Why not. Go ahead and surprise me. Of course, that's not a guarantee you will have a release."

"Understood. I want to surprise you for a change, no strings."

Chapter Three

Sophie departed to our office, where she had her large computer. Meanwhile, I carried on with the chores that needed doing. My wandering mind started thinking about tonight's adventure. Sophie turned me on just thinking about her and her alter ego, Ms. Circe, her Kink community name. It had been a couple of weeks since we had indulged in any play. The way she teased me got my juices flowing, and the thought went straight to my groin. My cock responded by filling the chastity cage. Here's hoping I will get a release tonight. What's that old saying? Be careful what you wish for. You might get it. Taking a break from the chores, I visited a craft store to pick up something I wanted for tonight's adventure. I stopped at a couple of other places, picking up additional items for tonight.

Returning home, I ran myself into a sweaty mess on the treadmill. As I did, my thoughts returned to Kenzo and the recent victims. I had a strong gut feeling about the religious connection. I had a shower. Refreshed and relaxed, I enjoyed an early afternoon expresso as I planned out the events of the coming night. My phone announced Sophie.

"Mas, let's do something light for dinner, sushi, and sashimi.?"

"Sounds good. Would you like me to order or pick up what you order?"

"I'll put the order in. You can pick it up."

"Okay, what's the pick-up time?"

"Seven."

Sophie arrived home about an hour later with a satisfied look and said, "Mas, you could be onto something- if number three is female. Victim number one, Frankie, was killed in the same manner as a Saint Wilgefortis."

"Who the hell is that? Never heard of him, it's him, right?"

No, a female. A strange story. The way it goes. A teenage Christian noblewoman named Wilgefortis had been promised, in marriage, to a Muslim king by her father. To get out of the wedding, she took a vow of virginity and prayed that she would be repulsive to the King. In answer to her prayers, she sprouted a beard, ending the engagement. In anger, her father had her crucified. Sound familiar. Anyway, because of her appearance, she has been described as a "transgender saint" and is sometimes seen as a patron saint of gender-fluid people. The perp made her up to be the image of the saint. Do you think this will help in profiling?"

"Can't hurt, every little thing helps."

"Good, now, Mas, I'd like to chat about tonight. You have something planned for us. I don't want to know the details, just the broad outline. I trust you."

Consent is a critical part of any relationship, especially in the BDSM world. It certainly was with Sophie and me. It's a two-way street, and everything has to be negotiated before any scene or play, particularly something new. A safe word, a word, when spoken, will immediately stop everything dead. Play may continue or not, but nothing happens until the issue causing the use of the safe word has been resolved. Yes means yes. Everything else means no, and that has to be honored.

"I promise it's nothing we haven't explored before, combined with a twist. Ms. Circe will still have the last word. If it's something you don't want, you say, and it ends. I don't think you will object to anything."

"Sophie smiled and said, "This is very different, and I'm curious to find out what you have planned."

"I'm sure Ms. Circe will be pleased. I will explain what I need from Ms. Circe when the time is right."

That sorted, we separated the rest of the weekend chores. We never had time during the week, so the weekend was usually crammed with us doing everything on a Saturday. We divided and conquered.

Sophie had dumped the dried wash on our bed while she put the next load in the dryer and got the next wash going. I separated his and her clothes and folded them in appropriate piles, ready to be put away.

After the chores, we sat on the back deck and watched the sun drop into the Pacific Ocean, a sight neither of us ever tired of. Sophie placed the sushi order and confirmed it would be ready at seven. I would leave at six thirty, taking my time. That gave me a timeline to prepare for Ms. Circe's surprise.

"Sophie, please don't enter the playroom until later. It's part of the surprise."

"Mas, you have aroused my curiosity. I promise I won't go in until you say."

"Thank you."

I left her on the deck to enjoy the encroaching evening and went to prepare the rooms for tonight.

Nothing too complicated, just knowing her tastes and what she liked. I had already put a vase of red roses in the playroom- her favorite flower, in her favorite color. I collected and readied the restraints I would be wearing later. Ankle cuffs joined with a short chain. Wrist cuffs joined with a short chain. All the cuffs locked, and I had the four locks open and ready to lock on the cuffs. Finally, there is a three-inch-wide leather collar, also with a lock. Ms. Circe had the keys, so once on, I would be locked in until she released me.

I placed scented candles in the playroom and our bedroom and would light them later. Choosing the music would be easy—something ambient or something like Tangerine Dream or Eno, soothing and dreamy.

The time to pick up dinner came around in a hurry. I asked if Ms. Circe could be available after I returned with dinner.

"Sophie laughed and said, "I'm sure that could be arranged. Any other requests of her?"

"If she would be only in her satin gown, that would be appreciated."

With a knowing smile, she said, "Oh, that request can be accommodated with pleasure."

Of course, it could. She knew what seeing her only in her gown did to me. It was teasing and, therefore, arousing. I left for Heian Sushi to collect dinner before I became too distracted. Heian means peaceful mind, but my mind was anything but peaceful, full of anticipation.

The ride over was slowed by early evening traffic, which was expected, and did not phase me. Ritsuke San, the owner, was his usual polite self, welcoming me, saying, "Hammett San, please have a sake. Your order will be ready very shortly. We are making sure it is perfect."

"Thank you Ritsuke San. Your food is always perfect."

He smiled and bowed, acknowledging my compliment, saying, "You are welcome Hammett San. We always do our best." While I waited, he left to attend to the other diners, sipping the ice-cold sake. Our order came out, and the server bowed and thanked me for ordering with them. I paid and returned home, thinking of the best way to execute my plan for the evening.

I got it. I had the order of events in my mind, now to execute. Quickly putting the food in the fridge, I went to the playroom and scattered the red paper rose petals I had got at the craft store and lit the sandalwood scented candles, they would infuse the room with a scent Sophie enjoyed. Next, I stripped naked apart from my chastity cage and applied the cuffs, ankle first, and wrist, and lastly, the collar all locked on. I was ready for Ms. Circe.

I called, asking, "Ms. Circe, are you ready for dinner?"

"Yes, Mas, I am."

Working with cuffs attached is relatively easy. It slows you down, and you have to be careful. I took the sushi out and placed the rolls and sashimi around the large plate as artistically as possible. Wasabi, pickled ginger, and soy sauce, each in their dishes. I picked up Ms. Circe's favorite chopsticks and took everything into the dining room, ready for Ms. Circe. A glass of chilled California Chardonnay was poured. It would be the only alcohol she would have until we completed our play.

She walked in from the lounge. This was supposed to be my surprise evening. She surprised me, wearing a robe I hadn't seen before, pale gold semitransparent. It flowed and shimmered like liquid gold. Her breasts moved under the fabric and made it move like a golden stream. I could see her darker aureole through the fabric. As she moved, the gown moved with her. She was covered and yet exposed in all her naked glory. She appeared as a Greek goddess. Stunned, I was speechless.

Ms. Circe broke the spell, saying, "I couldn't let you have all the surprises, could I?

All I could say was, "As you wish, Ms. Circe. Dinner is served."

She sat at the head of the table, slightly away, and turned from the table. The perfect position for me to serve her. Kneeling close to her, I could inhale her fragrance, and all my senses were being assaulted, and I loved it.

I picked up the chopsticks and asked, "Would you like to choose which pieces or let me choose for you."

"You may choose for me. You know how I like each piece."

I did. I knew which she liked with everything on and which with only ginger or wasabi.

The first piece was a spicy tuna. I added a little wasabi and a small piece of ginger and gently dipped it into the soy sauce. Leaning forward, I lifted the morsel toward Ms. Circe. She leaned forward to accept it. I was focused on getting the sushi to her, but my peripheral vision picked up that her gown had enticingly opened. Focus Mas, this isn't about you. This is Ms. Circe's night.

After I had fed her three varied pieces, she said, "Mas, you may have a piece of sushi."

I picked the piece closest to me and devoured it. The next piece for her was a salmon sashimi. We went back and forth, me feeding her on my knees. Toward the end, I finished up what was left of the feast. It was about half of the food, in different proportions. She ate more of her favorite and less of others. I liked everything. To end the meal, we each had two pieces of Toro tuna. It was expensive in relation to everything else but so worth it, it melted in your mouth.

Still on my knees, I asked, "Ms. Circe, was dinner satisfactory?"

"Yes, Mas, it was delicious, and the service exemplary. A good start to the evening, don't you think."

I didn't need to answer that. Quickly, I cleared up the dishes and left them in the kitchen to take care of later.

She finished her wine and asked, "Mas, what is next on the agenda?"

"If you will follow me to the playroom."

We moved to the playroom. The scented candles had done the job, and the room was filled with the exotic air of sandalwood. The paper rose petals scattered about, and the oriental drapes added to the enchantment. I pushed play on the CD player, and Tangerine Dream's music enveloped us.

As she entered, she said, "Mas, you have outdone yourself. This is delightful."

"If you would disrobe and lay in the center of the bed, your massage awaits."

Her gown floated to the floor in a puddle of gold, shimmering in the candlelight. She placed herself in the center of the bed. Ready for me to start. I had warmed the massage medium, a mango and neroli oil concoction. Seeing her naked aroused me as it always did, and I'd had a good start seeing her in the translucent gown. My cage was filled, and I was ready to start the massage. Starting at her extremities, I worked toward her center. Her skin felt like silk. As I spread the oil on her sun-kissed body, the tan lines around her hips drew me in.

The glow from the candles, the scent permeating the room, and the relaxing sounds from the CD player created an atmosphere in which Sophie and Ms. Circe could completely relax and let go, and I was the medium to make that happen. I massaged her gently to firmly, guided by the sounds emanating from her. Her back done, I quietly asked her to turn over. She complied, slowly rolling over, her eyes closed. She was almost purring.

I continued to oil her up. Her skin absorbed the oil, and I could see her visibly relaxing into a Zen-like state. I knew that wouldn't last, as Ms. Circe liked her pussy and breasts gently massaged with the oil. Even though it wasn't strictly massage territory, it was what she liked, and it aroused her. There's no downside to that, but I did leave those areas until the end. I could feel her body ready to my ministrations.

She rose to meet me. I gently oiled her neither lips, parting them like pink rose petals. She was wet. Her breasts were waiting for me as I worked the oil in and around each glorious globe. Her nipples hardened in a crinkled sea of aureole. Soon, she was breathing heavily and moving more distractedly on the bed.

She said, "Stop, Mas, I'm ready for an orgasm. Please change places with me."

Ms. Circe sat up and moved to the side of the bed, allowing me to lay prone in the center. As soon as I was in position, she sat astride me. Her hair was disheveled, and in the candlelight, there seemed to be an aura around her, almost divine.

I was ready for this, and it would pleasure me to please her. She eased up my body until she was above me. Placing one knee beside my head, then the other. She was drawing out the pleasure to come. Slowly, she descended onto my face, and her pink lips met mine. A groan escaped her, and I was in heaven.

She sank onto me, the relaxed weight directly connected to me. I could breathe easily, and looking up, I saw her tits jutting out, the nipples standing proud and pointed. My tongue started to make small movements, to which Ms. Cirec reacted. I knew this ride would be intense and over quickly. I knew her body and how it responded. I knew which buttons to push, so I did.

My tongue played with Ms. Circe, goading her on and bringing her back. Each time, a little further toward nirvana. Her labia, her outer and inner lips were attended to, as was her clit. She was getting to the point of no return. Her breathing and movement told me she was near. Another round of my tongue, and she went over the precipice. Her orgasm came crashing down on her. She stopped, trying to hold the feeling boiling inside her. That was not possible. She released herself into the waves of feeling and shuddered on my face, rubbing herself on me. The little earthquakes that followed gradually subsided.

Moving back down my body, she lay there, motionless, her breathing gradually returned to normal. For a moment, I thought she had fallen asleep. Taking a deep breath, she pushed herself upright and said, "Don't move. I'll be right back."

Like I was going anywhere. Laying still, I wondered what Ms. Circe had in mind. Whatever it was, I trusted her. She hadn't bothered to cover herself, and that vision I appreciated. What grabbed my attention were the keys she was twirling around her fingers.

"Yes, Mas, time for some fun for both of us. I liked your surprise. Simple and heartfelt, down to the rose petals. My turn to surprise you.

Ms. Circe returned to the bed. Kneeling beside me, she released my wrist cuffs, the ankle cuffs, and finally, the collar. She slipped the key into the lock of my cage. As she removed the lock plug, the cage separated with the pressure of my filling penis. The cage part was eased off my cock, and the retaining ring was opened and removed. This left my cock and balls completely unencumbered. Surprised, I remained silent.

"Mas, I love you and want you inside me."

I expected her to sit astride me and ride my cock as she had my tongue and face. I was wrong.

"Tonight, we switch places."

I couldn't believe my ears. This was a rare occasion, and I would make the most of it. Rolling to one side, I made space for Ms. Circe. She lay where recently I had lain. She was spreading her legs, openly inviting me in.

All she said was, "Love me, Mas."

I needed no second invitation. I moved between her

legs, drinking in the sight of her lying naked and open. Slowly, I lowered myself over her. She sighed and reached for my hard cock. She guided me into her waiting sex. There was no rush. I buried myself in her as deep as I could go. It felt like coming home, and I could feel her heat, cocoon-like enveloping me.

I was moving back and almost out of her and then thrusting forward. She let out a groan of pleasure. In, out, backward, thrusting forward, and listening to her responses. I wanted to make this feeling last as long as possible and urgently wanted to come. I was torn between two wants and needs. Ms. Circe was moving under me, synchronizing her movement with mine. We two became one. Her actions changed, becoming more vigorous and her breathing more ragged, alternately groaning and gulping breath. I was rising and could not hold out much longer.

Ms. Circe was quickly approaching nirvana, and she called out, "Mas, deeper and harder."

Following her instructions, I thrust and pounded into her, which made my need to come more urgent. She orgasmed, bucking to ram herself onto me, and as she did, I called out.

"May I come, please may I come."

She screamed out, "Yessssss." And continued to buck against me.

I exploded into her deeply and again, then again, and I was spent. She shuddered as her seismic waves subsided. We were sweaty and slippery, and it felt like we were the only two people in the world.

I asked, "Can we roll to one side?"

Without saying anything, she moved under me to the right. I rolled left and managed to stay inside her. I did not attempt to exit her, and she clung to me. Even as I deflated, we held each other. It couldn't last, and eventually, we broke apart. Still silent, basking in the joining we had enjoyed. We made our way to the shower, and even then, as we soaped each other, no words were exchanged.

Dried and feeling like the King and queen of the world, we went to our bedroom and fell asleep in each other's arms.

Chapter Four

Sunday was supposed to be a day of rest. At least, that is what I had been told, not for us. My phone went off, and I didn't answer it. Sophie's rang, she did answer it.

A sleepy, "Hi, who's calling at this ungodly hour?"

"Kenzo, and it's not ungodly. It's almost nine, as in nine a.m. Meet me at Wanatabe's. I have more information on number three. I want to get it to you without being compromised, so Sunday it is.

"Okay, be there. Give us time to wake up." She hung up and said, "Come on, faker, I know you are awake listening. Kenzo has some info for us."

"I am complying under duress."

"Is that a complaint? Because you need to lock up my property again."

Laughing, "As always, I will comply."

"As I expected. I'll put on coffee-go."

Putting the chastity cage back on was easy. I've had a lot of practice. Physically wearing the chastity device is no problem, it's between the ears, is the issue. The teasing, the frustration of pleasure, and the pleasure of frustration, and I wouldn't have it any other way.

Coffee was ready by the time I was dressed. We loaded coffee into travel mugs and went to Wanatabe's café. As we drove, making good time in the light Sunday traffic, we chatted about the case, knowing we needed much more data. Making a bet with Sophie.

"I'll bet the third victim is female. With the info you found on Saint Wilge-whatever her name was, the Saint Sebastian copycat, and now burning someone at the stake, this one has to be Joan of Arc. This killer has a religious agenda."

"Mas, that is a reach. The Salem witch hunts were religious as well."

"True. However, with the other two being saints, I figure this one would be a saint, not a witch. The only saint I know who burned at the stake was Joan of Arc. There may be more.

"I'll look into it. Not taking your bet either."

Parking was easy. Plenty of spots were available, but none were close to the café. Busy with customers enjoying the San Francisco weather and a relaxing Sunday. Wanatabe San was behind the counter, directing the seeming chaos. He saw us, bowed in our direction, and looked to the upper floor. I acknowledged him with a smile and took Sophie up the narrow stairs to the room where the 'Go' games were always available.

Kenzo was eating breakfast and stood up when he saw us enter.

"About time. Some of us have things to do on a Sunday." He laughed and hugged both Sophie and me, who asked.

"What couldn't keep until tomorrow."

"Me, I am up to my ass with this one, and I can't be seen with you guys. The new vic is a female."

I couldn't resist, "Ha, I told you so."

Sophie responded, "Mas, don't be an ass."

Kenzo said, "What am I missing?"

"I asked Sophie to do some digging for me. I have a theory-the killer has a religious agenda. It got me thinking when you told me the third vic was burned at the stake. All the vics are being killed in the same manner as old-time saints."

"What?"

"I know it sounds crazy. Listen. Sophie found a saint Wilge-something." Sophie took over the details.

"Saint Wilgefortis, a noble girl who was promised in marriage to some king she didn't want, by her father. She committed to being a virgin and prayed to be made repulsive. She grew a beard, it worked, the King called off the engagement. Her father was so pissed he crucified her. The first vic was a female made up like a guy, specifically the facial hair-right."

Kenzo skeptically said, "Right, she also had a fake dick, was that in the original crucifixion?"

With a chuckle, Sophie added, "Not documented."

I said, "Can we get back on track? The second victim is a copy of Saint Sebastian, down to the actual way he was killed. Most folks think he died from the arrow wounds-not so. He was nursed back to health. Then he accosted the Emperor with repent or die, and the Emperor told his guards to club him to death, which brings us to vic number three. I believe she was a copy of Joan of Arc, burned at the stake."

We were silent for a moment, all of us lost in thought. Kenzo broke the silence, saying.

"That's pretty fucked up if it's true. It doesn't explain the why, what's the motive for the killings?"

"No idea. None are not your typical saint if there is such a thing. Wilge-whatever was trans, Sebastian gay, and Joan of Arc rumored to be lesbian, that has to mean something. Kenzo, you have a Catholic school education. You should know this shit.

He laughed, "Trust me, no one ever went into the sex lives of the saints in school. You guys probably know more about this than I do. Your theory is worth following up on, and I'll leave that to you, but if you find anything, pass it on to me ASAP."

Sophie said, "Promise, the first two had KinkInc profiles and were involved in the LGBTQ kink community, which makes me believe this one will as well. Do you have a name yet?"

"We think so. Carol Freeman is the only person so far that meets all the criteria of the perp. Carol Freeman. Female, Caucasian, thirty-two, self-employed, an artist and personal trainer. She disappeared on Wednesday night and was reported missing on Friday by the gym manager where she works. The Gym owner said she missed three client appointments on Thursday, which has never happened before. Plus, she didn't come in for her own regular Friday morning workout. He tried both her cell numbers and emails, but there was no response, so he called us. The gym owner gave us as much info as he could. She's unpartnered at the moment and has played the field.

We got a warrant and opened up her place—no sign of her or her leaving in a planned way. We have access to her electronic life. Here is a list of her passwords. She had her passwords written down at home-not smart, but we'll take it. Here's a list of her clients, personal training, and art. Oh, and she does have a KinkInc account. No leads. The last anyone saw her was leaving the gym, South of Market, after her last client at 9:30 p.m. The last call on her phone was just before nine-thirty, confirming a training session the following day, which she missed. That's it for now. I will get the autopsy report to you when I get it. The damn ME is dragging her feet."

Defending the ME, I said, "Kenzo, you know as well as anyone, she is very thorough. If it's to be found, she will find it, and it will stand up in court."

"Yeah, I know, it's just frustrating. We need something to break. These murders are going to make all the media sooner than later, and my life will blow up. Fuck it. I'll let Marie know the drops when I have something for you."

"Breakfast is on us. It's the least we can do. Trust us. Sophie and I will be working on this case. We'll get him."

Sophie added. "Whatever you need, ask, okay?"

A wan smile and he left, looking tired, six weeks of process and procedure hadn't gotten the SFPD anywhere. We were fresh eyes and not burdened by the same rules as Kenzo.

Sophie would start digging into their lives. I would do the leg work, getting all the background we could. Sometimes, people opened up to us, non-officials, more easily than the police. A relaxed person remembered details they hadn't with the police. It's not a criticism of the police, just reality. With nothing planned for the day, we went into the office. Sophie started her process with Frankie, building an electronic picture of her life. I left her alone to do her thing.

I dove into the autopsy report, reading line by line, making notes on the pages, and re-reading parts until I had a complete picture of how Frankie had been tortured. As I expected, the autopsy report was comprehensive. Frankie, I always liked to use a victim's name it made them remain human, not just a case number. This girl had suffered a lot. I guess that was the perpetrator's point.

She was drugged, 'roofied'. The timeline from when she was taken till she was found was too long for blood or urine tests. She was extremely dehydrated, so her urine was out. People don't realize Rohypnol, to give its official name, could be tested in hair for much longer, and Frankie was a positive result. That explained how she was taken. The needle marks? Maybe the result of a sedative. To keep her drugged and compliant until the time of display in Golden Gate Park.

Things that didn't make sense to me yet. Where would you keep a person hung on a cross without anyone knowing? Frankie would have made noise, although the autopsy stated that breathing would have been difficult when crucified as she was. It couldn't have been easy moving her and the cross combined. The cross, constructed of aluminum tubing, was light and strong. Frankie was on the small, light side. Perhaps that is why she was targeted. Total weight together was one hundred and fifty-three pounds— Frankie at one hundred and twenty-one, and the tubing thirty-two. A strong male could handle the weight easily. What made it more difficult was that it was dead weight, plus the awkwardness of being a cross. There was also evidence of what were assumed to be metal shackles used on her wrists and ankles.

Next autopsy report. Sean, the second body displayed, was the first to be taken. He was alive when

Frankie was taken, according to the timeline from when he was taken to the time of death registered by the ME. Were both held in the same location? He also had to have had some medical treatment for his puncture wounds, antibiotics at least, as they had started healing well, with no signs of infection.

The wounds were through and through. The ME speculated they were made with a nail gun, from the size and type of injuries. The wounds had been carefully placed, painful and avoiding critical organs. Cause of death. Several blows to the head with a heavy blunt object, probably a hammer or some other similarly shaped heavy object. His skull suffered catastrophic damage. That part would have been quick. His wrists and ankles also bore significant evidence of metal shackles being used to restrain him, more than on Frankie.

Reading the reports didn't make me more confident that this would be a quick case. The perp was clever and meticulous in forensic countermeasures, leaving almost no trace evidence. The materials used, the concrete used at the dump sites, are available at any big box store. Same with everything else used, easily obtained, nothing out of the ordinary, paid cash, nothing suspicious. The roofies no one was going to fess up to that one, and they were probably purchased in Mexico, much easier than here in the U.S. Shit, no wonder Kenzo was stressed.

When we got the third ME report, I didn't expect anything different evidence-wise. Next on my list of things to get was the profiles from the SFPD and the FBI profilers. They were good at what they did, but it was not a perfect science, unlike the ME. She had the physical evidence in front of her, the profilers were working with shadows, smoke, mirrors, and experience, not to be dismissed but not exact either.

We worked the rest of the morning and then called it a day. Monday would be another day, and we would be fresh. We tried to relax for the rest of the day, but it didn't work for either of us.

Chapter Five

Monday rolled around, and it was one of those I don't want to get out of bed days, a heavy marine layer, damp and dreary. I rolled over and cuddled Sophie, who snuggled deeper against me. Bliss. It couldn't last, and it didn't. My phone went off like a fire alarm - damn, it was later than I realized.

A sleepy, "Hello, this is Mas."

"I know. You're the person I called." Marie, that got my attention. She rarely called me-us at home. "Get your butts in here. Kenzo left a cryptic message on the office line. I've picked up a packet of stuff from Wanatabe's and also treated us to a breakfast."

Click, call ended. Now I was wide awake, I gently nudged Sophie and said, "Sophie, more 'stuff' from Kenzo. Marie just called."

"Oh god, what time is it?"

"Nine twenty-three."

"What. Shit, I forgot to set my alarm."

"Me too. We must have needed it. Let's go, I'll put coffee on."

We were up and ready to go as soon as the coffee had brewed-yes that quickly. Marie was already well into doing the day's chores when we walked in. Seeing us, she picked up a large manila envelope and handed it to me, saying,

"I hope this is something we can use. You need to

see the paper and check your news feeds, and it's not pretty."

Sophia and I went to our respective desks, booting up our computers. Marie was right. The news was out, "Dramatic killing in San Francisco's Golden Gate Park."

I ate breakfast as I read. The media was going to have a field day with this one. When they did some digging and found the two prior killings, and they were bound to, the shit would hit the fan. All the outlets had the story, and most were reasonably accurate, as far as it went before speculation and theories based on imagination took over.

The SFPD had done an excellent job with the initial press release, keeping it basic and truthful. I didn't envy Kenzo on this one. This case was going to be a nightmare, even if Kenzo solved it tomorrow, and I would guarantee it wouldn't be. The newspaper had more details, mainly about the park and its history.

Kenzo's reports and data were just what I wanted—the SFPD and FBI profile unit's conclusions on the perp. Digging in, I first scanned both reports, then started over and read every word carefully. Both made interesting reading. Breaking for a coffee refill, then starting over again. I compared the two reports. They were remarkably similar, the FBI a slightly more lengthy and detailed report, but there was one hundred percent agreement on all the significant points.

Of course, neither guaranteed the complete accuracy of their report's content, but the more data received, the more accurate the profile would be. In other words, the more dead bodies that turned up and could confidently be attributed to this perp, the better the profile would be. Great. I condensed the two reports into one profile.

'White male, probably early forties. He is educated, precise, and meticulous in his daily life. A planner, not someone who does anything impulsively. Functions well in society and is accepted, not a marginalized person or loner. Healthy and fit, he looks after his body without being vain. Will have strength and endurance from the way the concrete was placed and finished and moving the bodies to those locations. The risks he takes are calculated and then implemented on his agenda at a time with the lowest risk of discovery.

The religious aspects are not as motivational as the obvious sexual motivations, and they may play a very minor role in his pathology. He will be a member of or convert to a fundamentalist Judeo-Christian denomination.

He is motivated mainly by a homophobic drive for punishment. He may be a suppressed homosexual himself. His victims are in the LGBTQ kink community, and he may be punishing them for his feelings. He has a calculated hatred for his victims, directly expressed in the way he tortures them.

He acts intellectually, not emotionally, although the trigger that started his killing was undoubtedly based on an emotional event. He is also projecting guilt onto his victims. The victims are paying for something they have no knowledge of. Simply by being who they are.

While I agreed with almost everything they proposed. The playing down of the religious part didn't sit well with me. It's too easy to dismiss when you have the obvious LGBTQ connection. I wondered if they considered it a coincidence all three were connected to the gay kink BDSM community.

This case had a religious connection and a sexual one. The two lines were too intertwined, especially after the third victim, Carol, not to be connected. That had to be too much of a coincidence, even for the PD and the FBI. Perhaps they hadn't got the details of the third vic and would revise their reports later. We couldn't wait for that. The clock was ticking down quickly till the next body dropped.

The question was, how do you find someone who doesn't want to be found? This killer was not one of the ones who wanted to be caught to stop them. No, this one would keep killing until he was forced to stop. Where do you start to boil it down to essentials?

Christian-based religion, victims of all sexual minorities, public display of martyred saints, why Golden Gate Park? What purpose do the killings serve? Is it for himself or the public?

He has a deep knowledge of Christian history, including how Saint Sebastian was actually killed. Is he a pastor/priest? Possibly, doubtful, lay preacher may be. Religious academic may be, although academics don't usually take physical action, does this mean there is more than one person involved? Doubtful. One person could do all three murders, just easier with two. Two people killing for the same motive is less likely. A cult-like Charles Manson is even less likely.

All the victims were connected to the kink community through KinkInc, but none connected to each other, at least that I could find. A deep dive into the KinkInc accounts, business, and personal lives of all the victims would hopefully give us a 'why' they were chosen.

Another thought. Using the three drop sites as examples, try to figure out where else the killer might have chosen for drop sites. If we could predict where the sites were, scratch that. The size of the park was against us. Then again, serial killers rarely changed their way of operating. I had suspicions this would not be the case with this one.

A thought popped into my head.

"Sophie, can you get a list or report of any deaths over the last two years that have any connection to the gay or kink community, accidents, murders, and specifically anything religion-related."

"Wow, you don't want much, do you? I'll see what I can come up with. It will mean trolling through the PD archives and all the media outlets. I can cross-reference the results. Marie will have to help sift through the crap. Once I have a decent data set, Fiend will help out. This sort of search will get his juices going."

Sophie had used her 'friend' Fiend in Philadelphia before, with excellent results. I had never met Fiend, he was, is a conspiracy theorist and computer wizard who shunned society. He lived off the grid as much as possible. I always thought he was enamored with Sophie. Surprisingly, she was oblivious to that thought.

"Whatever it takes—no disrespect to the SFPD or the FBI. I think downplaying the religious part of this is a mistake. I think religion's the driver behind all of this, and homophobia is definitely a critical part of his agenda."

"I don't know Mas. The FBI is good at profiling.

"Just a gut feeling that it's the driver."

"Uh oh, I don't like it when you get those feelings. One, they are usually right, and two, usually something bad happens."

"This time, it's already happened. We're only trying to stop more bad things from happening, and I don't think we can."

"Mas, that's not like you. Where's the positive Mas I know and love?"

"Serials are not easy to catch, and this one's brilliant, and unless he makes a mistake- unlikely, or we get really lucky, it's going to be a long haul.

"Then let me get going on your outrageous requests for data, and I hope we get lucky."

She blew me a kiss, twirled the key to my chastity cage on its chain around her neck, and winked at me. I smiled, knowing I loved her and she loved me. There was not much I could do in the present circumstances, so I took the opportunity to go and blow holes in paper targets. I couldn't get the idea out of my head. It was up to us to catch this guy, not the FBI, not the SFPD-ridiculous. With all their combined assets, they made our little troop look insignificant. Still, we could do things they couldn't and didn't play by the same rules.

Collecting my weapon from home, I went to the gun range. Two hundred rounds later, I was covered in GSR. The action and process of loading the magazines, setting the target, and taking my time shooting acted as a brain cleanser. I didn't think of anything, concentrating only on the procedure and letting go. Target shooting was as Zen-like as I got.

Feeling better, I called Sophie, saying, "I'm going home, and dinner will be ready for you, so don't work too late."

"Promise I'll be sensible. Getting the bulk data is all I am doing today, and I won't be able to get all of it today, so I won't be late.

"Good, I love you."

"I love you too Mas."

She hung up, and I arrived home. My first action was to clean my weapon, good habits die hard. Putting it away safely, I showered to remove the GSR. Fresh clothes, and I started to think about what to make for dinner. Beer or wine-wine led me to pasta and raid the fridge for veggies. Shitake mushrooms, and a change of plan, mushroom risotto with broccolini done.

Sophie arrived as promised-not late. She looked tired.

I asked, "Are you okay?"

"Yeah, just tired. These killings dredged up a lot of bad memories. I got a lot of data, too much already. We will need to review and shrink it. That's for another day. What's for dinner?"

"Mushroom risotto with broccolini, garlic bread, and a very nice Chardonnay from Three Bells winery."

"That sounds good, quick shower and I'll be ready."

We ate dinner on our back deck and chatted about nothing, avoiding painful memories and current horrors. We held hands as the sun went west over San Francisco. Lights replaced the sun and started to twinkle, illuminating our city.

Chapter Six

Sophie was awake before me. The sounds from the kitchen brought me around. Beating me out of bed was not the norm. Going into the kitchen, she was wearing one of my T-shirts, which barely covered her ass. Now I was really awake. Hugging her from behind, she leaned into me, and I Kissed her neck, asking.

"How come you are up so early."

"Woke up and couldn't get back to sleep. I keep thinking of what the partners and family of the vics are going through. It still hurts when I think of Suzanne."

"I know how you feel. It's gotta be worse when it's a sibling."

Sophie's sister had been killed as part of a corrupt tech scheme, along with seven others, in what the media called the 'Bodies in the Bay.' My partner in our investigation business was killed in a hit-and-run a few months before her sister, the offender, never found each had our demons.

"So, what's for breakfast?"

"We have time for huevos rancheros IF you leave me alone."

"No problem." How an East Coast girl learned how to make Mexican food so quickly and well was a mystery. I just appreciated the result.

A quick shower and I was ready, coffee and huevos rancheros demolished, we set of for the office. We walked and talked, I asked Sophie.

"How much data do you have for us to go through?"

"Too much already, with more to come."

"How much is too much?"

"We went back two years and covered San Francisco and the surrounding counties. There are a lot of deaths in that size catchment area."

"You were smart to do the surrounding counties. Just cos he drops bodies in Golden Gate Park doesn't mean he lives in San Francisco-good point."

"He probably does. I just wanted to cover all the bases."

"Why do you think he lives in SF?"

"He is employed and smart. He has planned and prepared his drop sites, which takes too much time to take off work without someone noticing. With all this city's traffic issues, getting in and out can be a nightmare. I think he is in the city."

"He could be self-employed. That would give him flexibility."

"Good point hadn't thought of that-damn."

"I agree with you. He is in the city, and I think he is employed, not self-employed. In the profile, they believe he is smart and meticulous, so what fields employ smart, meticulous people? Would that narrow down the data?"

"I guess it will still be a big pot. Tech, sciences of all sorts, accountants…shit, even car mechanics have to be precise and meticulous."

"Agreed, but you are forgetting the planning part. That will be a big part of this. Who are good planners?"

"Logistics folks, teachers, scientists again, even

priests have to plan. Event planners, anyone who organizes anything. We are going round in circles, but I get where you are going."

"Good, because we have to add in the religious part and the homophobic part and look into the backgrounds of all the victims. Why did I open my big mouth? This is a huge task!"

"That's why we have computers to assist. We will get there, I promise. It will just take time."

"That is something we don't have much of. We are already days into the timeline for the next body drop."

"I know, just trying to be positive."

"And for that, I love you."

"Ditto, Mas, I mean it, and we will get him."

Sophie said that with so much conviction I stopped in my tracks and asked.

"How can you be so sure?"

"Because we need to. You have your gut feelings. Well, this one is mine. Let's get to work."

"Has Fiend agreed to assist."

"Yes, he has. When I have the data sets, I will give him parameters and let him loose on it."

"That should keep him out of trouble for a while."

I said it with a smile, hoping to raise a smile with Sophie. It worked briefly. We reached the office, hellos to Marie and a coffee poured. Sophie disappeared behind her screens, and the rapid tapping of the keyboard was all I heard. Lunch came and went for Marie and me. We left a sandwich for Sophie on her desk. She hardly noticed the food. Several hours past a half-eaten lunch, I heard a sigh from Sophie.

"Mas, that's about it on the data dump. It's a lot of data and will take time to sift and sort."

"Did you include suicides in your data?"

"What?"

"Suicides-you know, people offing themselves."

"Shit, shit, shit. No, I didn't, and I should have. I'll be home late tonight. I will need to add that parameter into the algorithm and rerun it so it makes sense and will be easy to parse out. I must be getting old."

"But you are still adorable."

"Thanks, but this was a mistake I shouldn't have made."

"Hey, it's called teamwork. You'll fix it, no harm, no foul."

"Yeah, but it's wasted a day."

"Can't think like that, we caught it early, move on, better than finding out a week from now."

"I guess you're right, just frustrating."

"You do your thing. I will bring you dinner and make sure you get home at a decent hour. You will need your sleep to be sharp tomorrow."

"Okay, thanks, Mas."

Leaving her to do whatever she did to mine the data. I sat and thought about the perp and his victims, the profiles we had from the FBI and the SFPD. Something was bugging me. Dismissing the religious aspect of the crimes was part of it, but not all, and I couldn't pinpoint what it was. It would have to come to me when it did—no use trying to force it. Marie said goodnight, and I went home without disturbing Sophie.

As I prepared dinner, I kept an eye on the clock so Sophie didn't stay too late. I thought about the perps' actions and a question. Why the three-week gap in kills? That had to be significant, twenty-one days, more or less. Also, why start now? What's the trigger? It had to be a trauma, and that type of trauma can surface years later. The date of the first victim would mean a great deal to him. Him? I began to consider more than one perpetrator. Too complicated, it had to be one person.

More information was needed. He could move the vics more efficiently using a trolly or trucks. The photos of the drop sites would have that info if it existed, or perhaps he cleaned up afterward to disguise the fact he had mechanical assistance. With the lack of forensic evidence, he had already proven he was smart, and no one was that lucky to leave so little behind. Also, I wanted a look at a list of gay-lesbian saints to see if that would give us any clues, which I doubted. However, a review would be good.

Sophie called, "I am leaving the office now. Will see you soon. Do you need me to pick anything up?"

"No, we are good. Beer is in the fridge, and food is in the oven. Just need you to make it a perfect night."

She laughed, saying, "You are too kind, Sir. See you soon."

As promised, Sophie arrived, and we ate dinner, downed a couple of beers each, and talked through what we had on the case, what we would do, and what more we needed. That minor niggle was still there, I didn't tell Sophie.

Both tired, we went to bed early. No kink play, no sex, only each other nestled into each other. Sophie was out in seconds. I lasted until her soft, regular breathing lulled me to sleep.

****

The sun arrived with a new day I wasn't ready for. Even though I had slept well, I didn't want to face the day-I had no choice. Leaving Sophie sleeping, I started the coffee and dressed in that order. I tried to be quiet making breakfast, at least not as noisy as usual.

Coffee delivered to Sophie, waking her with a gentle stroking of her shoulder. She came around slowly. While her computer work was not particularly physical, it was mentally draining and took its toll. I hoped she would not have to do any all-nighters, as she had done on our last big case, What the media called 'The Bodies on the Bridge.' We needed a break on this one, and with Fiend on board computer crunching, it would be easier on Sophie, and that may be the break we needed.

Wearily, Sophie came into the kitchen and hugged me, saying.

"We'll soon have the data we think we require. If it's not enough, I don't know what will be."

"Hey, don't worry, we do what we do, and something will give."

Something always did give, hoping it was before the three-week timetable.

"Sure, Mas, you go ahead. I need to shower. I'm taking it slowly today. The data will be waiting for me when I get in."

"No problem. I am going to check in with Kenzo and have a chat with him. See if the latest autopsy report is ready and get any updated photos. I have some thoughts I want to run by him."

"Good, see you later. I love you."

I left for the office, calling Kenzo on the way. He answered on the first ring.

"Hi Mas, anything?"

"Not yet, still digging. Any news on when the

latest autopsy report will be available?"

"Soon, and I don't know what that means. You will get it as soon as I do. We are spinning wheels. We have followed every lead we have, and looked at every minute of camera footage. This dude is good."

"Sure, he is good, we are better. He only needs to make one mistake and we got him. Hey, will you get me all the crime scene photos for each site? There must be some missing, and I want to make sure I don't miss anything."

"I'll follow up and get you everything we have. Thanks, Mas. This one is getting to me. I'm afraid we will be getting more bodies."

"Agreed, I think so too. I know it's hard to be patient. Rush and hurry are good friends with mistakes."

"Okay, any news on the kink community front?"

"That's it, nice one, Kenzo. This case isn't about the kink community. It's personal for the killer. Get your guys to dig deeper into each of the vic's lives. There has to be a nexus between them-we just don't know what it is right now."

"How the hell do you figure that.? We haven't found anything in common between them, nothing other than KinkInc accounts."

"It's there. We need to keep looking. All the killings were specific and hands-on. That's personal. If it were just about homophobia or kink, the killings would be done at a distance or certainly quicker. These victims were made to suffer excruciatingly. That's torture for pleasure."

"Mas, I get your point. It doesn't mean it's not connected to the kink community."

"True, if it is, it's peripheral. The religious aspect is still the driver. Do you know a priest who would talk openly to me? They need to have good insight into the history of the saints."

"Yeah, I know a Priest. I'll get back to you today."

Kenzo ended the call, and I continued to walk to the office. He had given me food for thought. If it was personal, was all this about the perp or someone the perp knew? For the religious part, was he trying to absolve his own guilt or punish the vics for someone else? More goddamn questions, still, if you don't ask the question, you won't get an answer.

Marie was already in and cranking away at keeping the office running. Ever since she had persuaded her partner Chung to wear a chastity device-she had dressed more provocatively, without being trashy-it suited her. My chastity cage was now even more secure now that my PA piercing had healed. Sophie, or more precisely Sophie as her alter ego, Ms. Circe, had attached the piercing to the end of my cage with a small lock. No chance of escape now.

Back to the case. We already had the three victims' work-life details, so KinkInc was where I would start today, taking a thorough look into each victim's profile. I would search for commonalities, friends in common, anything that would tie them together.

Knowing it would be a slog, I loaded up with fresh coffee and started with Sean Costello, the first taken. Gay didn't mean kinky, and it looked like from his profile, he was monogamous with exhibitionist tendencies. He was proud of his body and worked out, but not in the same gym as the third victim, Carol. That would have been too easy.

I started a spreadsheet, noting the clubs he listed, gay and kink. The Cauldron was the one he visited most often-not a surprise. Sophie and I knew the Cauldron very well and had played there ourselves. He was a social butterfly with lots of 'friends', and this was going to take longer than I initially thought. KinkInc is a challenging site to maneuver around. Bring up the profile, bring up all the friends, and then go into each one. It was tedious and needed to be done with no stone unturned.

Sophie arrived, said hi to Marie and me, and disappeared behind her computer. The keyboard began to chatter, then silence, which made me look up and ask.

"Why did you stop?"

"The program is running again, and today, we'll have all the data the algorithm is set to look for."

"Great, when?"

"When it's done. I have self-defense class this morning, and the data should be ready for me when I return."

"Good, go kick some ass."

She smiled and said bye, and I returned to the tedious chore of looking at a seemingly endless number of profiles. Click, click, click-next, the same routine. Some of the profiles on Sean's friend's list were a joke, poorly written, had lousy grammar, and were just horrible. Some were excellent and a pleasure to read.

The sheer number was getting to me when Marie said, "Okay, Mas, lunchtime, you need a break."

She was right. Even with the computer glasses, Sophie got me, my eyes felt heavy; a break would do them and me good. We decided on a local watering hole. We were known and shown a small table, one of three, kept for regular locals. Usually open, if not the best seats in the place.

We ordered and enjoyed the bustle of the lunchtime crowd. The food was good. A simple California fusion food washed down with a local craft beer. We talked about nothing in particular, and the break was what I needed. I was refreshed and ready to tackle more appalling profiles.

The afternoon passed slowly, with me completing the review of Sean's KinkInc profile-nothing, not a damn thing to connect him with the other victims. Next was Frankie, which used the same process, although there were fewer profiles to review, thankfully. She was interesting in that her business was directly related to BDSM, corsets being a staple of the kink community. The business profile was a different matter that didn't concern me. I was convinced the killings were personal, and that is where I concentrated my efforts.

The day ended with all of us tired. My eyes were tired and scratchy. Marie said we were good for the month. Everything that needed to be done or paid was taken care of. Calling out goodnight as she left.

Sophie looked satisfied with her algorithm's results, saying, "Well, it took longer than I wanted. We have too much data to review, and it needs to be refined. I am sending it to Fiend for his comments and suggestions. Can we go home? I'm exhausted."

"You bet. I feel like my eyes are going to fall out of my head. I don't know how you do it with three screens all day."

"Practice-let's do take-out and crash. Tomorrow will be another busy one."

"No argument from me. Pizza?"

"Fine, no anchovies!"

"Okay."

I called the order into Gusto Pinsa Romana, who produced an excellent thin crust pizza. We left to collect our dinner. After a few minutes of wait, they were busy as usual. We were taking the opportunity to review the day.

I said, "The KinkInc review is a chore. I don't think it will give us anything useful.

"Then why do it?"

"I want to cover all the bases, in case there is something, and it's good at giving me a feel for them as individuals. Frankie is a bit different. She was in the community, twice as it were, business and personal. I'm concentrating on the personal. The business side can wait there's too much info to deal with. It's a female-focused business, and our perp is male."

"Men wear corsets, especially in the community, cross-dressers, sissies etc."

"True, but I don't believe our perp is in the community. He is outside looking in and religious -that I'm sure of. Shit."

"What is it, Mas."

"Kenzo was supposed to get back to me with the name of a Priest who would be willing to talk to me about LGBTQ saints."

"Call him tomorrow. That can wait a few hours. Dinners ready."

Paying for the pizza, we quickly reached home. We ate out of the box, too tired even for paper plates, with paper towels for napkins. Polishing off most of the pizza, we each had a second beer as we watched some crap on TV before crashing into bed and a deep sleep.

Chapter Seven

My phone went off when it was supposed to, and I didn't want it to. I felt hungover, even though I wasn't. Detective work has little glamour, and yesterday's slog through the profiles proved that. Today was another day to try to move forward.

Sophie would be catching up with Fiend. He was three hours ahead in Philly and had probably been up all night looking at what Sophie had sent him. That would keep her busy. My first call would be to Kenzo regarding the Priest contact. It was unusual for him not to get back to me. Something must have happened, not a good sign. I have almost completed reviewing Frankie's profiles, and next would be Carol's.

Coffee on and a quick shower for me. We decided to pick up breakfast on the way. It would be faster and more efficient.

Kenzo answered on the first ring, "Mas, I know. I promised to get back to you yesterday. With the media splash on the body in the park, now the second one hit the media. The news is bringing the loonies out. There were two idiots yesterday, both claiming to be the perp- not a chance on either. We had to do interviews to make sure they didn't do it, and they didn't have any useful info-they didn't, and it made for a long, frustrating day. Call Father Benedict at St Thomas, the one near the park. Father Bededict's waiting for your call. Heads up, he's not what you would expect. I'll text you the number. Good luck, and call me with anything, yes?"

"Thanks, that's a promise."

He hung up and left us to continue on our way. Picking up breakfast, we made good time to the office. Looking up the church address, as I ate, I dialed the number Kenzo had texted. A rich, deep voice answered.

"Good morning. I wish you peace. How may I serve you today?"

"Hello, Father, my name is Mas Hammett, and Kenzo gave me your number."

"Mr. Hammett. Kenzo mentioned that you had a rather unusual request, which was most intriguing. I will be happy to help you if I can. I have a fairly flexible schedule. However, if you would give me some specifics, I could do some research before we meet."

"Father, it's kind of a delicate nature, and I don't want to offend anyone, at least not deliberately."

"As you wish, this morning is taken until eleven, and then I am at your service until two. Is that acceptable?"

"Great, make it noon, and lunch is on me."

"Wonderful, I am a pescetarian, so anywhere with seafood is a treat."

"I will find somewhere and pick you up at noon. Thanks again."

"Peace be with you, Mas."

With that set, it was back to profiles. Carol was all over the place and played the field, at least women-wise. That made it easier as there were fewer men to deal with as potential perps. I didn't expect to find the perp in the profiles anyway. I sought connections between the three victims to lead us to the perp. There was a connection we just hadn't found yet.

"Mas, we need to talk. I have Fiend on the line."

"Okay, what's up?"

"It's what I thought it would be, the volume of data. Fiend agrees we have too much data to review on our timeline."

"How do you mean?"

"In San Francisco alone in the last two years, there were over a hundred homicides, two hundred suicides, and almost seven thousand suicide attempts. Deaths ruled as accidents by vehicle, at work, and residential compound those numbers."

"Shit, you weren't kidding about the data. Let me think."

Fiend said, "The more specific you can be, the more efficient we can be. We can do this, but it will take much longer than needed, and those numbers are for San Francisco only. Going out to the surrounding counties, we get bogged down in data, you know, can't see the trees for the forest."

"Got it, Fiend." I had to figure out a way to cut the numbers. "Okay, keep it to San Francisco only for now. San Francisco is obliged to investigate all violent, sudden, or medically unattended deaths within their jurisdiction. Cut out the suicide attempts. I don't think an attempt triggered the perp, and stick with all the deaths. Does that help?"

Together, Sophie and Fiend said, "Yes." Sophie continued.

"Give me a minute." Keyboard clattering. "That still leaves us with a rolling two-year total of 351 deaths due to homicide, suicide, and medically unattended for San Francisco. The medically unattended could mean suicide, accidental or natural. It's still a better number."

"Good, and look for any death with religious connections or overtones."

Sophie asked, "Such as?"

"No idea."

That brought a gruff laugh from Fiend, who said, "Leave that part with me, and I'll scan for any religious aspect in the deaths. I can adjust the existing program and run it for that."

I said, "Clarification, Christian only. No other religion. This perp is using Christian saints."

Sophie commented, "Could that be a deflection or decoy?"

"Not a chance. He's a Christian of some denomination. He knows too much about the history of the saints, and we need to catch up. Don't forget everyone was Catholic before Martin Luther."

"Okay, let me sort this out and resend it to Fiend."

"Sophie. Don't worry about a resend. Please give me your new parameters and the algorithm you are using. I'll take care of it this end, and you take care of yours."

"Thanks, Fiend, I owe you one,"

"Any time for you, Sophie, you are always interesting, and Mas. Chao"

I was an afterthought on that one. He also confirmed my suspicion that he had a crush on Sophie, and no, I wasn't concerned.

Without a word, Sophie closed the call and started tapping away on her keyboard. Back to finish Carol's profiles, which would take me to lunch. The time to pick up Father Benedict came quickly. I said goodbye to Sophie, but there was no response, and Marie, who promised to make Sophie have lunch, which probably meant a sandwich at her desk, was better than nothing.

'*The Daily Catch*' didn't open until noon. I called and left a message for a table for two. Hopefully, they weren't busy today and this early. It was reportedly the best seafood restaurant near the church. The traffic wasn't too bad for San Francisco.

A tall, rangy man was waiting at the curb as I pulled up at St Thomas church. Long grey hair pulled back in a ponytail. Multicolored T-shirt, worn shorts, and shod in battered sandals. I stopped with the window down.

He asked, "Mas?"

"Yes, Father Benedict?"

As he climbed in, he said, "Call me Benny, everyone does, except the senior Priest." He laughed, deep, generous, and genuine.

Kenzo was right. Father Benedict was not your typical priest. He looked more like a stereotypical hippie from the sixties, confirmed by his Grateful Dead T-shirt, rather than a Priest.

"I hope '*The Daily Catch*' Has a table for us. I left a message before they opened."

"They will."

I looked at him, his serene face looking forward.

"How can you be sure?"

"They know me, good choice by the way."

"Oh." That was all I could say to that. I found a parking space close to the restaurant. Benny walked quickly with purpose, and I had to hurry to keep up with him. The restaurant opened as we arrived. The hostess immediately recognized Benny and said, "Hello, Father Benny. Here for lunch or just visiting."

"Hi Jenny, wishing you peace. I'm having lunch today with my friend Mas."

Jenny showed us to a small booth near the kitchen and seated. Benny took the seat, looking out into the restaurant. That was what suspicious people do, and he noted my quizzical look.'

"No, no, Mas, I am not worried about being attacked. I want to be seen so people can approach me if they want to. You have a suspicious nature, Mas."

"You must know something about that if you recognized what I was thinking."

"A different life, a lifetime ago." He laughed again, the generous laugh of someone with experience.

"Fair enough." The waitress came and took our drink and food orders. "Kenzo said I should talk to you about a sensitive matter. I-we need information."

"Kenzo is under a lot of stress. He told me of what has happened, is happening, so anything I can do, without breaking the confessional, ask."

"The FBI and the SFPD profilers believe it's rooted in homophobia. That is part of it, for sure. To me, the religious aspect is more integral to catching this person."

"Why do you think that, and what do you need from me?"

The food arrived quickly. We talked as we ate our lunch. No one could overhear our conversation.

"These victims were sacrificed, each in a very particular way, all up close and personal. If it were just homophobia, the killings wouldn't be one here and one there, it would be bombing an LGBTQ club or shooting up a gay meeting or festival. These crimes are committed by one person with an agenda, triggered by an event in his life."

"Can't say I disagree with you on that summation. What exactly do you need from me?"

"Information on all the gay, lesbian, queer, and trans saints you can identify."

He chuckled, "Mas, there are many more than you would think. I can get you a list of the most famous and well-known and some of the less well-known. How will this help you?"

"I don't know if it will. I-we have to gather as much information as possible and put it together so it makes sense if we can."

"Who do you think the three current victims represent."

That brought me up sharp. "Current victims? You are expecting more.?"

"Unfortunately, I agree with Kenzo and you. This person is not done and won't be until they're caught. Which Saints do you think you have and why?"

Explaining the sequence of body drops and how the victims were presented, starting with Saint Wilgefortis.

"Well, that is one saint I haven't heard mention of in a long time. You were clever in discovering her."

"My partner did the digging. Comments on these three."

"Using Saint Wilgefortis, and then killing Saint Seb in the actual manner of his death not the common incorrect version, not found in your average bible study class. St Joan everyone knows about her, replicating her martyrdom with a live person, which is very disturbing. Whoever this person is, they have a better-than-average knowledge of the history of the Saints and how they were martyred. It's almost academic. The study of the LGBTQ saints is not encouraged, not even here in San Francisco. It is discouraged everywhere."

"How did you get interested in the subject, or subjects?"

"I lived through the summer of love, and I still appreciate the Grateful Dead, survived Vietnam, indulged in the *me* eighties, worked here in the AIDS epidemic, and seen all the changes in San Francisco. If you want to reach people, you go to them, where they are and live. Don't expect them to come to you. A lot of Priests shunned the dying in the AIDS wards. I believe that everyone deserves whatever solace they can get. I started looking for anyone in church history they could relate to. When I started researching, I was surprised at the number of questionable saints." He laughed at his comment. "I was not encouraged by the higher-ups, and I don't mean the ones in Heaven."

He was silent, and I let him drift, not wanting to disturb his memories.

"Right, Mas, I will get you a list of the questionable saints as soon as possible."

"Thanks, you always said this 'person' you didn't put a gender on them. Why?"

"Because I don't know if it's a man, woman, or both."

"You think it's a couple?"

"I am open to all possibilities, and you should be too."

"I will be, thank you. You have given me something to think about."

We closed the lunch with me dropping Benny back at the church with his reiterated promise.

"You will have the list of appropriate saints today. May peace and success be with you. I will be praying for you.

That was a first. I don't think anyone had prayed for my success before. I would take prayers, tarot cards, or crystal balls if it would help us. As I drove back to the office, I thought about what Father Benny had said about two people.

Most serials are men. That's a given, historically and statistically. Sure, there were some women, but there were very few in comparison. The same was true with couples, but there were very few. What couple would be religiously whacked out enough to kill so far, random people? If it was a couple, what could trigger a couple to do this?

A single male, fit male could do it—a single woman, not a chance, with the weight and awkwardness of the body drops. A couple could work it, or one could be the lookout at the drop sites. It still didn't make sense for two people to be doing this. Back to data, we needed to figure out the trigger. Then, we would be making progress.

When I walked in, the office was eerily quiet. Marie was buried in whatever she was doing, and Sophie's desk was quiet. I could see the top of her head over the monitors but no sound of a keyboard, which was unusual.

"Hey Sophie, what's up?"

Looking up, I saw her eyes were red. I was not sure if it was tiredness or if she had been crying.

"So many deaths. What a fucking waste. I have only just started looking into them, and it's depressing. What makes it worse is that I'm still unsure what I'm looking for."

"Hey, it's okay. The more we do, the closer we get to answers. We go through this tedious crap to get what we need. It's the same in every case."

"This one is worse, stirring up some bad memories."

"Why don't you let Fiend handle the data end?"

"No, Mas, this is OURS, and I will do what's necessary. We have to."

"Well, Father Benedict was a piece of work. Kenzo was right about him not being the norm. He looked like an escaped hippie, which he is. Tall, rangy, with long grey hair, and wearing a Grateful Dead T-shirt. Very sharp, he promised a list of saints that may be useful to us. He is also praying for our success." That comment raised a smile and comment.

"That's a first."

"Exactly what I thought. Benny also suggested we keep an open mind about the perp."

"In what way?"

"He kept saying person, when we assume the perp is a male, he would not make any assumptions. We shouldn't discount it being a couple or two-person team. Food for thought."

"That would be an anomaly."

"Agreed, but we shouldn't dismiss it out of hand. Let's build different scenarios.

We can discount a single female due to the physicality of the crimes. One male only, top suspect. A couple, male and female, would be my next pick. A two-male team leader and acolyte is possible but not likely, and I would bet, if so, not Gay. Lastly, a two-female team between them would have the physical capabilities to do the crimes, again, not Lesbian. I'm still convinced these are religious crimes, first and foremost not sexual, at least primarily religious. Like with rape, it's not about the sex, it's about the power and control." Sophie was pensive, and a frown creased her forehead before she spoke.

"Rape is still a sex crime. I'm not sure you're right yet. We still don't know enough. I'm not saying you're wrong, but you sound like you're becoming fixated on the religious part. Remember what Father Benny noted, an open mind. A lot of the Christian iconography had sado-masochistic and homo erotic overtones."

"Where do we go from here? The clock is ticking."

"Thanks for giving me something to think about other than dead people. There are a lot of them."

"Can you break down the mass of data into smaller bites by gender, age, ethnicity, homicide, suicide, and, if possible, religion?"

"You forgot unattended medical deaths."

"Shit, can you separate accidental deaths from suicides? If it's an OD, was it deliberate or accidental? What I am asking is, can you break down the bulk data into bite-sized pieces that will be easier to review and investigate if it requires it?"

"Yes, I was thinking about that myself. The trigger doesn't have to be a major incident to set someone off."

"True, in this case, I think it was a big thing, combined with religious extremism."

"Oh, hell, Mas, get off your religious fixation, will you? You're going to drive me nuts."

"Okay. Do you need Marie or me to do anything to assist you?

"Not yet. Now I have a plan. I'll let you both know. When it's time, I will need you both to do a lot of leg work, computer-wise and out there in the real world."

"Just name it."

With Sophie's mood lifted a little, I returned to profile land and continued to Carol. Frankie's and Sean's profiles on KinkInc had not produced anything tangible, and I didn't expect anything from Carol's either. Down the road, something unrelated may connect to something I'd seen and reviewed in the profiles. God, it was boring doing it.

Each with our tasks, the afternoon passed quietly as the clock ticked relentlessly toward evening. The sun was dropping to the west, the fog began to appear, and we all felt drained. None of us had achieved as much as we wanted or would have liked.

Happy hour was in order. Marie called her partner Chung, who was not traveling, to meet us for drinks. Chung not traveling would mean he was also locked in a chastity device. Marie had persuaded him to try it out after she had accidentally seen mine. I had been attacked and ended up in the Hospital. I was a little out of it, and the gown opened, and she couldn't miss it. That and a conversation with Sophie set her on the kink path. They seemed happy and were looking for a house. The monies from the Bodies in the Bay case were steadily coming through.

We met at the Lipo Lounge for a Mai Tai or two and then an early dinner in one of China Town's many great restaurants. The dinner lifted all our spirits, and Chung entertained us with stories of growing up in a Chinese family in America. He should have done stand-up. Saying our goodbyes, Sophie and I slowly walked back home, no rush.

I asked her, "Do you feel up to playing tonight."

"Mas, normally I would be delighted. Not tonight. I want to relax and crash."

"Good enough for me."

"Besides, it hasn't been that long since your last release, feeling horny?"

"With you around-always."

She laughed, "Good answer that will not get you out any earlier than I have planned."

Arriving home, we each had a beer, watching a Discovery program on the Elephant seals that made our coast home. Then, bed, spooning, and sleep.

Chapter Eight

The days blurred into one another, then the weeks. Sophie was in regular contact with Fiend. He had been working on the data, specifically looking for religious connections, and had come up with the same as us. Nothing concrete. I had been through Carol's profile and her contacts—nothing to connect her to the other two vics, as I expected. Still, I was sure there was a connection between all three victims.

Father Benny delivered as promised, and as promised, the list was longer than expected. The list covered individual gay, lesbian, and trans saints and couples. There was no way to predict which saint would be chosen or who the next victim would be. The list was currently of little use. If another victim showed up, we would probably be able to identify the long-dead martyred saint, and that would be about it.

Sophie had dissected all the data into smaller sections, and we had all been working through the homicides, suicides, and other deaths.

Having our back door into the police systems was a huge asset, and we dredged it for information on each death we investigated. It was depressing work. Some were just as listed -unfortunate accidents. The suicides were the worst emotionally. Homicides were the most difficult logistically. Often, the perpetrator had escaped justice. We could have stumbled over the trigger incident and not know it. Trying to get the puzzle pieces was not easy, and when we had what we thought were pieces, none would fit together.

No one and nothing we saw connected back to the three victims we had, only the fact they were murdered in a historically religious manner with homophobic overtones and had KinkInc accounts. We were running out of time. This coming weekend would be telling, and I wondered if the perpetrator would stick with their previous timeline. We had agreed that we needed to keep it as a gender-neutral person. Being fixated on a single male only as the perp would be a mistake, even if it were a single male. We had to follow the evidence we didn't have.

If the timeline stuck, was the victim already a missing person? We had discussed that possibility with Kenzo, and he'd already thought of that and had a team jumping on all missing persons' reports as soon as they came in, with nothing to report so far. People were always going missing, juveniles running away, and Silver-Alerts for missing seniors, mostly innocent and happily resolved, but not all ended well. We were all on edge as Friday rolled around.

We were all frustrated with doing the work and getting no results that made sense. For Kenzo, it was worse. He had the department higher-ups, the mayor's office, and the media breathing down his neck, especially after the news leaked about the St. Sebastian death. When they discovered that, a feeding frenzy would be a good description of the media. Speculation and conspiracy theories ran rampant, none of which helped find the perpetrator. San Francisco was perhaps more sensitive to serials than some cities, having lived through the Zodiac killer, who was never caught.

Thankfully, the media did not get most of the details surrounding the deaths. Kenzo had done an excellent job of restricting most of the information to his team, letting out only enough of what he wanted to release, keeping the media piranhas at bay. I didn't envy him or miss this crap, and I'd also had to deal with it as a member of the SFPD. We were about to close up for the night when Kenzo called.

"Hi Kenzo, you are on speaker."

"Mas, we have a missing person and the only one that fits the MO. All the other missing's are either accounted for or not following the MO, non-LGBTQ, or connected to the BDSM community. He's Jeremy Hale, a male in his late thirties, gay, and partnered. A successful Realtor. He and his partner own several rental properties in the Castro district. Clean record, no speeding tickets, several paid parking tickets, not surprising in this city, nothing suspicious. His partner, Ashton Oka, is an investor and financially secure. We haven't been able to contact him since Thursday late morning when we took his statement and checked their home."

"When did the report come in?"

"Wednesday evening, late by Ashton. The Real Estate office was looking for him. Jeremy was last seen at a house showing. When the next client arrived, he was not there for their appointment. The client called the real estate office, and they tried to contact him but couldn't get an answer. They called Ashton. Ashton tried calling, texting, and e-mail no result. That is when he called us. We checked the client who called Jeremy's office: clean, pissed-off client, nothing else.

We have the records of all his client showings for the day, except the prior appointment to the one that reported Jeremy missing the appointment. We can't find a record of that invisible client, and the name in his calendar was not traceable. Fake name and details. I think he was taken on Wednesday, which is pretty ballsy, it would have been in daylight."

"How about the partner, Ashton? Anything on him, has he disappeared as well?"

"We aren't sure yet. We are still following up on Ashton. I'm not sure if they are connected, but two may have gone missing. I'm hoping it's not an escalation."

Sophie asked, "Any forensics at the house showing?"

"Too much, lots of fingerprints. We are working as quickly as we can to eliminate as many people as possible. Some areas had been cleaned thoroughly, too thoroughly for a casual clean-up. I'm sure it was a forensic countermeasure. Another reason why I think he was snatched at that location."

Jumping back in, "What about his phone records?"

"We are going through those. We don't have Jeremy's cell, but we have accessed his calls from the carrier. Several were from a downtown Hotel, which is a dead-end-lobby courtesy phone. I had to give you a heads-up. I think we will be getting another body dump this weekend."

"Can you get Sophie and me access to the snatch location? I assume it's still a crime scene."

"It is, and it's a vacant possession. The owner has already moved and is obviously upset. The lock box access code is one, nine, two, five. Please make sure you put the keys back. Call me with your observations, ideas, or anything, yes?"

"You got it. We will get over there. It will take time with Friday traffic."

"Don't I know it. Just call me. It doesn't matter how late."

"Promise."

We looked at each other, knowing Kenzo was probably right about a body dropping over the weekend in Golden Gate Park. Not if, just when and where. We grabbed our bags and headed out to my SUV. Marie said she would close the office and call if we needed her.

The ride over took as long as I had expected. Traffic was Friday night lousy. There was nothing we could do about that. We used the time to discuss what Kenzo had told us. The snatch had to have been well planned and executed. There is nothing random about the selection of Jeremy. Damn, this bastard was clever. However intelligent someone is, perpetrators eventually make a mistake, always. Unfortunately, the innocent suffer until that happens.

Parking in the Castro on a Friday night was almost impossible. The streets started to bustle with people looking to relax after a week's work. We were on a different mission. Finally, I squeezed the SUV into a spot, barely. Quickly, we walked the three blocks to the property address.

The house was typical, with a garage under the house and an entrance to one side up some steep steps through a wrought iron gate. The realtor's lock box was where Kenzo had said. Sophie accessed the keys. The property looked in great shape, with good paint, and should be a quick sale. I followed her up the steps. The two locks opened easily, and we entered after putting on latex gloves. We moved freely about the empty house. Most surfaces were covered in fingerprint powder, especially where you would expect fingerprints to be. Some surfaces were clear of any prints but not the annoying powder. The perp had cleaned up, which meant they felt comfortable there timewise, and nothing rushed. They had known Jeremy's schedule and worked accordingly.

How was Jeremy taken? Drugged? Unlikely, physically overpowered-maybe, if it was two people, certainly possible. The perp surprised Jeremy and held something over his nose and mouth, not chloroform, which is not as effective as TV makes out. Taser, more likely, quick and effective in most cases, the perp would have time to restrain the victim. How do you get him out of the house unseen, idiot? The garage.

I called to Sophie, "Meet me in the garage."

Sophie was there before me, asking, "What is it?"

"I know how Jeremy was taken."

We entered the garage from inside the house, careful not to touch more than we had to. It had been cleaned out, and the only things left were the things that should be there. On examining the floor, there were two sets of tire marks, one for a car, the other for something broader, SUV, minivan, or truck.

"Look at the tire marks. My theory is that the perp makes an appointment with Jeremy, nothing suspicious, so they had the real estate talk. The perp uses a Taser on Jeremy that puts him out, and once he is out, the perp restrains him, opens the garage, backs in a vehicle, closes the door...back to privacy. He loads in his victim, cleans up, and drives out, closes the door, and is away, no one the wiser. One person could do it, and it would be even easier with two.

"Jeremy would not suspect a single male, male-female couple, or female couple. Zap, he wouldn't see it coming- no reason to."

"That is a good theory and one that holds water. It doesn't get us any closer to the perp, does it?"

"Nope. Jeremy was not picked at random. We must get into his life, social media, everything ASAP, and his disappearing partner. Do you think his partner could have been taken as well?"

"Wow, Mas, that's a stretch, possible, but why? All the other vics were single saints."

"True, maybe he's after both these guys. Sean and Frankie both had partners who weren't touched, so why these guys? The two of them have to mean something to the perp. The list Father Benny sent has multiple pairs of gay and lesbian saints on it."

"If Ashton has been taken, and he wasn't taken at the same time, maybe he saw something or knows something about Jeremy's abduction. That's a more likely scenario-right."

"Could be. We can guess, speculate, and theorize all we want and keep the ones that make the most sense and fit our evidence. We must wait and see how it all plays out this weekend."

"We will be on call all weekend, right?"

"I don't think we have a choice."

"No, we don't."

We closed up the house and put the keys back in the lockbox. Strolling back to the SUV, the area was beginning to get packed, happy faces out for an evening of fun and frolics. All the bars and cafes were busy, and soon, the restaurants would be as well—a regular Friday night in San Francisco. If Kenzo was right about Jeremy, and I thought he was, all these people were at least safe for the next three weeks.

Sophie drove as I called Kenzo. He picked up immediately.

"Well?"

"You are on speaker. Our theory is that Jeremy was surprised, probably tased, restrained, and abducted via the garage. It's the only scenario that works without someone seeing something suspicious."

"That is exactly what we think happened. The perp would have to know Jeremy's schedule and work accordingly. I wouldn't take long to open the garage back in a car or van, load him in and out, gone no one the wiser. I'm glad we are on the same page on that one. Any ideas on the vehicle? Due to the wheelbase, we think it's a van, minivan, or truck."

"Agree on that. Our thought was a minivan rather than a truck, but either would work."

"Thanks for confirming my thoughts. I'll call if anything breaks."

"Hey, Kenzo, don't second guess yourself. You don't need us to confirm your ideas. You're a good cop and don't forget that."

"Tell that to the mayor's office and the PD brass. It's a pressure cooker, and more to come next week."

"Kenzo, Mas, and I are here for you and working on this priority. What are they gonna do? Take you off the case, the one that knows the most about it, even they aren't that stupid."

"Thanks, Sophie, it's got nothing to do with stupid. It's all politics and perception. My Captain has my back so far, but he also has to take orders. I'll call if anything breaks. Thanks, guys."

We could hear the weariness in his voice, and it saddened me to hear it. Kenzo was one of the good guys. With all our efforts over the last three weeks, we hadn't moved forward. We were still processing a lot of data, but nothing you could hang your hat on. Frustration-I let out a loud.

"Goddamn it." Hitting the dashboard with a clenched fist.

"Mas! I've never seen you like this."

"Sorry, frustration, we have to be smarter than this perp."

"We are. Like Fiend says, we are coming in at the end of a movie, and we don't know how it starts, and we need to fill in the story backward.

"How do we get back to square one? We have data, and we know what we have is accurate, not the detail. So far, it's too broad. Let's see what happens this weekend."

Sophia quietly said, "I don't think I am going to like this weekend."

"Me either. Let's go home. I need a drink."

"Take out, or eat out?"

"Yes, I don't feel like cooking."

Chapter Nine

Waking with a start, it was Saturday, and no early call from Kenzo, a small mercy. Sophie was still sleeping. I rolled over and spooned, and she snuggled back into me. My metal chastity cage poked her in the ass, but she didn't seem to mind, and didn't wake up.

I was now wide awake, and my cock filled the cage to full. I must admit any BDSM play was furthest from my mind right now, but I would need a mental release soon. When I was an SFPD Inspector, I used kink play as my stress release. I had managed to stay away from the usual PD pitfalls of drink, gambling, and screwing around.

Most detective work is mental before the physical, and this one was a significant stressor. Now was not the time for play. Now was the time to focus. I would know when I needed a stress release, and getting it always gave me a new perspective on a case. We had been having monthly massages since our last big case, which helped the physical.

People not in the kink community don't understand the release you can get from giving yourself up to someone else entirely. The closest I can come up with is a Zen moment- letting go to emptiness, a sense of peace that can't be described in words.

Being this awake, I had to be doing something, first brewing the coffee. Next, I would get to the farmers' market before it got crowded and I'd be back before Sophie woke up. A safe bet, as the market was close, and she was still sleeping deeply. The market was already bustling with customers enjoying the weather and the variety of produce.

I hoped I was back before Sophie woke. Opening the door as quietly as I could, the house was still silent. Good. Breakfast would wake her.

And it did. Sleepily, she came into the kitchen asking, "Why didn't you wake me? I like going to the market."

"You needed the rest. I was awake and couldn't go back to sleep. Coffee?"

"Silly question, and it was thoughtful not to wake me. I love you, Mas."

"Love you too. Breakfast?"

"Yes, please."

Together, we made a breakfast fit for two hungry detectives. As our meal ended, Sophie said, "One day down, only tomorrow left for the body dump if they stick to the timetable."

"I'll put money on getting a call from Kenzo tomorrow. Jeremy will show up somewhere in the park, killed in the manner of a saint."

"I agree. If we had a concrete starting point, we could use the data we have more efficiently. We have done a lot of work in the past weeks, and it's too general."

"Agreed, we need a break in the case, and we need a break ourselves. How about a stroll through a park? NOT Golden Gate."

That comment raised a chuckle and her agreement. We dressed for a day in one of the many parks in and around San Francisco. The drive was easy, and the fresh air did us a world of good. Our stroll turned out to be a more strenuous hike but worth it. Blowing away mental cobwebs and making our bodies work, pumping our blood. In the end, we were healthily tired and hungry.

Stopping at a café on the way home, we ate and talked about everything and nothing. We talked about Marie and Chung and how they seemed happier over the last few months—looking for a house and bidding on one, yet to know if they were successful. That subject brought Sophie around to say that Chung seemed to have adapted to his chastity device very well.

I asked her, "How much input did you have in that situation."

"Enough. Marie asked me about it right after seeing yours in the Hospital, and she researched online, which only confused her with so much contradictory info."

"And her dressing more provocatively?"

"Oh no, that's all on her. She does look good, though."

"Yes, she does. I thought you had a hand in that as well."

"Nope, I had enough on my mind. This brings me neatly to us now that your PA piercing is healed. You haven't said much lately."

"Nothing to report, healing right like the piercer said. Wednesday will be thirteen weeks and three since you changed out the ring for a lock, so we are good."

"Oh, I have some ideas regarding that, and when we get home, we can explore."

Her laugh was light and frisky, and that was good to hear. The day had succeeded in taking our minds off the potential for another body dump.

When we got home, we first did shower off the hike sweat and dust. Sophie, as promised, told me not to bother dressing yet. Curious about her plan, I obliged, sitting on the end of our bed. Sophie returned with a small bag and sat next to me in front of me. She started by saying.

"Mas, you have been amazing. You have consented to almost everything I have brought up. You get me, and it takes a strong person to submit and surrender as you have."

"Sophie, a two-way street. We have given each other what we each need. And now?"

She laughed, "Right to the point as always, well, mostly. Your chastity device is a pretty secure one. With the integrated lock, it won't come off until I say so. However, before you could probably pull your, or as Ms. Circe would say, her cock, out of the cage having unauthorized fun. Now, with the PA lock, it's more secure. However, I know you could pick the locks."

"I wouldn't do that. That would defeat the bond of trust between us."

"Mas, I believe you and trust you. My ask will add a layer of difficulty to the chastity experience and your actual release."

"Ask away. I can always say no and negotiate from there."

"Hmmm, I don't think you will object."

Smiling, I said, "Then tell me, tell me."

"Okay, the reason I asked you to get a PA piercing was so I can attach your cock to the end of the cage as I have."

"That's it?"

"Yes, but not quite."

"Now I am curious. If all our other consented agreements hold, then I consent."

"Yes."

"What will you change?"

"Oh, Mas, it's easy. I was hoping you would say yes."

She showed me what looked like ordinary pliers, except when you closed the grips, the jaws opened, the reverse of the usual pliers. The same ones as when she removed the original piercing and inserted the lock. She was prepared.

"Have you done this before?"

"Only once, the piercer detailed the process. I have to be careful, that's all.

"Yes, please be careful!"

That brought a giggle from Sophie. She handed me the key to the lock through my cock piercing and cage. As I released the lock, she knelt in front of me, and with a little lube, she slid the lock out of my flesh and put it aside.

Sophie said, "That was easy." She cleaned the pliers and a ring with alcohol. The ring was a complete circle.

"I asked, "How does that work? It's a closed ring?"

"It's called a segmented ring."

This process was not going to be easy. I was already getting hard.

I pushed my dick around in the cage using Q-tips. The cage filled as I pushed and prodded. Sophie gently held the cage, assisting me until the end of my penis was at the end of the cage. Sophie put the pliers in the ring and squeezed a section fell out. She lubed up the end of the ring and manipulated it carefully into the open piercing easily accessible through the end of the cage.

I questioned, "You close it the same way?"

"Yes, using the pliers, this type of ring is more comfortable for what I intend. It will turn completely."

She pulled my penis tightly against the end of the cage. Sophie had drawn the ring so it protruded through the end of the cage and included one of the end bars of the cage within the ring. Putting the pliers in the ring and squeezing, inserting the missing section of metal, the ring was now a neatly closed circle. I was physically attached to my cage. Happy with the process, Sophie wiped away the excess lube. No escaping without removing the ring.

It didn't feel much different. The weight was the same, with only a slight tug at the end of the cage. So far, so good.

"Mas, remember, if there are any issues, you must tell me immediately?"

"Yes, any issues, I'll let you know ASAP."

"Good, this has to be fun for both of us, two sides of the same coin."

Sophie looked like the cat who had got the cream, satisfied and happy, and why wouldn't I want her to feel that way? I loved her. We spent the rest of the day pottering about doing the domestic chores every couple did. Cleaning, doing laundry, and sorting out bills.

Toward evening, a feeling of dread crept up on me because I expected a call announcing the arrival of another murder victim in the park. Sophie looked at me and noted my face.

"I'm thinking the same Mas. We are going to have a bad night. Can't Kenzo get more people patrolling the park tonight?"

"I'm sure he has, but it's a fucking big park. You would need an army, and even then, it probably wouldn't be enough. This drop has been planned for a while. They just have to execute."

"I hope it's not another one like Carol-the torture is what gets me. I don't understand it."

"Until we get perp, we probably won't know. It could be any number of things. The killer or killers could be using the victims to relive the saint's martyrdom, substituting them for their guilt, warped revenge for something imagined or actual, who knows. It's very personal."

"How do you mean?"

"I think they are going after these victims specifically, not because they are LGBTQ, although that does play into it somewhere. We need to find the why."

Sophie had pulled me back into the abyss of this case, and in a way, I was glad I would be expecting Kenzo's call when it came, and I was sure it would.

Chapter Ten

The phone burst into life, and its strident tones were what I had been expecting. Sleep had not come easily and was undoubtedly not restful. I was fully awake on the first ring, seeing Sophie was also awake.

"Yeah, Kenzo? You're on speaker." I looked at the clock-five twenty-seven.

"Yes, we got another one. I'll text you the details and location. It's Jeremy, and he's a mess. Don't need to bring Sophie."

"Screw that, Kenzo. I am in."

"You'll have to do with scene photos. Sorry, Sophie, no disrespect."

"None taken, thanks for thinking of me."

"Mas, look for my text. Wait until most of us are gone before you start poking around. I'll leave instructions to allow you in, and make sure you bring your professional IDs.

"Got it, what's your timeline?"

"Give us another hour to clear out. We got a call at two twenty that one of the patrols had found a body. We set up cameras at each entrance to the park. We are reviewing all the camera recordings to see if we can identify the vehicle and perp."

"Good luck. I hope you get it."

"Yeah, me too. We are also interviewing all the foot traffic. They may have seen something."

"We will be there. I assume the ME will be doing this one top priority?"

"She's already on her way in."

"Catch up later. Breakfast is on us if you can get away."

"Huh, doubt it, but thanks anyway."

He clicked off the call. We looked at each other. Sophie frowned and started to get dressed. I shrugged, checking the clock for a timeline to leave for the park. We couldn't do anything until we saw the crime scene and got the data on Jeremy. His partner still missing was an anomaly. There were several options. Ashton was responsible for Jeremy's death and on the run, or he was scared and in hiding—neither of those made any sense. Ashton was taken and would be next unless we could find him.

Dressed and ready to go, we carried our coffee, not bothering to eat. I didn't feel hungry. Sophie felt the same way. The location directions Kenzo texted took us to the area on John F Kennedy Drive known as *'Portals of the Past.'* A folly if there ever was one, an old Greek-style building on a small lake.

JFK Drive is one of the main arteries through the park, but no one takes it unless it's for the scenery. Fulton Street is parallel and much quicker. We pulled over a hundred yards short of the crime scene tape and walked up to the closest officer with our creds ready for inspection. He said he had been authorized to let us through. I thought I recognized one of the other officers and nodded to him. He came over, and I was right. He said he remembered me for my days in the SFPD. He looked older and had three stripes on his sleeve. His only comment was.

"Don't fuck up our crime scene."

We didn't. There wasn't much to 'fuck up.' The body had been dumped on the side of the road. There was no significant blood in the area. Killed elsewhere and dumped here in the park. The location was interesting. Approximately halfway between Great Highway and Stanyan Street, the east and west ends of the park, and close to Crossover Drive. We didn't bother taking any photos. We would have access to the PD's photos. Taking our time, we walked the entire area around the scene, looking for anything. We didn't find anything the PD hadn't already discovered, but I wanted to get the feel of the place.

As we returned to the SUV, Sophie asked, "Do you think the location, *'Portals to the Past,'* has any meaning to the perp? Or just a coincidence, a convenient location to easily dump a body."

"I think everything they do has some purpose. Everything they've done has been thought out, deliberately and meticulously. I'd be surprised if there are any forensics."

"Tire tracks, maybe, but I agree with you. Let's get out of here."

"We will have to wait for the PD reports and the MEs. I guarantee she will do this one in record time."

"Call Kenzo and get breakfast."

"Yes, he'll probably beg off."

Surprisingly, Kenzo accepted our offer of breakfast at La Promenade Café. Sunday hours were eight a.m. and Balboa Street was near the park's northern edge. Parking was easy on a Sunday morning, and we had time to spare. We waited in the SUV until eight rolled around.

Being the first customers in, we had our pick of the tables, choosing one toward the back of the café. Kenzo arrived a few minutes after we had ordered. His order was.

"Just coffee for me."

Sophie said, "That's not breakfast. You have to eat, Kenzo. Remember, this is on us." That raised a tired smile, and he reluctantly added a breakfast sandwich.

I asked him, "How are you holding up?"

"Not as well as I want or should be. I want this one. What he does to the vics is brutality for pleasure. The pressure from everywhere is getting worse. It's like they think I don't want to get this solved."

"Spit it out, you can talk to us, rant at me and Sophie. You need to get out the frustration. We can take it."

"You guys are the only ones I can talk to. I am the team lead, so I have to be calm and collected and deflect all the crap so the team can do the work. I've never had a case like this one, with almost no forensics to track. This dude hasn't made any mistakes."

I said, "Yet. You know killers always make mistakes. Besides, he may have already made a mistake, and we haven't recognized it yet."

"Nice pep talk, Mas, and bullshit, other than the part about them always making a mistake. This one is very good."

Sophie said, "We have a lot of data and are still dredging through it. Something will give."

Kenzo stared into his coffee before saying, "I know, but how many more bodies have to show up first? When you have nothing to work with, it's hard to work. All the guys are good investigators but need something to work with. We'll see how this one adds to the profile."

I said, "I'll put money on them, adding to the Homophobic angle, not the religious."

"Mas, you still going on about the religious part being the primary reason for all this? Give it a break. Jeremy was wearing an evening dress, so yes, the kink theory is still valid."

"Well, Father Benny is praying for our success, and I feel he agrees with me. By the way, he is out there for a priest, and I liked him."

"You don't know the half of it. He arrived in the summer of love, tripped out, followed the Grateful Dead for a while, and then stayed here. He volunteered for Vietnam as a medic, the only way he would go. Purple hearts, I know he was injured at least twice, commendations for bravery under enemy fire, etcetera. He comes home and is vilified for going to that shitty war. Somehow, he managed to get ordained and worked in all sorts of shelters and Free clinics before they were called non-profits. Managed to pry open the wallets of the SF high-fliers to fund AIDS research. Worked through the AIDS epidemic doing stuff no one else would do, like holding the patients and caring for them, giving them last rights. I know he's pissed off a lot of church higher-ups. He's one of the good guys and almost makes me believe."

I added, "We have all seen too much to believe, although I agree, he's one of the good guys."

"Thanks for the distraction. I have to get back. You will get the reports as soon as I get them, photos, the whole enchilada. Still didn't come from me-right?"

Sophie said, blankly, "What didn't come from

you?"

"Exactly. I'll call Marie and let her know the drop."

We said our goodbyes and separated, us to home and Kenzo back to his office. That part of Police work I didn't miss. We didn't have anything planned for the day and had completed most, if not all, of our domestic chores the previous day. At a loose end, I said I was going into the office. I didn't know what I would do there. I had to get out and think with no distractions. Sophie said OK and would call me later. I was walking to the office on a bright sunny day, surrounded by all the Sunday people out and about enjoying the day, while we had the dark shadow of another murder victim hanging over us.

We had all been working hard on this case. Kenzo and the PD, with all their resources, were on it twenty-four-seven. Our little troop was also committed to assisting, doing whatever we could. Nothing is enough until the perp is caught. You have to realize what you have control over and what you don't. You can't just wish a case closed. Thinking we needed to be more efficient in what we were doing, the volume of data was too much for us, even with the help of computer genius Fiend. Computers can only take you so far. The old saying about computer programs is if you put crap in, you get crap out.

We didn't have crap, we just had too much data to go through efficiently. Think Mas, how can we work smarter, not harder? Convinced these crimes were personal and that the victims were all somehow connected. We needed to make a connection. One connection would be a start, and that would lead to another.

To get into the right frame of mind, I reread the three autopsy reports. Frankie and Sean…I almost knew by heart. Carol, not so much. The autopsy revealed that she had been burned alive. Her body was severely charred, and there was no evidence of her being restrained with shackles- it didn't mean she hadn't been.

The data we did have would lead to the answer. How to use it to our advantage. Murder is usually a good motive for revenge killings, but we haven't found anything so far to link anyone to a revenge motive. Suicide is not usually a motive for revenge. Suicide is a solo endeavor, and it crushes the suicide's family, who often blame themselves incorrectly in most cases. Fuck I needed something to hang an idea or theory on. Doodling, I began listing ideas, theories, motives, and anything that popped into my head, and it didn't have to be logical. How logical is it to kill people in the same manner as ancient saints?

My list was all over the place, distilling it down to what we knew and was a fact in one column against all my wacky ideas in another. We knew the victims were not randomly chosen. No, we believed they were specifically chosen. They were all Kink, most partnered, one not. Both genders had been targeted. All were successful in their professional life, a mix of employed and self-employed.

They were all held for several days before being killed. The shackles and the associated overtones of bondage persuaded the PD into thinking the perp was targeting the Kink community. I didn't think so. Rope was more popular in the kink community for bondage.

Metal shackles were employed, because they were secure.

The victims were held in a location where the perp felt confident enough to torture and kill them without discovery. There would have been a considerable amount of blood and cleanup necessary. How many properties in San Francisco would meet the isolation and soundproof criteria? Torturing people was not a quiet pastime.

In the other column, my wild ideas and theories are most improbable or outright wrong. Someone who was cleaning up SF of LGBTQ folks, one by one. Revenge for an unsolved murder. Killing members of the Gay community for a slight or imagined slight, maybe they got hit on by a gay person. They were told to do it by god. Perhaps by killing people in the manner of the saints, they would be redeemed- that was a bizarre one. Atone for something they did or didn't do using the chosen victims as a sacrifice.

Whatever the originating issue was, the origination was an explosive mix of religion, homophobia, and death. We had to find the initiating cause, which was easier said than done.

The next step for me was the police reports and the ME's report on Jeremy. Then hope we would have enough leads, or any leads, to find his partner before the three-week pattern repeated. Not a satisfactory outcome to my thinking, but it was what it was, and I felt better for having done it.

The rest of the day was spent with Sophie and a neighbor's family who was celebrating the return of their oldest son, safely back from an overseas tour in the military.

****

Monday crept around, and we woke to a marine layer that would last too long into the day. The choice was to stay in bed and be depressed or get up and go to the office and be miserable until the sun did its job. What a choice, I decided the office would be the best course. Sophie was awake with me.

She said, "I need to get in and look at what we have and consult with Fiend to see if we can develop a better way of doing things. Would you bring breakfast to the office?"

"Yes dear, of course dear, it will be my pleasure dear."

"Careful, Mas, sarcasm could misplace a certain key."

At least she said it with a smile, and I knew she could and would play with my head regarding my release from chastity- and I loved it.

"Anything in particular?"

"Avocado toast would be good."

"Done."

She left, and I pottered about, slowly getting into the day. I made breakfast and had another cup of coffee. Now, I felt ready to meet the demands of the day. The marine layer was not my friend, and it affected my mood just as a sunny day got me up and out, ready for anything.

Sophie's breakfast request was called in and ready for me when I got to the café.

I greeted Marie as I entered the office. Sophie was already deep in conversation with Fiend. I placed her breakfast on her desk, and she blew me a kiss. She didn't miss a beat with Fiend.

From the previous week's data, Marie and I had been reviewing the death certificates, looking for anything odd or unusual, and no, we hadn't found anything to raise any suspicions. Back to that tedious chore, but it had to be done. We had to cover all the bases thoroughly, and that took time, which meant slowly. Rush and hurry are best friends with mistakes. Marie mumbled she was going out. I waved and returned to reviewing dead people.

Marie returned quickly and dropped a large envelope on my desk. "Present from Kenzo."

That got my attention immediately. Ripping open the sealed envelope, I found the ME's report. Damn, that was fast, she must have broken all records to get it done that fast. Her standard MO was days, if not weeks, with every 'T' crossed and every 'I' dotted. I was glad she'd broken the pattern.

Starting with the photographs, Kenzo was right. Jeremy was a mess. The dress was torn and blood-stained. He had been severely tortured, with bruises and lesions all over his naked body. Broken bones in his hands and feet were not life-threatening but excruciatingly painful, which I assumed was the intent. The exterior damage indicated that Jeremy would probably have some serious internal injuries to go along with the external.

The torture was systematic and thorough, almost clinical, and it was a means to an end…the replication of a dead saint. I would review Father Benny's list after I had read the autopsy report. Dressed in women's clothing, added to the victim's humiliation, and in this case, I would bet there was evidence of shackles on Jeremy's wrists and ankles. Where the hell was

Ashton?

For sure, I would not be showing Sophie these photographs. Reading the autopsy report was like Jeremy had been in a major auto accident. His list of injuries was significant, and none were accidental. They were inflicted callously and deliberately by another human.

The ME concluded Jeremy had died of blood loss and shock. The report was clinical in its description of the damage Jeremy had suffered. That was the ME's job. Reading between the lines, it wasn't anger. She was outraged that another human would do this damage to another and leaped off the page. In my time, I had seen some nasty corpses. Only the worst car wrecks were equal to what had been done to Jeremy.

Father Benny's list was my next stop. I looked down the list, and then again, nothing stood out as a match for this killing. The only saints that came close were a couple of pairs of saints, and the closest of those were two third-century Roman soldiers, Sergius and Bacchus.

Converted to Christianity, their conversion was discovered when they refused to join in what they considered pagan rituals. They were arrested and beaten, forced to wear women's clothes to humiliate them. Bacchus was tortured to death, and Sergius survived the torture for several more days before being beheaded.

Oh shit, that is why Ashton couldn't be found. The killer had taken Ashton as well. I was sure he would show up in Golden Gate Park, his head separated from the rest of him and possibly in the same area as where Jeremy was dumped. That would be a considerable risk;

I had to get hold of Kenzo. He didn't pick up. It must have been significant.

Wait a few minutes before the next dial. What could the Police do? Set up cameras on motion sensors, like the ones used to record wild animals, to back up the ones at all the entrances. Kenzo and his team had to be running all the license plates through the DMV database. Which should be an easy get for Kenzo.

Suppose the perp used the exact vehicle as the one used for the Sunday drop. Match the plate, and they would be caught. The camera idea was our best chance so far at getting the perp. Redialing, still no answer. Sent a text, and an e-mail, where the fuck was he?

This idea was too important to wait on, and we didn't know if Ashton was still alive. If he was, he was on a short timeline. Sergius survived Bacchus by several days, that was more than two. Wednesday night would be the first possible drop if they were going to follow the story of the two saints, which is what I expected.

God damn, where in hell was Kenzo. My phone buzzed-Kenzo.

"Where's the fire? I was getting my ass chewed off by the police commissioner himself, no less. What's up?

"Listen, I think Ashton will be the next body to drop, and it won't be in three weeks. I was going over the list of saints from Benny and."

"For god's sake, Mas, will you leave the religious crap out of this."

'Shut up and listen, Ashton will be dumped, probably in or near the same spot as Jeremy. Wednesday night, at the earliest, he will have been tortured and beheaded. Look up Saints Sergius and Bacchus. Get motion sensor cameras at Jeremy's drop sight. You can thank me later."

"Mas, this is crazy. You got to let this obsession go. The profilers agree religion is part of this, but not the main driver."

"Just set up the cameras. I'm wrong, no harm, no foul. If I'm right, you may get the perp. See ya around, Kenzo."

Ending the call was not what I wanted to do. I wanted Kenzo to set up the cameras and succeed for multiple reasons. Well, if the PD wouldn't set up cameras, we would. We still had the motion-activated cameras used in the Bodies on the Bridge case. Looking up, Sophie stared at me, and Marie stood in the doorway.

"What?" I asked.

Marie was the first to comment. "You were shouting."

Sophie continued, "You were loud, saying that Ashton would show up dead. Explain, please."

"Marie picked up the ME's report, and I read it. You don't want to. I tried to reference the killing to the list that Father Benny sent over, and two sets of male saints kinda matched, but only one where the saints were killed days apart. Ashton is missing, and I think he was taken and will show up in a few days-not, three weeks. I tried telling Kenzo, but he didn't want to hear about the religious part. The profilers still think it's more about homophobia and kink, with Jeremy being in a dress, etc."

Sophie said, "Okay, so what do we do?"

How I loved this woman. No questions just

unconditional support.

"You don't think I'm crazy?"

Marie and Sophie laughed and commented, "I wouldn't go that far, but you are usually right with this stuff."

Sophie added, "If you are sure, what can we do that the police can't?"

"We still have those motion-activated cameras, right?"

"Of course, what are you thinking?"

"If the PD won't set up cameras, we will-actually you will."

"Not a problem. Do you want a live feed, recorded, or both?

"Both, if we miss them on the live feed, we will have evidence to follow up on."

"How will we work this?"

"We will be parked near the site looking at live feed. We can't be too close, or it may spook the perp. These are going to be long nights. If I'm right, it won't be many."

Marie nodded and said, "I'm in."

I started to protest, as did Sophie. Marie held up her hand. "Enough. I am a partner in this business, and I can watch a screen just as well as you guys. Besides, Chung is traveling, and the nights get lonely, so how does this stake-out work with the three of us?"

God bless Marie. Three people with one always resting on a stake-out is much better than two.

Next, Sophie would pick up the cameras. We would install them at the crime scene, and then it would be a matter of waiting. Patience would be vital in catching this psycho, which was the primary mission.

We had to hurry up and wait, and by that, I mean we had to quickly install the cameras and then wait. Sophie left to collect all the equipment. We would need to place the cameras securely.

I paced the office, thinking maybe this was the break we needed. Just to confirm I wasn't crazy, I called Father Benny.

The church receptionist answered, "Yes, Father Benedict is available. One moment, please."

"Mas, is everything alright?"

"No, not really. I need to run something past you. Got a minute?"

"Yes, of course."

I ran the scenario past him. I wanted his opinion on my theory of Sergius and Bacchus.

"Mas, I think you have a good theory, and I agree with you. The next victim will be Jeremy's partner, which will be soon—certainly not in three weeks. No one in Roman times lasted three weeks of torture. God save their souls."

"Thanks, Benny. It helps to know I'm not too far out there."

"Sadly, I think you are correct. I will pray for you, wishing peace on you and yours, Mas."

"Thanks, Benny."

As I ended the call, I could hear the sadness in his voice. His sadness could not dampen my energy for the plan to trap the perp. Sophie returned with everything we needed to install the cameras.

Arriving at the site on JFK Blvd, it was almost empty. Crime scene tape was still in evidence. Sophie and I scouted the area for suitable locations to put the cameras. There were enough trees, lamp posts, and bushes to install our four cameras. I followed Sophie's lead on where we installed them.

Two facing one way, two the other, making sure one in each direction was angled to get license plates. Thankfully, California vehicles had front and back plates. The cameras were secure. Sophie checked the feed on her laptop, and all four were up and running. She didn't like the angle on one, so I adjusted it until she gave me a thumbs up.

Sophie had switched them off and would reactivate them at midnight on Wednesday. There was no point having them on any sooner. We left the site and drove to Fulton Street, the closest road to that area of the park. When we started our vigil, we would try to find a parking spot between 25th and 30th Avenues', the two closest entrances to the park. On the park side, 25th Ave split into Crossover Drive and Transverse Drive. Transverse Drive was the nearest intersection on JFK Blvd to the drop site.

With this location, the perp had multiple choices for entry to the drop site and various routes to escape. We had to prepare to quickly adapt to which direction they chose for their getaway. Catching them at the drop site was unlikely. Getting info on the vehicle and following them was a better bet, but not foolproof.

I wish Kenzo had believed me. If the perps escaped the containment area, using the PD resources for containment and helicopter coverage would be much better than our unofficial team of three.

On the way back to the office, I asked Sophie, "Would you pull the Police reports connected to this last drop? I want to see if they got anything off the cameras they placed at all the entrances. By now, they must have run all the plates."

"Sure, that's an easy one."

Our back door into the police department computer system had been a godsend, and we protectively treasured it. We still wanted everything Kenzo gave us and could provide us with, and it didn't hurt that we had our backdoor access. Sophie was surprised that it hadn't been discovered and nullified.

Bad news. All the plates that had been caught on camera had come back as kosher. There were no red flags there. I wondered if they had matched the plates to the vehicle. If you used stolen plates that hadn't been reported as stolen, it would not be in a report or show up against a check. More work for Sophie.

She sighed and agreed to look into the plates and the vehicles they were registered to. The list was manageable, using the drop's time parameters. Although the park was open twenty-four hours, there was little traffic that late at night or, that early in the morning, even on the main thoroughfares. That was another day done.

Chapter Eleven

Sophie was up and had the coffee on before I surfaced. We made good time getting to the office. As Sophie booted up her computer, I thought about the coming night and how we could use the three of us most efficiently on the stake-out.

The body drop would probably be a late-night, early-morning event. Fewer people, tired park rangers. That puts the timeline between two a.m. and four a.m. when the body is at its lowest ebb—putting Marie and Sophie on the early shift. I would relieve Marie. Sophie could crash on the back seat of the SUV while I monitored the cameras' live feed.

We briefly met at lunch to review what we had and the upcoming stake-out. Both Sophie and Marie agreed to be on the early shift. That settled, we planned for food and coffee breaks. The bushes in Golden Gate would have to make do for a restroom, which is easier for me than the two women, life on a stake-out.

Marie said, "I'll take care of snacks. Nothing too heavy. We need to be awake, right?"

Sophie and I chorused, "Yes."

That sorted, we went back to work for the afternoon, on the understanding we would be closing up early, going home, getting ready by having a timed nap, and dressing for the night. People who don't live in NorCal think that all of California is always warm. Not here. Once the fog rolls in, it gets chilly really fast. We all had a jacket or sweatshirt in our vehicles, always.

I hoped being parked on Fulton Street late at night as a couple, we would not have any issues with the Police. Sophie had packed a spare power source for her laptop as a backup, just in case. We didn't need to dress for a covert operation. Our timed nap passed quickly. I had slept, if somewhat fitfully. Ready to roll, Marie would call for Sophie and pick up my SUV. When I switched shifts, I would take Marie's car, and she would go home directly from the stake-out.

Marie was on time and looked anxious, nervous energy. She rarely was involved in the active part of our investigations. Whenever she had been, she held up her end.

Kissing Sophie on her way, we had agreed if anything happened before I arrived, Marie was to call me, and Sophie was to call Kenzo immediately. They were to follow the perp if they could do so safely. No crazy driving. Sophie had her weapon on her, not in her purse, hoping she wouldn't need it. This was primarily a surveillance operation. If the perp was seen, we pass the info on to the police and let them do what they were paid for and very good at.

There was no way I was going back to sleep, not with the adrenaline going and knowing Marie and Sophie were out there working the case. Running myself into a sweaty mess on the treadmill helped. I kept my phone on loud while I showered in case I got the call.

Feeling better, I dressed for the night...warmer than needed. I could take the sweater off. My weapon had been cleaned after my last visit to the gun range.

Cleaning it again, I loaded it with hollow points instead of the full metal jackets I used at the range. I didn't expect to need it tonight, but as the old saying goes; it is better to have it and not need it than to need it and not have it.

Waiting time is the slowest time in the world. Seconds feel like minutes. Eventually, it was time to move. I picked up Marie's car from my parking space and drove to Fulton Street, calling Sophie as I did.

She answered. "Nothing so far, a few cars and a couple of pickup trucks, some runners earlier, nothing in the last half hour."

"Good. Be with you shortly."

Driving east to west on Fulton, there was less parking on the park side of Fulton, so Sophie parked on the residential side of the road and luckily found a spot between 25th and 30th streets. I called to say I was on Fulton and would double park to switch with Marie. Marie was ready as I pulled up just in front of them. I got out, and Marie got in and moved off in seconds.

Joining Sophie, I asked, "How're you holding up?"

"Tired and bored. I am happy to see anything on the cameras. We had two trash pandas visit."

Laughing at how Sophie picked up the local slang—trash pandas were also known as raccoons—we settled in for more of nothing. Sophie had moved over to the passenger side and had her laptop on a stand on the central console so we could both observe the nothing that was happening. Lights coming, we sat up, eyes glued to the screen. Only a park ranger, the vehicle continued past, and the screen descended into darkness once again. The minutes turned into hours with only the occasional vehicle passing in either direction, and the return of the park ranger in the opposite direction on their regular route.

The day began with the sun coming up. Thankfully no marine layer this morning. The chill dissipated, and we both exited the SUV and stretched out. We were feeling good moving after sitting so long, even with breaks. This stake-out was as bad as I remembered them to be, and sadly, this was still our best shot at getting the perp. Nothing was going to happen in daylight, and we were both hungry.

Rather than trying to find somewhere around Fulton, we figured we would head back to North Beach and hit up one of our local favorites, Roma Café. Roma also opened earlier than most and would be by the time we made it back. True to form, the aroma of roasting coffee welcomed us. We chatted briefly with the manager and found seats outside to enjoy the waking up of San Francisco.

Marie would be the one holding down the fort today. Sophie and I would head home and crash, which we did. All the other work could wait until we had proven my theory, or not, regarding Ashton as the next victim. I was betting Ashton's body would show up within the next two or three nights. If it didn't, I was wrong, and he would appear on the three-week cycle.

The alarm volume was set lower so I would hear it and not disturb Sophie, who had done the longest stretch of surveillance. When I surfaced, it was early afternoon, with little on my phone in the way of messages.

I dressed and made it to the office for a late lunch with Marie, who said, "Nothing much happening. I've kept the office running between looking at license plates and checking them against the registrations. There are a few checks to sign, and that's about it. No results on anything else."

"Great. I'll sign the checks when we get back from lunch."

"No, Mas, you can sign them before we go. If you get a call or text, you'll be gone, and no signed checks for me."

"Okay, okay, slave driver. How do you feel today?"

"Not too bad. I had more sleep than you two. I assume nothing happened?"

"No, a few vehicles, the park rangers, and a few early-morning runners."

"Maybe we'll get something tonight."

"Maybe, if they stick to the pattern."

"Mas, you may be weird and drive me nuts, but I trust your judgment on shit like this."

"Thanks. I think there is a compliment in there somewhere."

"Seriously, Mas, I mean it. Whatever you need from me, ask, and it's yours."

"That's appreciated, Marie-honestly, without you, and now you and Sophie, I'm not sure I would have kept this shop open."

"What? You never said anything. It was that bad?"

"Yeah, pretty much. Simon's death hit me harder than I expected. I'm much better now. and looking forward, not back." Marie had been there when my business partner was killed in a hit-and-run. The grief was changing. I don't think it ever goes away, but it changes over time.

"Shit, I wish you'd told me."

"Not something I was ready to do then, not sure I am now. Anyway, we have bigger issues to solve. You up for another late night?"

"You bet your ass I am. Same as last night?"

"Yup, same as, and thanks for everything."

"Family Mas, family."

She turned away from me, and I knew she was also thinking of Simon."

I broke the spell, asking, "And those checks are where?"

"If you looked on that trash heap, you call a desk, you'd see a folder marked signatures required."

Now, that was the Marie we knew and loved! Quickly, I signed the checks and handed the file back to Marie, and we were off to lunch. We went to one of our favorite watering holes, and were quickly seated, catching the tail end of the lunchtime rush. We chatted about everything, and I brought up the subject of house hunting. Marie went off on a rant, declaring that San Francisco was conspiring against her and Chung to stop them from buying a house. They had lost five properties, being outbid, even though they had gone over the asking price.

Then I had a thought. My partner, Simon, had left me his house in the will, and I hadn't gotten around to clearing it and selling it. Sophie and I certainly didn't need two properties, not with the taxes I paid on both.

"How about you buy Simon's old place? I've been putting off selling it. If you are interested, it will stay in the family, as it were. But not if the memories are too sharp.

"Mas, are you kidding me?"

"Now, why would I do that to my second favorite

partner."

"Because you could. Can I talk it over with Chung when he gets back? This is not something for a phone conversation if you are serious."

"I am as serious as a heart attack. No rush. We can even do it over dinner if you like."

"I like. Do you think Sophie would object?"

"About what, keeping our partner and her partner, all of us, happy? I don't think so."

"You are the best, Mas." It looked like she was about to tear up when our food arrived. We attacked the food, which was always good here. The chef/owner cooked what he liked from whatever was good at the market that day, with just a few staples. Sated, we made our way back to the office. I sat thinking about the case and the probability of catching the perp tonight or whenever they showed up with another body.

There was still too much data. We had to narrow down the focus. Needle in a haystack, we had to make the haystack smaller and the needle bigger. Nothing came to me, and I was getting wound up for tonight's vigil. Marie would pick up the snacks as she had done the previous night. It was still too early, but we closed the office, and Marie went to the post office.

Arriving home, I found Sophie in the shower, which got me going and filled my chastity cage. The monthly massage sessions were working, keeping the physical stress down. The kink sessions did the same for our heads. We hadn't had a kink play session for a while, and I was thinking one would be suitable for both of us to decompress sooner rather than later.

My mind was wandering, and Sophie brought me back to reality. "Mas, got an eye full, enjoy the visuals?"

"I could show you if you like."

She chuckled and shook her head. "Not now, I have other things on my mind. We will need a play distraction soon."

"I was thinking the same thing."

"Patience is a virtue. I can't believe the difference between the work Mas, who can be patient as needed, and the outside of work, impatient horny Mas. I think chastity is good for you."

"I wouldn't change a thing, not a thing. I love you."

"I know, and I love you too, Mas, and you were worth waiting for. Now, let me get dressed for tonight."

Dinner was homemade pasta with a jar of a local restaurant's red sauce, topped off with some meatballs I had made a while ago from the freezer and needed eating—no alcohol tonight, coffee for later in thermos jugs. Sophie was getting itchy feet and wanted to start early.

"Take your time. It will probably be a waste of time and a long night. Chill out."

"Stake-outs are new to me. I wish I had more active experience. I was always stuck behind computer screens, and you are right. I didn't-don't know the results of a lot of my work. Here, I see it in real-time."

"Yeah, well, reality can be overrated."

We did chill, watched some crap on TV, which thankfully distracted Sophie. Marie called and said she was a few minutes out.

Sophie left with a kiss, saying, "I'll see you later."

She went to meet Marie in the reserved parking spot for the SUV. Switching cars, she was on her way to surveil the cameras from a parking spot on Fulton Street near the park entrance.

Me...? I had six hours to kill before I relieved Marie. The previous evening's regimen was repeated, running on the treadmill. Tonight, I cleaned an illegally purchased weapon, a long story. I showered and dressed for the night. Driving to the rendezvous was easy at two in the morning, with very little traffic. I made sure to obey all traffic signs and signals. The last thing I needed was to be pulled over for a stupid traffic violation.

Marie was ready, waiting for the switch. I double-parked, and I was out, Marie was in. It only took seconds before she was on her way. Sophie slid over to the passenger seat. I got in and adjusted the mirrors.

As I took the offered snack bar from her, I asked, "Anything going on?"

"Not much. Earlier was a little busier than last night, but nothing for us. Getting to know the park rangers' vehicles, one has a slightly off headlight. Not even wildlife so far. Do you think you could be wrong about the timing?"

"Maybe, possibly. I am sure the perp took Ashton and he is dead, or if they keep the three-week schedule, he will be."

"I don't get it. I...we aren't normal. Our Kink life is consensual, something we both need. No one gets hurt, well if one is counting a spanked ass as hurt. The killing is a pathology I just don't get."

"Good, that means you aren't mentally sick. The perp is over the edge, a psychopath, or someone who has had a psychotic break. We may never know the whole story. They may not understand the motivation, only the compulsion to continue."

"Great…wait vehicle coming."

The car passed the camera site, not stopping or slowing down, then everything went back to the dark screen. The screen was as dark as the previous night. The marine layer and cloud cover blocked out the moon. A slight reflection of the water by the folly was our only light. The cameras would work in low light but not very well in no light. We relied on the vehicles' lights, as we didn't have night vision cameras.

Vehicles came and went. The park rangers did their patrols, and the intervals between vehicles became longer. After three o'clock had passed, I wondered if I had been wrong. Sophie was dozing off, and I struggled to focus on the dark screen. Lights coming, I nudged Sophie, and she was immediately awake. The lights went out, and there were no turns for the vehicle to disappear.

"Quick which direction were they heading."

"Toward the 30th Street entrance."

A dark shape appeared near one of the cameras. Stopping, it seemed to wobble.

"Shit, it's them. Get ready. Call Kenzo. We have to try and follow them."

Starting the SUV, we were facing toward 30th Street, two blocks from the 30th Street entrance to the park near the Buddhist Association of San Francisco. They would have to put their lights on to drive on the streets. It was too risky not to put them on. They wouldn't want to be stopped by officers with nothing to do on a quiet night.

Sophie was talking to Kenzo. I wasn't listening. I was hyper-focused on the entrance to the park. YES, a white minivan. Lights went on as they paused at the intersection and turned up Fulton. They passed us, and I didn't get a good look at the driver, hoodie up, and a scarf over the lower part of their face. My impression was that the driver seemed small, certainly not what I expected.

Then again, I wasn't sure what to expect. Serial killers never look like what you expect. You build a picture in your mind of a monster the size of the Hulk with the looks of Freddy Kruger, and they turn out to look like the person next door, and you wouldn't give them a second look.

Doing a careful U-turn, I put my lights on and hung back, following them. Damn, they were turning back into the park at 25th Crossover Drive. I picked up speed, trying to keep them in sight without getting too close. They had multiple options going that way. South on Traverse Drive and Crossover Drive, through the park to Lincoln Way, to continue further south on Rte. 1 to Rte. 280. I didn't think they would be heading that far south. I thought maybe North on Crossover, drive into neighborhoods, or even stay in the park on JFK and out through to the panhandle and into those neighborhoods.

Careful. I didn't want to spook them. As I turned into the park, I killed my lights, moving closer to keep them in sight. No turn on Traverse Drive left. Crossover north and south, which? We would have to find out. Driving with no lights in the pitch-black night is not easy. I was afraid I would lose them as they approached the Park Presidio Bypass traffic lights, the north-south route. I had no choice but to turn on my lights.

A vehicle appearing didn't seem to faze the

minivan driver, driving carefully within the speed limit. As they approached the lights, they slowed down and then, as the light turned orange, sped up and made a left turn onto Park Presidio bypass. Shit, I couldn't follow them through a red light. That would be very suspicious. I waited until they had gone out of sight, then took a chance. There were no vehicles in sight, not even lights. I made a turn on red and floored it.

Sophie said, "Kenzo is sending a car to check the park site. He wouldn't believe it was a body drop until he had proof."

"Fuck him, we got to do this ourselves. Did you get the license plate of the minivan? I got some of it. We can use the camera data for the rest if I can't get it live."

"No, I couldn't make it out. Your partial is better than nothing."

The good thing about the Park Presidio bypass was that there were only turns once it left the park and crossed Fulton Street. The set of lights I saw up ahead had to be our target. Slowing down to the speed limit, I kept the same buffer distance between us and steady does it.

I asked, "Sophie, call Kenzo on my phone, on speaker."

His phone answered immediately. It wasn't him, a male voice asked who we were."

"Mas Hammett. Where is Kenzo?"

Lieutenant Otake is busy with police actions. May I take a message?"

"Screw that. We're following the minivan that did a body drop in the park, same site as before. Heading north on Park Presidio bypass, get some unmarked cars to help us and a chopper up."

"No, Mr. Hammett, You are not in charge of this operation. We do not take orders from civilians. We do this step by step by the book. If what you say is true, we will follow up and follow any and all leads."

"For Christ's sake, listen, *WE ARE FOLLOWING THE PERP,"* I was shouting, and I knew it. This was not going well.

"Mr. Hammett, you believe you are following the perp. When we have proof, we will follow up. Stay out of this and let the Police department do its job."

He hung up on me, fuck, what the hell just happened. Oh well, we were on our own. I stole a quick look at Sophie, and she had a puzzled look on her face.

"What?"

"Kenzo's in trouble. I think he is being watched, if not monitored and surveilled himself. He is going to be the fall guy if this perp escapes. I've seen it happen in other government agencies I've worked with. They couldn't mess with me because I was a contractor, and most of my work was way off the books anyway. We need to get him a burner phone ASAP tomorrow or rather today."

That made sense of someone else answering his phone. Son of a bitch, Sophie had to be right on this.

"Text Marie and get her to drop off a burner phone to Wanatabe's or the dojo, whichever opens first. Do we still have a couple of burners at the office?"

"Yes. I'm on it. You drive."

Hearing Sophie text a message for Marie, I concentrated on driving. We were heading north and trying to catch up with the minivan without appearing to hurry. Lights ahead showed me, it was the minivan. I hung back, slowing to match their speed.

Crossing Fulton Street, heading directly north toward the Presidio, and making a late right on Balboa Street. I was far enough behind when I signaled a right so it didn't look like I was tailing them.

None or very little traffic was a blessing and a curse. A blessing because I could see the minivan from a distance, a curse because there was little traffic to hide me if they were vigilant, and I expected them to be. A left on 10th Ave, then a right on Anza, they were taking precautions, with the zig-zag route, now a straight run, good move, it would be evident if anyone was following them.

Taking a chance, I turned left on 3rd Avenue, raced up to Geary Blvd, made a right, and then slowed down. It was a risk that paid off. They had made a left on Arguello Blvd and were now crossing Geary. I waited until the two cars coming in the opposite direction had passed, and I turned left just in time to see them turning east onto Euclid. I made the same turn. They were pulling ahead, little by little.

As soon as they turned left several blocks up on Parker, I raced to make up some distance. It was a traffic circle, not a stop or light, and that was good as it didn't slow me down much. As I turned, I saw them make a left onto California Street. When we got to the intersection, they were gone. Shit, I didn't see them left or right. I had to guess they made a right and then a left, no idea which one, or a right, and doubled back.

Gone, the closest we had been, and we fucking lost them.

"Please tell me you got the entire number plate."

"We never got close enough for me to see it clearly. I took photos, and maybe I can blow them up enough, and we still have the camera footage to go through. Even with lights off, hitting the brakes would give some light. Give me some time when we get to the office.

There was nothing to be done now except hope we had enough to get a full plate. We had a shot at getting them if we got the plate. We started to make our way back home.

Marie called asking, "The Dojo opens at six a.m. and Wanatabe's at six-thirty. Which would you prefer?"

"Wanatabe's. Then leave a message for Kenzo at the police department. Just say your order to go, emphasizing the word GO. Will be ready as soon as you arrive. He'll know what it means. How come you answered the text, you should have been asleep."

"I was, no problem, Mas."

"Well, thanks anyway for this and sorry for disturbing your night."

"All part of the job, right?"

"Yes, partner."

At least that raised a smile with Sophie. "We need to rest, or I will have to get data from the camera and scrub it along with the photos I took. No promises, Mas. At least you were right about the drop."

"Great. That means I was right about another murder."

"And right about the link to the saints. Hey, credit where credits are due. You need to tell Father Benny about this. Now, perhaps the profilers will change the emphasis of their profile to include more religious emphasis."

"We still don't know if there was a body dump. We assumed it was because that vehicle stopped at the site.

They could have been crime scene fans."

"Sophie, way to pop my bubble, but you're right. We don't know if Ashton was dumped. We're returning to the park, and it's still too early for the Café."

"Mas, I believe you're right and onto something with the religion part. I didn't at first, but now I'm all in."

"Thanks. That means a lot. Let's get there and hopefully the scene hasn't been messed up. We should probably recover our cameras as well. They won't be using that site again.'

"That's for sure."

We were both tired and lost in our thoughts as we returned to the park. No need to zig-zag, so I took the quickest, and most direct route. Several police vehicles had a cordoned-off area right where we expected them to be. When Kenzo saw me, he shook his head in the negative, which I took to mean he couldn't be seen with us. Parking away from the herd of police vehicles, we observed a hive of activity. When the ME's van showed up, we knew there was a body. That vehicle did not show up for the injured, only the deceased. The question was, was it Ashton or a completely new victim?

We couldn't do anything. All our cameras were within the large, cordoned-off area, and the PD was not taking any chances of missing any forensics. They would surely find the cameras—nothing we could do about that. We would tell Kenzo about them when we had a chance.

Time to move on. I was starting to feel the effects of the long night. The adrenaline rush of following the minivan had worn off. We needed food and rest. The café was open when we arrived, and I had decaf for the first time in a long time. I wanted to sleep, not to be jittery. The breakfast sandwich hit the spot. The decaf was good for what it was. Hot, wet, and tasted like coffee. At home, we crashed, not bothering to undress.

Chapter Twelve

Our alarms went off in unison. I was up first. I'd had more rest than Sophie, although she was more used to doing the silly late-night hours. After a shower, I began to feel more human, especially after the first cup of real coffee. Sophie stirred and followed suit with a coffee and then a shower.

Marie had texted me that the burner phone had been dropped off at Wanatabe's and a message left for Lt. Otake at the precinct. Kenzo would get the reference to Wanatabes and hopefully would use the phone to call us unless he had completely flipped out.

The next call was to Father Benny. The office said he was busy with parishioners for at least a few hours. Leaving a message to call me at his convenience. It wasn't urgent.

We were ready to get to the office, the walk did us good. Marie was up and at us, hugs all around. It's good to know someone cared. I began by pulling up Google Maps and following the route the minivan had taken from the park to where I had lost them. Looking at it in the cold light of day, they had used tailing countermeasures. In case anyone was following them. They must have had several routes planned where they could lose anyone following them, which they had successfully done anyway.

The driver had to know that part of San Francisco

probably lived in the general area, which included the affluent neighborhoods of *Presidio Heights, Pacific Heights, and Cow Hollow*, with Cow Hollow being the newest and trendiest—too many ways and places to lose a tail. If Sophie could pull a complete license plate, that may give us a lead to work with. Even if we got a license plate, would the experienced perp not have thought of that, or could they be so arrogant it didn't matter? Every criminal makes a mistake sometimes, and this could be our big break.

The afternoon was dragging, and I felt an all-nighter's effects. My eyes felt heavy. A call with no number rang. I answered, "Kenzo?"

"Yes, sorry about last night. I have to be careful. I am being closely watched. One wrong step, and I'm media fodder and the fall guy on this one."

"Who answered your phone? It's always attached to you."

"Officer Ryan, supposedly to assist the investigation, and keep tabs on me. Just department politics."

It was Sophie who figured you could be in trouble. I was so pissed off I wasn't thinking. How did you find out you are being watched?"

"I still have a few friends in low places. A friend left an internal envelope on my desk- anonymously with a warning note."

"Anything we can do?"

"Yes. Help catch this fucker. We are out of leads. Everything we had has been investigated and reinvestigated, nada."

"We assume it was Ashton you found in the park this morning?"

"Yes, and I agree with you now. The religious part is much more important than we thought. It's a bastard that I couldn't do anything to assist you when you were following that van. Where did you lose him."

"We are not assuming it's him. Father Benny said don't assume. We thought it was a solo him, now after last night, a couple."

"That's a troubling thought. Are you sure the vehicle you were following was the perp?"

"Nearly one hundred percent. We lost them on California, I didn't want to get too close. They turned onto California and, by the time we got to the intersection, they were gone. There's very little traffic at that time of the morning."

"That was bad luck. Any idea where 'they' were heading?"

"I figure somewhere in Presidio Heights, Pacific Heights, or Cow Hollow. Those areas seemed most likely, I don't think, as far as the marina district."

"That covers a lot of ground."

"Better than the entire forty-nine square miles of San Francisco."

That got a laugh and comment, "True brother, true. I'm sorry I got you involved with this shit show."

Sophie, who had been listening, said, "Shut up, we volunteered and are in till the end."

"I like it, trust me. I want this one caught. Stops the killing and gets me out from under."

Sophie added, "When can we get the reports and photos of the scene."

"As soon as I can get them to you. The ME is already doing her thing. Seems this case had gotten under her skin. She completed her report on Jeremy in record time. That and anything else I have, I will drop off at one of the two usual spots. I'll use this phone to let you know when and where. Thanks, I gotta go."

The phone went dead. Well, that explained a lot. When we caught the culprit, I was going to visit Officer Ryan. That could wait. There are bigger fish to fry. Firstly, Sophie was going to attempt getting the entire license plate. Then, we could track that to the vehicle and on to the registered owner.

She disappeared behind her computer array, and I soon heard tapping away, and soon after that obscene language, then silence. An hour or so later, she asked, "Didn't you say that Kenzo had set up cameras at all the entrances to the park?"

"Yeah, why?"

"Because I just can't get the resolution on our recording clear enough to pick up the rest of the numbers, I have the first number and the letters, but no chance on the last three numbers. I want to review the PD's recording of all the vehicles entering and exiting the park. Starting with the exits the perp used last night, the PD cameras should have picked up the perp's plate. That should identify the one I need."

"That sounds like an excellent idea. Can you use our back door?"

"That is where I'll start. I'll ask Kenzo if I can't get it."

"Get to it then."

"I beg your pardon?"

That key magically appeared and was twirling around her fingers, with a sinister smile on her lips.

"I'll have dinner ready when you get home."

"Excellent response, Mas. I think it's playtime, and

we both need it." We laughed and kissed deeply.

"We're two sides of the same coin."

"Yes, Mas, we are. We are both tired, and I think tonight will be an easy one for both of us. If you consent, I would like you to try a new item."

"Happy to look and see, as always."

"Good, now leave me alone to finish my tasks."

"Yes, Ma'am."

The day was looking to have an interesting ending. My cock was responding, filling the cage, and my mind was wondering what Sophie's new item could be. I would find out when the time came. She had never asked anything of me, kink-wise, that I had not agreed to. Her requests ranged from the simple ones to ones that pushed my buttons. She stretched my limits and boundaries, always with love and care.

Until Sophie had the data from the PD, there was nothing practical I could do at the office. Visiting the gun range for practice was my only option. It was not busy, and one side was empty of patrons. The owner agreed to rapid fire, as no one else was on my side. Otherwise, he did not allow rapid fire. Two hundred rounds went quickly, but I felt better covered in GSR. The shredded targets went into the recycle bin, and my brass was swept into a pile.

Home, I stripped down my weapon and cleaned it. Cleaning was a process that was second nature to me. My weapon had never let me down—not the one I used in the PD or this one. They say cleanliness is next to godliness, and I say cleanliness is next to your weapon working perfectly when you need it to. Taking a shower to remove the grime from the range and clean clothes, I felt tired but refreshed, and it would still be an early night.

Right dinner. Something light, baked fish, with salad and garlic bread. A quick trip to the local fish market for the protein and the bakery for a sourdough loaf for the garlic bread. We had everything else.

Timing called Sophie, "Sorry to disturb you. What time are you expecting to be home?"

"Soon. I have the recordings from the PD, but I'm going cross-eyed reviewing them. I'm too tired to concentrate on that much detail. I'll pick it up tomorrow."

"Good move. We have over two weeks until we get another murder. At least, I'm hoping they stick to the pattern."

"I was so focused that I had forgotten we were still on their timeline. I was looking back, not forward. I'll be home soon. I love you."

She hung up, wishing I hadn't reminded her about the perp's timeline. Knowing how Sophie worked, she would start pushing herself and probably too hard. I would have to take care of her and make sure she took care of herself.

Dinner is prepared and ready to go. Salad made and fish ready to go in the oven, it wouldn't take long. Bread toasted and ready for the homemade garlic butter.

I was thinking about how Sophie and I had met, the tragedies that brought us together, and how we were moving forward together. I had never met anyone like her—not in the PD, civilian, or the Kink worlds, and she was worth the wait. Kink was part of me as it was her, but not all of us. We meshed so well on so many fronts, and of course, we had our differences, and those made everything else better.

Sophie arrived looking tired. I handed her a glass of chardonnay.

"Thank you, kind sir."

"Take your shower, and dinner will be ready when you're done."

"Excellent, and after dinner, we can have dessert."

And by that comment, I knew Sophie's alter ego, Ms. Circe, would be in attendance for playtime.

Freshly showered, Sophie came into the kitchen wearing only her dark green satin robe. Her tits jiggled as she moved, nipples hard under the shimmering fabric. Oh hell, the sight of her set my dick hardening in its cage again. I could never get enough of Sophie. We kissed, and she tasted fresh.

She asked, "How long for dinner? I'm hungry."

"Everything is ready but the fish and garlic bread. Minutes."

She walked over to the dining room table with her half-finished glass of chardonnay. Her robe moved as she walked, her leg exposed, then covered, exposed, and covered again. The satin made subtle sounds as she moved. All my senses were receiving signals, and it was almost sensory overload. Sometimes Sophie did this deliberately, sometimes not. Not that it mattered. The effect on me was the same. I wanted her, all of her.

Dinner was served, and we enjoyed the food, conversing about generalities and San Francisco. Sophie couldn't get enough of the stories about her adopted city, and I knew a lot of stories. Food consumed; a silence descended over us. Anticipating what was to come, two individuals joining, giving, and receiving, we became one.

Sophie asked, "I would like to try something different if you will indulge me?"

"What did you have in mind?"

"I thought we could try a single glove on you. A different feel with a similar effect as the hogties. Would you be willing to try it?"

"Under the usual safety rules?"

"Of course, all safety measures."

"Then I am in. Anything else I should know about?"

"Oh no, Mas, I must keep you a little off balance. Tonight, there is nothing that we haven't done before. You, go into the bedroom and strip. Ms. Circe will join you presently."

The feeling of submitting was starting to rise. The sensation? A letting go. For the next however long it was, I was no longer in charge of me. I was someone else's responsibility, and I could do nothing about it but accept the situation and what would happen to me. Sophie, in a way, was freeing me, and the tension started to melt away. No thinking, just feeling. People not in the kink world seem to have a hard time understanding that being bound or submissive to another can be very freeing.

By focusing and exerting her control over me, Sophie found her release. In a trusting relationship, it works and is intensely satisfying. Two sides of the same coin, a mantra we lived by.

Entering the bedroom, she dimmed the lights and lit scented candles. Ankle cuffs, joined by a short chain, awaited me on the bed, along with my leather posture collar and a red leather single glove. Quickly, I undressed. Naked except for the cock cage, I attached the ankle cuffs, locked them, and knelt, waiting for Ms. Circe to join me. Not knowing what she would require of me added to the uncertainty and excitement. Hoping she would want me to go down on her, a pleasure for both of us. The bedroom had not been set up for that.

Ms. Circe entered with a swish of her satin robe, demanding, "Mas on your feet, please."

I stood, trying to control my breathing, waiting for the next instruction.

"Now, bring your hands and arms around behind you."

Done, I felt the cool leather slide up between my arms and my back—the actuality of what was being done meshed into a surreal vision. The right front strap was crossed over my chest, pulled snugly over my left shoulder, and buckled closed. Ms. Circe repeated the process with the left strap. My arms were encased in a leather tube with no means of escape, and Ms. Circe was not done with me.

She stood behind me, drawing the laces on each side of the tube a little tighter. With each pull, my arms were pulled further behind me. This action forced me to push out my chest. The feeling of restriction was heady, and my arms were to the point where I could not move anymore.

Ms. Circe asked, "Is this too tight, or can you go some more."

In my submissive role, I was mute unless I was asked a direct question that required a response, and my answer had to be succinct.

"A little tighter, Ms. Circe."

"Excellent. I instruct you to use your safe word immediately if it becomes painful. Understood?"

"Yes, Ms. Circe."

Still not finished, a strap was fastened around my wrists. With this last action, I was genuinely trussed until Ms. Circe released me.

One more item to complete her wishes, "Kneel where you are, facing the bed."

Complying, I knelt, and once I was in the correct position facing the bed, I felt a tug on the end of the single glove and the chain between my ankles. Ms. Circe had clipped the single glove to the chain between my ankles. I would not be going anywhere.

"Now for the show. An easy night for both of us, as I said."

Watching her every move, I wanted to touch her. I always did when I couldn't. She arranged the pillows on our bed so she could sit up more. She turned and smiled at me, pulled at the bow holding her robe together, and the satin parted. I viewed a slice of her from neck to feet. My cage had filled as soon as she started putting me in the single glove. Now it felt as if I would burst the cage. The contrast between her tanned flesh and the dark green of the robe emphasized by shimmering satin had me exhaling slowly.

The robe dropped to the floor, but I didn't notice. All my senses were riveted on Sophie in all her naked glory. Everything about her, I wanted to drink it in, as if it were the last drink I would ever have. My heart was pounding, and my penis throbbed in its prison, bouncing with every heartbeat.

Ms. Circe, naked in front of me, knelt and attached something to the end of my chastity cage, not heavy. I had felt this before, and it was a remote vibrator. Shit, I would get a release of sorts, not the way I wanted, it rarely was, but I would still enjoy every second.

Ms. Circe climbed onto the bed facing me, sitting almost upright with her legs spread. Reaching the nightstand, she picked up a vibrator. Already glistening with lube, she applied more.

She smiled at my predicament and said, "Time for our fun."

She would vibe herself off in front of me, and I couldn't do anything about it. Moving my arms was out of the question, but I tried anyway. I was trapped. I had consented, and I loved and hated this simultaneously. Wanting to be with her, in her. She knew exactly what she was doing and how it would affect me. She reveled in her power over me, and I surrendered willingly.

Ms. Circe slowly moved the vibe down over her mound of Venus, staring at me, sliding the vibrator between her legs. Her eyes closed, and her head tilted back. She was ready. Her left hand gripped the sheets as she teased herself, playing with her body. All I could do was watch sweet torture, and I was aroused. There had to be precum at the end of my dick; I couldn't look. I didn't want to take my eyes off her.

Watching her was watching someone who knew their body intimately. She understood what to do and when for the maximum extended pleasure. At this point, each movement had a purpose.

Suddenly, I was aware that the end of my cage was vibrating, low and slow. I didn't even see her pick up the remote. She was lost in the vibe between her legs. I knew it would not be long before feeling and instinct took over. The vibe attached to me had been intensified. Now, I could hear the buzzing. She was still working her outer lips and, occasionally, her love button.

Each time the intensity of her vibe increased, so did mine. My eyes were fixed on her, and my body responded to vibrations feeding into my core. My cock was rigid and pushing against the restraining bars of the cage.

An explosive breath as she pierced herself with the vibe, holding it in place and holding her breath. Slowly, her breath escaped between clamped teeth. She had been working herself by thinking. Now, it was all feeling. Her right hand pushed the impaling member inside her, and her legs closed to hold it in place. Using her free right hand to massage herself, nothing hurried. Circles and strokes, her breathing transitioned from even and slow to ragged and intermittent, and the vibes on my cock followed her.

Her hand moved slowly up her body, cupping her breast, squeezing and releasing, squeezing again. Index finger tracing her crinkled aureole, circling and teasing herself before moving to her nipple, hard and pointed. She pinched it between her finger and thumb, gently at first, then harder until she gasped. She repeated the action on her other breast, all while the vibe pulsated inside her. She was rising.

Recognizing the signs of her arousal, I knew that she wouldn't be able to prolong the inevitable and surrender to her orgasm. I hoped I would match her timing, and if not, she could deny me my release, and if I came before her, I would be punished. The intensity of the feelings in my cage increased and was magnified by the sound, like a swarm of angry bees, and the visuals in front of me.

Ms. Circe tried to suppress her release—an impossible task. She began to tremble. Her legs opened, and her hand went back to hold the vibrator buzzing inside her. In a rush, the tsunami of her orgasm released. Crying out unintelligible sounds of pleasure, she bucked against the vibe still in her pussy, pulling it out in one swift movement. Laying back still, her breathing slowly returning to normal.

The only sounds were her almost purring satisfaction as she stretched out with the ease of a big cat, along with the sounds of her vibrator and the one attached to me, which now had to be at maximum. The vibrations flooded me and enveloped me. I was trying to move, and I could bounce my cage up and down a little, anything to make me come.

Mesmerized, I was silent. There was nothing to say. The show had been a sensual banquet for me. For all my frustration, I had loved every minute of it. I hoped I would also get a release, which was never guaranteed. My arms and shoulders were starting to ache, not severely, just enough to make me aware of my predicament.

Languidly, Ms. Circe rolled on the bed and looked at me, utterly comfortable in her nudity. She stared at me, considering what came next. I was hoping she would let me come. A smile spread across her face, like the cat that got the cream, and the vibrations in my core began to subside. No, this can't be happening. I was ready to burst.

"I hope you liked the show, Mas. Now, our turn."

Like I had a choice. This rig was more restrictive than the hogtie I was usually placed in. Kneeling with the end of the single glove attached to the short chain between my ankle cuffs, it would be difficult to move, possible but challenging and slow. Hearing a buzzing behind me, I wondered if she was going for a second round herself.

Still naked, Ms. Circe returned. Standing in front of me she showed me a vibrating butt plug, and that was the buzzing I heard.

"Your turn, my way, Mas. There's no need to let you out tonight. I'll let you come in the cage. We can shower and crash. You can clean up tomorrow."

An inward groan, I wanted to get inside her, but I wanted to come more than anything. This was what I had consented to and was getting.

Kneeling behind me, she said, "Rise as much as you can."

She was in charge of my release, and that turned her on as much as the orgasm she had given herself. In her kneeling position, she lubed up the plug, and I felt its cool slipperiness against my ass. Sink down was her next instruction. I did, and she pushed upward, and the plug entered me easily. Nothing, just fullness. My cock was being kept hard from the low continuous vibrations through the cage. My ass started to vibrate. Surprised at the intensity, I jerked against my restrictions, which made Ms. Circe chuckle.

"Careful, Mas, I might take that as a sign you don't want a release."

Now I understood what she meant by our turn. She slowed the vibrator in my ass as she increased the intensity to the one on my cage, I was ready for it, and it felt good. The vibrations seared into me. She was varying the intensity of the pulses, back and front. Intense, not so intense, she played with me. With a remote in each hand, she moved the controls from intense to less intense and back again. I would try to move to maintain the intense feeling, but she would not allow that. Ms. Circe was in control of my release. I wouldn't last long. I was horney and primed before tonight, and the show Ms. Circe had put on raised my level of intensity to almost unbearable.

The vibes sang to me in their varied buzzing. My cock was hard in its cage, and my ass was pulsating. The two sensations met at my very core. My eyes closed, and I was transported. My entire being was focused on the vibrations coursing through me and my need for release. Ms. Circe now kept the cage vibe on maximum, as was the vibrating plug in my ass. Feeling a rising, soon I would not be able to stop my orgasm. The pressure rose, and the feeling became so intense I cried out.

"May I come, please? May I come?"

"Yes, Mas, you may come."

Shuddering as I felt myself ejaculate into the end of my cage, again, I pushed out more cum, and a third time. Then, I was done. Suddenly, all the tension in my body was gone, and I felt exhausted. The vibrators suddenly ceased, and I was back to reality.

As I returned to the present, Ms. Circe returned as Sophie, releasing me from my restriction. First, the vibrator at the end of my chastity cage was removed, and then the piercing ring. My arms relaxed as the single glove laces were released. The wrist strap was removed, and the cross-chest straps were undone. The leather glove peeled off my back. It had stuck to me. Freed of the glove, I stretched my arms and shoulders. The feeling of restriction had felt good, and it was just as good to be free and stretching. Sophie tossed me a box of tissues to clean myself and the cage as best I could until we showered. The keys to my ankle cuffs landed between my knees. Quickly, I removed the cuffs.

She had soaped up ahead of me. As I entered the shower, Sophie handed me the keys to my chastity cage. Once removed, I cleaned it, top to bottom, inside and out, and put it on the vanity to dry. Of course, the cage would then be placed back on me, and my cock imprisoned once again—no complaints. The butt plug popped out as I pushed against it, cleaned and sanitized, ready for the next time.

Sophie said, "That was fun for me. How about you."

"Seeing you, I wanted to be in you. I treasure every time I am. It was tantalizing and frustrating. The totality of you bringing yourself off had me ready to burst the cage. I guess that's a yes, especially my release. I am not sure I could have lasted another day if you hadn't let me have a release."

"I know it's a fine line. I want to push you right up to the line and sometimes push you over with care. Tonight was necessary for both of us, and I feel better for it...you?"

"Yes, I do. Let's finish up showering and get to bed."

"Not forgetting to lock up."

"Of course."

Dried off and locked back in the cage, the piercing back in place, Sophie checked the cage and approved. I joined Sophie in bed.

Turning off the light, she said, "I love you, Mas, for always. Goodnight."

The only answer I had was, "I love you."

Chapter Thirteen

Sunlight came through a crack in the blinds, and dust particles danced like diamonds. I felt good, relaxed, and ready for a new day. I stretched out, and my arms and shoulders were a little sore from being held in that unusual position. It was not a complaint, and I would submit to that again in a heartbeat.

Sophie was still asleep. Quietly, I got out of bed and put the pot of Joe to brew. Eggs on to boil, and bread in the toaster. Breakfast would be quick, and back to the office and the grindstone of this case. If what Sophie had done yesterday with her search algorithm had run correctly, we would have new leads to follow.

Not being a quiet person, I had disturbed Sophie, and she came into the kitchen a little bleary-eyed but smiling, saying, "The last thing I heard last night was that you loved me."

"Your hearing is perfect, and breakfast is almost ready."

Laughing, she returned to the bedroom to dress.

We consumed breakfast quickly, and left for the office. We were planning our day, with options if the algorithm had run correctly or not. We talked it out and had plans confirmed.

Sophie disappeared behind her computer array. Within seconds of her machine booted up, and I heard the sound I wanted to hear. "Yes."

"Mas, we got some hits from the DMV, and we now have a list of full plates with the beginning number and letters we had. The list is not huge, but bigger than I expected. Now, I must run it against all the number plates Kenzo's cameras picked up. We will have to share the review of the recordings. Looking at number plates is tiring."

"You said that you were going cross-eyed looking at the recordings. The PD should already have a list of all the plates that entered and exited the park themselves. We used to collate and condense everything from surveillance recordings to avoid precisely what you are doing. Sorry, I should have said something last night. I wasn't thinking straight.

"Shit, and I should have thought of that. Never mind, I'll get on it.

Marie arrived and was surprised that we were both in earlier than usual and asked, "What's up? Has something broken?"

Sophie answered, "Maybe. Mas and I had a brain fart, and I'm changing that to something positive."

Marie looked Sophie then me. "You both got some last night. Good for you."

I shrugged. "What makes you think that?" Sophie and I looked at each other and burst out laughing.

"Oh, come on, Mas, I work with detectives and read people. Both in early, you two are way too relaxed compared to yesterday, and neither of you has made a sarcastic remark about my arrival. Ergo, you both got some."

"*Ergo*, where the hell did that come from."

"It's called improving one's vocabulary. Now, let *me* get on with my day. Thank you."

She turned and returned to her desk, leaving us looking at each other. Sophie smiled and went back to look into the PD for the list of license plates. While she was doing that, I reread the timelines that the ME put as a time of death for each victim. I wasn't sure what I was looking for, if anything, just another angle.

Comparing the approximate times of abduction with the ME's estimated time of death, how long each one had been kept alive. Other than Saint Seb, all the other victims seem to have been taken and held for approximately the same amount of time before being killed. Saint Seb, who the perp needed to injure— torture was a better word, heal, then kill. He was the outlier.

Sophie said, "Got it. You were right. The PD does have a list of plates. It won't take me long to get a comparison between their list and the one I've built from the partial we had. That comparison should kick out any number of plates in common. Hopefully, only one, and that is the one we want to follow up on. That should be the perp's vehicle."

"How long?"

"As long as it takes me to run it. Minutes."

I went over to her desk and stood behind her. For this I could be patient, at least for minutes for minutes. She tapped away at her keyboard. Suddenly, data started to run on her left-hand monitor. It didn't run for very long.

"We got them, a perfect match, one of our plates against the PD cameras data, and only one. The time stamp on the PD camera puts them in the park at the correct time. Let's nail them, call Kenzo."

"Not so fast. It can't be that easy, not with this

perp. Let me think."

"What's to think about? We got a match."

"Sophie, this is too easy."

"This has not been easy. I'll run the plate against the DMV registration, we will have an address, and then we can get Kenzo and his team on it."

"Okay, run the plate against registration. We are looking for a newer minivan in white. Go for it."

I had a suspicion we were going to come up empty. The one thing everyone agreed on was this perp was careful. They would not be tripped up and caught on a license plate. While waiting for Sophie to do her thing with the DMV, I refilled our coffee mugs. The wait wasn't long, Sophie exploded.

"Son of a bitch, you were right, Mas, the plate comes back to a red SUV. No record of the plates or vehicle being stolen. Damn we needed that break."

"Another piece of the puzzle. We are building a picture, and every piece is a good piece."

"When we get this bastard, I hope they fry them."

"This is a non-capital punishment state. No death penalty."

"Usually, I would agree. However, this case is an exception for many reasons."

"Agreed, that is not our call. They are going to jail or a secure mental facility for life. Unless they choose suicide by cop, a good alternative, I think."

"Whatever. Let's just catch them. What's next?"

"We give Kenzo the info, and he can put a bolo on the license plate. Which I expect will never be found or show up on a completely innocent vehicle."

"Have you told Father Benny about the latest body?"

"No, on it's on my list for today."

Sitting at my desk, I was not surprised at the outcome of the license plate issue, but It gave us more information about the perp and how they operated. So many license plates are floating around, on people's garage walls, in junk yards, or stolen. The stolen ones are the easiest to recover if they are reported.

However, if they are switched out in a parking garage for a set of plates that are not hot or somewhere else, the owner will not usually notice the switch for some time. Why would they? Their vehicle has plates. No problem until you put the new tag on the plate, by which time, the reason they had been switched would have been long past—a clever way of keeping their vehicle anonymous.

Another factor in their favor is that a quarter of all minivans are white. No one has time to check all the minivans in San Francisco against their plates. Another dead end. It's time to call Father Benny and give him the bad news.

The church office said Father Benny was out and would not return for several hours. Would I care to leave a name and number? I did, and they promised to give the message to him.

That done, I called Kenzo on the burner but there was no answer. Texting him a message reading, *wanted a 'to go' order. He* would get the message and get back to me when he could, and it would be safe.

Back to thinking about our perp. This would be a great case to puzzle out, except for the body count, which is five to date, and I expected more to come. They had not made any mistakes so far that I could discern. We had a ton of data, information, and many bits, none of them tied together, which was frustrating.

We had told Kenzo we would work on this case full-time, and we did. We also worked on our other cases in between when there was nothing to do with the bodies in the park case. We were good and could handle multiple cases at once. We were also aware of our limitations as a three-person team.

Two cases had come and gone in the meantime, a missing person and a runaway. That one was easy. We tracked the credit card trail. Teenagers may be tech-savvy in many ways, but the real world is different. That one was a happy ending, with all parties crying and hugging.

The second one, not so much…a messy divorce. We didn't usually touch divorce cases, not with a ten-foot pole. That one intrigued Sophie due to the intellectual property theft associated with it. That one took some work but was sorted, and the lawyers were happy with the results we provided, and it closed our part of the mess. None of this impacted what we did or didn't do regarding the bodies in the park.

We had to rethink our next move, with the license plate issue being a dead end. We were already into the three-week timeline, and by days, it was not a good sign. My phone went off, and not a number I recognized. I answered anyway.

"Mas Hammett, how may I help you?"

"Mas, it's Benny, you left a message." I could hear what I thought was an old rock band in the background.

"Yes, Father—"

Father Benny interrupted me, saying, "Benny, please."

"Okay, Benny, we had the second part of the

Bacchus and Sergius duo show up."

I let the comment hang, and Benny continued in a quiet voice. "Was he in the same condition as the original?"

"Yes, he was. Ashton was dumped in the same place as his partner, Jeremy. We thought we had a good lead. It turned out this perp outsmarted us again."

"Mas, you have always known they are clever. I have spoken to Kenzo. He is certain that between the police department doing all the official things, and as he puts it, you doing all the less official things, you will be successful in catching them."

"I wish I had that kind of confidence."

"Kenzo has great faith in you, and from our brief interactions, I would say he is justified. Have you thought any more about what I said in not assuming it's just one person?"

"Not as much as I should have. I saw the driver of the minivan that dumped Ashton, but not clearly. Hoodie up, and it was dark on a computer screen. It was only a quick look when they passed us on Fulton Street. We never got close enough after that to get a better look. We were more interested in following them.

"And your first impression?"

"The person did not seem very large, especially for the effort it would have taken to move any of the first victims. Judging from the height through the window, it could have been a woman or a man on the smaller side. I assumed neither would be able to manage the first three murders independently. So, good point, Benny. I need to think on this some more."

"If you need anything from me, please don't hesitate. I will continue praying for you. Wishing peace to you, Mas."

He was one weird dude for a Catholic priest. That was San Francisco for you, a left-over hippie, Grateful Dead-loving priest. I wondered what sort of sacrament he preferred. He certainly was not the weirdest person I had met, that was for sure.

What Benny had done was make me analyze the size of the driver in the minivan. Considering the size of the minivan compared to an SUV or regular car, the driver was on the small side, which didn't mean weak. Put the size together with how long it took to dump Ashton.

Two people, it had to be two people. One person couldn't have stopped, parked, opened the side door, pushed out the body parts, closed the door, and driven off. Shit. Parking. The brake lights didn't go off. One to drive, and one to open the door and push out Ashton. Quick and easy with two people, they are off in less than thirty seconds. I would have Sophie break down the recording to get the time they arrived and left. It would be seconds.

Now we were looking for two perps. What combination and what was the motivation for two people to do this? Cult? I didn't think so, and this had always felt more personal. So, a couple. Male-male? Didn't think so with the homophobia aspect. Male-female, possible and most likely. Female-female, unlikely, the homophobia aspect and the physical requirements.

To really think this through, I need some thinking time, and then I should run it by Sophie, Kenzo, and Father Benny. Benny. First, Sophie for the logic and logistics of my theory, then Kenzo to pass on all the info we had, and my new theory of couples. Lastly, Benny, for any insights into the religious part of my theory. Busy day. I told Sophie and Marie I was going for a walk.

Sophie waved, and Marie said, "Please bring back some lunch. I won't be getting out till late."

"Sure, no problem."

Walking around San Francisco is usually a pleasure. Today was no exception. I had never been to Europe, and from what I had seen and heard, I always viewed San Francisco as the best of Europe and America in one place. The pace is more akin to Europe, with all the cafes and bars, all the amenities of the US and the weather. Can't beat the weather…well, most days. Thinking was the point, and that is what I did.

New thoughts crystalized and didn't seem too out there, at least not to me. I was sure Sophie would manage to poke holes in my ideas, and that was always a good test. Next would be Kenzo, another hole poker. If it all held up, I would get Benny's input on the religious part, hoping he could offer some insight.

****

As I walked back to the office, I almost forgot Marie's request for lunch. That would have caused some caustic comments from Marie and Sophie wouldn't have even noticed. Sandwiches for all, and large sides of guacamole and coleslaw for us to share.

The food was welcomed by Marie and Sophie, who had exhausted all avenues regarding the license plates. We lunched together as I laid out my thoughts and theory about the perp being a couple, not just two people. Explaining in a logical extrapolation of all our information and data. In the end, Marie and Sophie looked at each other. Marie spoke first.

"Mas, your theory makes sense about really fucked up people, and I can't find any holes in it. How about you, Sophie?

She was quiet, and I was sure she would have something that would put a hole or two in my latest theory. She shook her head, saying. "Can't fault your logic on this one. Everything we have or have seen could relate to a couple, especially the last body drop. The part of the body drop you asked me to time out. The time from brake lights going on to driving off is seventeen seconds. It was a fraction under. I rounded up."

"You don't think it's a crazy theory."

Sophie said, "Not the way you laid it out. Until we can prove it, it's just a theory. Better than anything we've had so far. All the facts fit as we have them. Let us know what Kenzo thinks.

"I haven't heard back from him yet. He's under a shit load of pressure. Maybe something in what we have will help him. You haven't found anything in the PD reports that we don't already have?"

"Nothing, they seem to be spinning their wheels until there is another victim or victims. Were there a lot of gay saint duos, as well as singles?"

"Unfortunately, more than enough to keep the perps going for quite a while."

"Well, that's depressing."

"I'll text Kenzo. Hopefully, he can update us."

"Get me a copy of the body drop. Kenzo can get it to his forensics department to verify the time and how it's not possible for one person to drive and do the drop in the time."

"Consider it done."

My phone dinged a new text. It was Kenzo.

"Got your message; Wanatabe's tomorrow lunch is the soonest I can make it unless you can deal with the night visit at home?"

I texted back. *"See you tonight after six. We'll be home, come and have dinner."*

I told Sophie the gist of the text, saying, "We'll be having a dinner guest."

The rest of the day was, so what? What did my theory get us? Not much further, only that we were looking for two psychopaths. They had to be connected. Were they brother and sister? Man and wife, or some other relative? Those were good questions we didn't have the answers to yet. I called Benny again, wanting to pick his brains on the religious aspect. The church office answered, confirmed he was in, and would see if he was available. He was.

"Hi Mas, what can I do for you?"

"Your knowledge of Christian history and how it relates to this case."

"Gotcha, fire away."

"We now believe it's a couple, not a solo killer. I'm convinced that religion, I should say Christianity, plays a big part in the motivation for the perps. What form of Christianity, I don't know. That's why I called you."

"Good question. It won't matter if they claim to be Catholic or any Protestant denomination. They are so far outside of true faith that it's irrelevant. They are broken souls."

"I didn't think God gave you more than you can bear?" I asked with cynicism in my voice, and Benny picked up on it.

"That's bullshit, I've seen too many broken people to believe that. Your cynicism is well noted in that particular phrase. The reason I am a priest is to help the broken souls." He paused, and I remained silent. "Many only need a helping hand or even knowing someone is there to hear them. Sadly, there are also some souls so broken that nothing will help, and nothing can be done for them. It doesn't stop me from trying."

"What happens to those people?"

"Many things, some commit suicide, some are killed, and many end up in mental institutions—particularly the dangerous ones. Many end up rotating through jail, being released, and end up back in jail. They are not criminals, and the system is so broken it can't give them what they need. Sorry, I didn't mean to go off on that tangent."

"I don't think our perps fit that description."

"No, I'm sure they don't. It would be best if you talked to an expert in that field. I would say, and it's a guess, that the male is a psychopath, and the woman is under his influence."

"Why do you think that?"

"Simple, in Christianity, particularly the more esoteric versions, it's extremely patriarchal. The women are brought up to follow without question the men in their life—first father then husband."

"This is good food for thought and more puzzle pieces."

"Any time Mas. Still praying for you and wishing you peace."

"Benny, you as well."

With Benny's observations, I called out to Sophie,

asking, "Any updates on the FBI or PD profiles?"

"I haven't checked recently. I'll do it before we leave tonight."

"Great, I'm going to do a chili for dinner. If Kenzo shows up for dinner, we will have plenty, and if not, we will have dinner tomorrow and probably the day after."

Sophie laughed at that. She knew I couldn't make a small chili however hard I tried. I would need to leave early to make it how we liked, picking up fresh ingredients from the market. My mouth was already watering. I do make a good chili.

Chapter Fourteen

Chili was almost ready, the aroma wafting around the kitchen. I had cracked a beer. To honor the meal, it was a dark, very drinkable beer. Sophie came home about an hour after me, waving sheets of paper.

"The FBI and the SFPD have updated the profiles, added comments about religion being more significant than originally thought, and the possibility that it's a couple, not a single perp. You are good at this, Mas. You were, are ahead of the profilers."

"Thanks, save the congrats for when we catch them."

"Okay, okay. We're getting closer."

"I hope so. Will you set the table? Just the rice to do, and Kenzo to arrive if he's coming for dinner. We can start without him if need be."

"Sure, gimme a kiss. You deserve it."

We kissed, and again deeply, we melded into one another. Sophie felt good. I could feel her heat through our clothes. Damn it, she always had this effect on me. Dinner...complete dinner, that was what I needed to do, without distraction. Sophie knew what impact she had on me and enjoyed my discomfort as much as I did.

The doorbell chimed, and Sophie went to answer the door. It was Kenzo. He looked tired, and it didn't help that he knew he was the scapegoat if everything went sideways. We hoped to avoid that and get him kudos for solving the case.

"Hey Mas, thanks for the invite. I need a friendly face. Thankfully, Sophie is here."

"Very fucking funny, Kenzo."

We all laughed, setting the mood for the evening, friends joining together. The chili disappeared along with the rice and beer. The conversation over the meal was light, avoiding any mention of the reason we invited him. That didn't mean we were not going to get to it. With dinner done and sitting on the back deck with post-dinner coffees, we addressed the elephant in the room and the bodies in the park.

I started, "We have some new theories about the killings." I let that hang.

Kenzo bit, "What have you come up with?"

"We have been reviewing all the data and facts that we know for sure. We believe it's a couple doing the killings, or at least involved. A single strong male could have done everything so far?"

"Yes, that is still our main supposition."

"Except that one person couldn't have done the last body drop. Sophie, show him the recording." Sophie opened her laptop and ran the recording from before the arrival of the minivan until it left. "That timeline doesn't allow for the driver to do the drop. There has to be two people involved.

"Good point, and I get that, and what about all the others?"

"All possible as a solo agent, but much easier with two."

"I can agree with that, but two psychopaths working together, that's stretching it a bit."

"I talked with Benny, and he told me that some of

the more conservative branches of Christianity are very patriarchal, with the women are completely subjugated to the men."

"Still a stretch. Why are you so fixated on the religious part? You aren't religious, are you?"

"No, not really. Organized religion turns me off, and it's a long story. Let's say I'm suspicious of any organization that wants that much control over its population."

"Fair enough, I suppose, but it still doesn't answer my question."

"Okay, the killings, as I said before, are up close and personal. The victims are all part of the BDSM/LGBTQ community, murdered in the same manner as reportedly LGBTQ saints from history. The last two, Jeremy and Ashton, go back to Roman times. I have never heard of these saints, sure Sebastian and Joan of Arc, but the others—gimme a break, I'll bet you hadn't either."

"True, I only knew of Saint Sebastian and Joan of Arc, not the others."

"You don't believe in coincidence any more than we do. Five murders, everything about them screams serial killer. A psychopath with a serious case of homophobia."

"You are laying out a good theory, but no concrete leads as to who is doing it."

"If that asshole who answered your phone the other night had done what was right, they would probably be in custody right now. Not a reflection on you, Kenzo."

"Thanks."

Sophie joined in, "We have all the data you have sent us, and more we gathered. Mas has broken it into more focused areas, but we need a key to unlock the motive. I can crunch data all day long without getting anywhere if I don't have direction to what we need. We have a haystack, and we know the needle is in it. We just don't know where. Is there anything you have that we don't that would narrow it down more?"

"Nada, you have everything we have. I think this case will end my career, unless we get lucky."

I had to answer, "Better be lucky than good, best to be both. We are good and will make our own luck."

Sophie added, "Kenzo, we will get these perps. I guarantee it."

He said, "Nice, Sophie, your mouth to God's ear."

"Nope, I have faith in Mas and you. It'll work out, trust me."

The conversation was getting maudlin, "We have the recording of the minivan. Sophie has sent you a copy. The license plates were stolen from an SUV. You may want to check the registered owner. They may not have noticed their plates were changed, and it will probably be a dead end. The white minivan is a lead of sorts, with too many white ones to check all of them, but it adds to the pile of facts. We now know it's a couple.

"Mas, I wished I felt that way. This one is getting to me, not only because of the brass breathing down my neck. Justice for the vics, that's what I want."

Sophie added, "So do we, and to help you get it."

We chatted more about the methodology of the perps, what the forensic teams had and didn't have, and all the interviews with the victims' families and friends. This case was a big PD operation, and a lot of resources were being thrown at it. There was nothing to bite on.

Patience and diligence were going to be needed. We were down to between thirteen and fifteen days until another body would be dropped. That was a lot of days and no time at all.

As Kenzo left, he said, "Thanks for the meal. It was good, and so was the company. I appreciate all that you guys are doing. I'll let you know if anything breaks."

Together, we chorused, "Same here, take care."

He left, we looked at each other, and I said, "We need a break to end this quickly."

"I agree, but I don't know what more I can do. Like I said, I can crunch data all day, but it's useless if I don't know what I'm looking for."

"That's why we make a great team. You do what I can't, and I do what you can't.

"I love you for that, Mas. Let's go to bed and get a new start tomorrow."

"Agreed."

****

Morning arrived, and I was ready to go. The previous evening's conversation with Kenzo and Sophie had given me the impetus to reengage. Coffee brewed while I made toast. We would pick up breakfast on the way into the office.

I had no idea what I was about to get involved in, just that I had to take another look at the facts as we knew them, review them, and think outside the big shitty box we were trapped in. Sophie was not so enthusiastic, slowly coming around. I left her a cup of joe and two slices of sourdough toast with local honey.

My toast disappeared, and I put the empty coffee mug in the sink, shouting out, "Bye, Sophie. See you at the office later today."

No response...I chuckled to myself. I would probably pay for that comment, and I didn't care. Today, I felt good, and I hoped nothing would change that.

The walk to the office helped me think. I mused on the case as I walked. I needed a jump start, an idea, or a change of perspective. Then it struck me...we had all been looking at this from one perspective, the victims only without finding a connection, which there had to be. We had the data to start with the police files and reports. We would get what we didn't have from Kenzo's investigation or on our own.

If the connection was not obvious, it had to be some levels down. We had to build up a profile of each of their lives, which the PD had superficially done. What we needed to do was dig down several levels.

Sean Costello was the first one taken. Question. Do we use the timeline of when he was taken or when Frankie, the second person taken, was killed and put on display in the park as the first victim? Maybe Sean being the first one taken was significant, maybe not. To me, Frankie's body drop date was more important, but we would start with Sean.

Sean partnered with Adolfo. There were no problems there, friends confirmed. The two were as happy a couple as Adolfo claimed. Sean was doing well in the investment firm and was a rising star. He was openly gay, and that was not a problem with the firm or his direct upline. Sean's KinkInc account was not very active, and seemingly, he had not played the field since meeting Adolfo. If and when they played, it was with each other as play partners, and almost nothing in public BDSM clubs or spaces.

Working on down, we needed to find all those people who worked with Sean in the company one year ago on the dates around Frankie's body appearing in the park. Colleagues, administrators, support staff, and anyone who came in contact with him or him with them. Especially if they left or were fired from the company around that time. The SFPD inspectors had made a good start. Now, we needed to spread the pool to more peripheral folks who had some contact with Sean but not necessarily every day. Everyday contact would just be better.

Follow up with Frankie and so on. The same drill. If we went far and deep enough, there would be a connection to all the vics. All I had to do now was get Sophie and Marie's buy-in.

I arrived at the office, and it was already open, suspicious. I called out.

Marie said brightly and happily, "Good morning, Mas."

"How come you are in so early?"

"Chung isn't traveling for two weeks, so we had a chastity cage lock-up party last night. That always energizes me."

"Lucky Chung."

She laughed and went back to her chores. Having seen my cage, it must have triggered something in her. She had somehow persuaded Chung, her partner, to wear one. Chung now wore the chastity cage when not traveling on business. The following two weeks would be fun for them, or at least Marie.

"Hey, Marie, I want to run something by you before Sophie gets in. I've been thinking."

"Don't strain yourself, Mas." She said it with a smile.

"Very funny. Regarding these killings."

That took the smile off her face, "Okay, what do you need?"

"Just listen and give me your opinion after."

"Got it."

Explaining what I was thinking to another person helped me by verbalizing my idea, and having Marie talk back to me, clarified it in my mind. I gave her as much detail as I could. She came back at me.

"Mas, great idea, but a ton of work. We can start with all the reports that the PD has done, interviews, etc. I bet Sophie can build a matrix, or her friend in Philly, to cross reference all the contacts, a bit like a Venn diagram, where they intersect is the connection, just a lot bigger, of course."

"You think it could work?"

"Better than what we have now, which ain't shit."

"How brief. I'm not sure Sophie will be as enthusiastic, and it'll mean more work on her, maybe Fiend, and us, and it'll be a boring in the trench's chore."

"I know, but I'm good at that stuff. You know that."

"Okay, then back me up with Sophie when she gets in."

"Deal."

To be proactive, I started re-reading all the PD reports on Sean, noting all the names of the people the PD had interviewed or listed. That list grew fast and long with Sean. The investment company was not a large one, but it still employed a good number of people, from brokers to janitors and everyone in between who made the company function.

Sophie arrived, and Marie and I corralled her as soon as she walked in the door.

"Whoa, hold on. I need coffee first, then you can attack me."

I stood. "Sit, I'll get the coffee."

"What brought this on? You both seem too excited for a regular day.

Marie answered, "Mas has a great idea." She let that hang, Sophie bit.

"And?"

"Well, Mas isn't sure if you will be as enthusiastic as we are."

"You mean it will be a shit load of work for me?"

"And probably your friend, Fiend."

"Coffee up," I said. "Marie and I think we have another way to attack the lack of progress. We, and by that, I mean everyone, including the PD, have been concentrating on the vics themselves. What if the connection is not so direct."

"What do you mean, not direct?"

"What if the connection is more peripheral, someone they all met or knew but not necessarily every day? So far, we have five victims and four situations. If we look at them individually, there is nothing in common other than KinkInc accounts, and even there, none are connected. The closest would be Sean and Ashton on the financial investment side, both in the same field but not connected. So, what if the connection is someone they all knew but in different parts of their life? We must scour their lives for everyone they knew or came in contact with."

Sophie looked at me, then Marie, before saying, "Are you fucking crazy? Do you know how much work that is? It's not a lot. It's a goddamn ocean." She groaned, "This will not be a good day."

I had to ask, "Can this be done, and can we do it?"

"Yes, and I don't know. This is a huge job, better handled through official channels for many reasons. More manpower and the authority to do it, we are civilians without access to a lot of places we would need. If we can get Kenzo's buy-in, we may be able to do it with Fiend's assistance."

Marie asked, "Sophie, do you agree with the idea?"

"I don't know. It's an avenue no one has been down yet...so, worth a try. I'll talk to Fiend and see what he thinks. Mas, you talk to Kenzo. Without him, we won't get the level of access we need, which is on you. Good luck."

"I'll take care of Kenzo. Do you think this is a viable route?"

"Yes, I think so. The workload scares me, and we are talking about a lot of people, possibly in the hundreds, unless we get lucky."

"Sophie, I don't want to investigate each person. We need to get a mass of names and cross-reference them against each victim, seeing which one all the victims have in common. There may be more than one, but there can't be many. They all worked and lived in different circles."

Marie asked, "What about all of them having KinkInc accounts?"

"The KinkInc thing is a distraction, but not a surprise when you consider how many kinksters there are in San Francisco. I'll bet it's over fifty thousand in

San Francisco alone on KinkInc, never mind the surrounding locations."

Marie looked surprised, saying, "There are that many kinky people in San Francisco?"

Sophie and I laughed. "Don't forget you are included in that community now."

Marie looked surprised at Sophie's comment, saying, "Me?"

I responded, "You, being a keyholder, and Chung wearing a chastity device, even part-time, would be considered kinky."

She looked embarrassed and blushed, and that didn't happen very often. She dropped her head and said, "I guess I hadn't thought of it in the bigger picture. This is something just for Chung and me."

I added, "And that's fine. For many people it's just something between two people. Usually, it takes time and trial and error to find a partner who compliments you. It took me ages to find my first kink relationship partner. Then, there was a big gap without anyone. Meeting Sophie was a blessing."

She looked at both of us and said, "Like I said, you two are weirdly good together. If it works, it's good. Right?"

Sophie and I echoed together, "Right." And that caused us all to laugh.

"Back to the issue at hand. The more names we get, the better our chance of finding the common denominator; that person who ties them all together."

Somewhat mollified, Sophie said, "That's a bit different. Looking at large numbers of names in a matrix is much easier, not easy, easier. We will be recruiting Fiend on this, and he will eat it up. Go call

Kenzo."

"Yes, Ma'am."

Rather than call Kenzo, I texted him on the burner. That way, he could call me, text me, or whatever. He would know I needed to contact him in a safe place. With nothing productive to do, I took the opportunity to go to the gun range. My usual two hundred rounds later and covered in GSR, I headed home. On the way, my phone buzzed a new text. Pulling over, I opened it. Kenzo wanted to meet for lunch. Damn, I would not have time to get home, shower, and change. I texted back, 'to go.' Immediate response. 'Yes'.

Making a U-turn, I headed to Wanatabe's Restaurant, Café, and Go parlor. The journey sucked. Thankfully, parking wasn't a problem. Wanatabe motioned after his greeting bow that the upstairs was open, and Kenzo was already there.

Kenzo was sitting at a Go table. As I entered, he greeted me, pointed to the game board, and said, "This will be a good game. Your meeting, oh, and I took the liberty of ordering."

We hugged. What I was about to ask Kenzo was a big ask. He may want to avoid taking the risk or being able to. It could end his career if it came to light.

"Before you say no, hear me out."

I explained the theory I had laid out for Marie and Sophie. He nodded in the positive. Then, I got down to what we needed and wanted from the PD and him. That brought a different reaction.

"Are you out of your fucking minds? No way. I can't let you or anybody into my department computer. You're nuts."

He was fuming at my audacity for even asking. I

let him stew, remaining silent. He would have to break the silence. He was thinking. He was hooked on some parts of the plan but not all. His career was on the line anyway. If the perp weren't caught soon, he would probably be replaced. Damaging and probably stalling his career. Or worse, he would take it personally that he couldn't get justice for the victims.

"Okay, Mas, I knew I needed help from day one, and I came to you first for the kink stuff, not for this. If we can do a workaround, it may work. Would you get Sophie on the phone?"

"Sure." As I dialed, the waitress came in with what Kenzo had ordered: our usual pot stickers plus an order of tempura. My mouth started watering. When Sophie answered, I had a mouthful of tempura shrimp.

"Sophie, I have Kenzo here, you're on speaker?"

"Hi Kenzo, what's going on?"

"Your asshole partner is trying to give me a heart attack with his request."

Sophie chuckled, "That's why he's asking you, not me."

"As crazy as he is, if you can help, we might have a chance to bring this off without me losing a career I love and you guys not going to jail."

"I like the not going to jail part. What do you need?"

"There is no way in hell I am giving you or Mas access to my computer. If you can supply me with a laptop, I will put a copy of all the lists we generate on it and files of all the names related to each victim. Can you arrange to have access to that laptop?"

Sophie replied, "Yes, I will get you a clean laptop and a large-capacity thumb drive. Save everything to where you normally would. Also, please save it to the thumb drive and transfer the data to the new laptop I will access remotely. That way, you haven't sent anything anywhere. Suppose anyone asks, comments, or checks either of your computers. Tell them you want to keep the data separate from what has already been gathered, as there is so much of it."

"Yeah, that works for me. How soon can you get me that laptop?"

Sophie was quiet for a moment before responding. "How long will you be with Mas."

He looked at me. I shrugged. "I'm easy, you decide."

"Sophie, I can stretch it, forty to forty-five minutes."

"Good. I will have Marie bring the laptop to you. I have a spare laptop here at the office. It won't take me long to prep it, and we always have extra thumb drives. Traffic may be an issue, and of course, if you can put up with Mas for another forty-five minutes."

She said the last with a laugh, and Kenzo joined in. I just smiled, whatever it took to get Kenzo on board. Besides, I liked his company. With that settled, I hung up, and we returned to enjoying the food. The conversation was light, and we reminisced about our past life in the PD, and the people we knew in common. Kenzo mentioned Big Boots, a motorcycle officer well-known to me in the PD and the kink community.

I asked, "Was that the connection, BB to me and Sophie and the kink community?"

"No more a confirmation. I'd had my suspicions for ages."

"Why?"

"Easy, you didn't party hard, didn't gamble, that I could see, and didn't screw around. What did you do to decompress? Didn't go fishing, hunting, or any other relaxation usually used? After a few comments by you and other officers, I put two and two together and came up with four. Mas, I'm a detective too, ya know."

"And?"

"Hey, no judgment, I was curious. I wanted to make sure that my partner was reliable and had my back. That was it."

"I passed the smell test?"

"Flying colors, everyone I spoke to had nothing but good things to say about you as a partner. Your private life, none of my business as long as it didn't impact us doing our job or my safety."

"Good to know. Being out of the norm in the PD is not easy, even in San Francisco."

"There is nothing normal about the PD, and the politics are getting to me. I just wanted to do my job and catch the bad guys."

"Don't sweat it. Once you get these perps, you'll be a hero again, and they'll forget about how they were going to shaft you."

"Don't BS me. Police work is always a team effort, and you know it."

"Yeah, but you are their fall guy on this one. You face the media, but they don't. Be the hero and take it for what it's worth."

We chatted about families, at least on his side, what Sophie and I had been up to in the cases we'd had, the sordid one and the others that were bread and butter. There was a knock on the door, and Marie came in, a little out of breath, carrying a laptop bag.

She sat and handed the bag to Kenzo, saying, "Sophie gave me some instructions for you. The computer is a blank slate and charged. All the accessories are in the bag. It also has some good encryption to protect you from prying fingers. Here is the thumb drive, it should be big enough for whatever you need. She wants you to use your full name as the login and this password exactly as she wrote it." Marie handed Kenzo a sticky.

Kenzo looked at the sticky. "You have got to be kidding me."

I knew Sophie had done one of her, '*No one is going to get this password.*' The password would comprise seemingly random upper and lower case letters mixed with numbers and unique items.

"Hey, it could be worse. Sophie had me memorize three sets of those passwords so I could get into her computer if needed."

"No way I'm going to remember all that lot. I'll take a picture to be sure." He looked at me. "No one would guess this is a password even if they get my phone."

"Whatever you need to do to get the stuff to us."

"Wait," Marie said. "Not finished yet. Sophie wants you to make sure the laptop is always plugged in, on, and connected to Wi-Fi so she can access it when needed, especially when you are home. That's it, I gotta run. Good luck, Kenzo."

"Thanks," Kenzo said and turned to me. "Where did you find her?"

"I didn't. Simon did. I wish I could take credit for the hire."

"I need to go. I will let you know when the new

reports start coming in. I will need to reorganize the teams. That will be easy. At least it will look like we are doing something."

We said our goodbyes, and Kenzo left. I waited until he was sure to have left the area. Paying the bill,

Wanatabe quietly asked if everything was okay with Officer Otake. I told him, "No, but we're working on it."

He smiled and bowed, telling me that the room was always available if we needed it. I thanked him and left.

Back to waiting again until we had the data to scrub. Time was running and I wasn't confident we would have enough to collar the perps before another body dropped. It would be in the park, and they wouldn't use the same vehicle. We were back a square, but not to square one.

Chapter Fifteen

The ride back to the office was slow, traffic sucked, and I didn't mind. The time was well-spent. Thinking about the case, I wondered if we could approach it from a different angle. We had just initiated a new program and would have to let that run to get any new results. This was a frustration I'd learned to deal with when I was an inspector. It didn't mean I had to like it or accept it without trying to change it. Opening the office door, Sophie assaulted me.

"Where the hell have you been?"

"Traffic, dear, can't do anything about that in San Francisco. What do you need?"

"Oh, nothing really. I was concerned about you being so long. Anyway, I have already built a matrix with Fiend's assistance. We have already loaded as many names as we can from the reports we have. It's pretty bare right now. Some victims have more name connections than others."

"Great. Kenzo protested, but did see the potential of this avenue."

"Oh, I forgot to tell you. He has already loaded in some more information we didn't have, not much, but more."

"He is reorganizing the teams to go back out, revisiting all the contacts, and expanding on the name base, just as we requested. He said if he gets pushback from anyone, he will threaten search warrants and subpoenas, which usually gets people cooperating if they don't have anything to hide."

"Good for him."

"I'm hoping we can pull this off. I'd hate to see him get screwed over."

"Me too. We can't do much until we get the data into the matrix. We have an inquiry about our availability to look into a case of potential fraud. Are you interested?"

"Maybe, depends on the circumstances and the estimated time commitment."

"Got it. I'll look into it and give you the run down when I have it."

The day was spent doing chores and meeting with a potential client. We took the case. It fit our profile of interesting. Signing them up as clients and getting all the information needed took time, and we took the time because we had to be thorough for both sides of the client relationship. That night, we both crashed early.

****

We took the new case because it was interesting, but mainly because it wouldn't impact our work on the park killings. A lot of the new job would be handed off to Erin, a forensic accountant whom we also knew as Ms. Double Entry in the kink community.

Kenzo's team poured a mass of information into the reports. The names of work associates, friends, and anyone who touched their lives, dry cleaners, suppliers, cleaning services, and fitness memberships. We wanted a picture of their personal, business, and social lives and looked at everything. Every name went into the PD pot and flowed through to us.

Sophie and Fiend managed all that data. Marie managed the office, and I did whatever needed doing for either of them. I felt a bit like a spare dick at an orgy. Knowing my limitations, and technology was one of them. I was frustrated and patient because I also knew I would need to put something into action at some point. I hoped it would be soon.

Another day passed, and I was getting antsy. I needed something concrete to do. The date for another body drop was getting uncomfortably close, and we didn't have anything to bring us closer to catching the perp.

Sophie called out to me. "Mas, we may have something—somethings actually. Got a minute?"

"Of course, what is it."

"Fiend and I have been scrubbing the data. We have four maybe five names connected to most or all the victims. Two businesses and two individuals."

"Who are they, and what is the connection to the vics?"

"The two businesses are current and active, a dry cleaner and the other is a pharmacy."

"Scrap them, no interest. We are looking for a personal connection from one to two or more years ago. This is personal, not business."

"I get that. Couldn't they be working for one of the two businesses?"

"Possibly, but I doubt it. You know what that means, right? Checking out all the employees for both businesses, going back the two years we want."

"Why can't I keep my big mouth shut."

"Okay, let's start with two individual names, and if they don't pan out. Then we can go after the business?"

"Yeah, I guess that makes sense."

"Who are they?"

"The names first, then I'll get into the connections. Angela Marinelli and this is the odd part. There are two women both named Ruth, different surnames. Coincidence?"

"Don't believe in coincidence. The connections for Angela, please."

"Okay, Angela Marinelli, VP for a biotech company. She used Sean as her financial investment advisor for approximately seven years and went to his partner Adolfo for her hair-dressing needs. She's connected to Frankie by purchasing one custom corset. I am still checking to see if she has a KinkInc account. She bought two pieces of art from Carol, and it doesn't seem to be a gym or training connection with her, just art. Jeremy is the Realtor she used when she bought her apartment. There don't seem to be any ties to Ashton, his partner, at least not that we can find so far."

"Any religious affiliation listed?"

"Not that we could see. We will be doing a deeper dive now."

Good, and the other names?"

"This is where it gets a little strange. I have some ideas, but I want your input, okay?"

"Sure, go for it."

"Ruth one, Ruth Stevenson, worked for the same investment firm as Sean. She was an analyst with no connection to Adolfo. She worked part-time at Frankie's shop and was on the list of custom corset customers. She used the same gym as Carol and was trained by Carol when she joined, being shown how to use the machines and getting the three complimentary training sessions. She has no other connection to Carol. That's it for Ruth one. Ruth two, Ruth Stonewall, also worked as an analyst for Ashton. Also, on Frankie's list of custom corset customers, her purchase was later than Ruth one. There is no connection to Carol that we can see yet. She rented an apartment from Jeremy and Ashton in one of their investment properties until about a year ago. No religious affiliation was noted. That's it."

"You think Ruth, one and two, are the same person."

"Damn it, Mas, how did you get that?"

"You were too obvious, and it makes sense. However, changing your name, social security number, and other documents is difficult unless you are in the witness protection program. Or have a documented history with an abusive partner or stalker."

"You mean legally. In Philly, I could have gotten anything I needed, including a passport that would fool most official scrutiny. Here, I don't know all those folks yet."

"I hadn't thought of that, I guess. I still think like law enforcement, sometimes."

"We came from different worlds."

"Agreed. We need to investigate Angela and the two Ruth's. Don't stop inputting the names. These two could be nothing."

"Planning on it."

Sophie printed out all the info she had on the three names. Marie and I would start digging. Marie took Angela, and I had the two Ruth's. We only had the basic info from the police reports, so it was up to Sophie and Fiend to get into their social media accounts. That would tell us a lot about them if they had KinkInc accounts, any religious affiliations, and more. We checked police archives for arrest records or records of any sort-nothing on any of them.

Sophie came through fast and credited Fiend for the quick response. Angela was busy on social media, work-related, and vacation, nothing regarding KinkInc, which meant she wasn't on the site or had hidden it very well. We would keep looking.

Ruth Stevenson was on KinkInc, inactive for over two years. Ruth Stonewall is not on KinkInc. Everything I could find so far regarding Ruth one stopped about two-plus years ago, around the same time as her KinkInc account went dormant. All of Ruth two's information was just over two years old, give or take, and nothing for the past fifteen months. It would have been nice to be able to check the rental records of Jeremy and Ashton, for when Ruth two stopped paying rent and disappeared. That would now be on Kenzo and his crew to dig into.

Sophie had hit it on the head with the limited info we had on these two Ruths. I agreed with her. These two were one. Now, all we had to do was find out why, and if they were connected to the bodies in the park. Just because they connected to most of the victims, that didn't mean they were connected to the killings. I had a gut feeling they were, and we had to find it fast.

I confirmed with Sophie that Fiend would keep loading the names into the matrix while she concentrated on Angela and the two Ruths, digging out anything on them. She agreed these were the best leads we had and would follow them.

We were still missing the motive for the killings. If

Ruth was a connection, was she the trigger that sent the perps over the edge? We needed to find her. She had put a good deal of effort into hiding herself if the two Ruth's were one. There was no record of her past her disappearing act of fifteen months ago.

Did she change her name again or leave the area, and if so, why? Good questions. Her social security number would help there unless she had a fake one, which was not unheard of. If she really wanted to get off the grid, it was possible, not easy, but possible, and that would not be good for us.

Sophie ran the social security number for Ruth's one and two—lots of info on Ruth one, until two-ish years ago—almost nothing on Ruth two. Her social security number came back to a deceased African American man. Fake ID. Now, this was getting interesting, not an official ID change like the witness program. What or who was she afraid of?

We had something to get our teeth into. Two Ruths, this was the lead I wanted us to concentrate on, wherever it led us. Marie would run down all our hard facts for confirmation purposes. Sophie would do the electronic digging for any background still out there. I would hit the KinkInc account for more clues about when Ruth Stevenson changed into Ruth Stonewall and perhaps why.

Ruth's profile was short and sweet. She identified primarily as lesbian, with switch tendencies and very little other personal information. Her age was listed as twenty-seven, which automatically changed with the years. That put her name change at twenty-four or five, two-plus years ago. She had a good number of friends on the KinkInc account, nothing exceptional, few followers, and she didn't follow anyone. She listed a few groups, primarily Lesbian, feminist, and support groups. Her interests were select and clean, detailing bondage and domination, and those were broad definitions.

None of her friends were linked to any names in the PD reports, which didn't surprise me. Many aliases are used on KinkInc. The friends were an eclectic mix of males and females. The photos in her profile were mostly images that interested her, some with religious overtones. None showing her face, some showing her body, mostly clothed, with a few well-done nude or partial nudes credited to a friend, not on KinkInc. A lover? Nothing really, I could hang my hat on.

Ruth two, Ruth Stonewall. What an idiot. Stonewall, of course, I should have recognized it earlier. The Stonewall Bar in NY was a Gay Icon, one of the initiating factors in the Gay rights movement. Taking that name for hers was a statement in itself.

Ruth Stonewall appeared approximately at the same time Ruth Stevenson disappeared, with only a slight overlap. Ruth one had carefully planned and prepared to disappear, leaving one life and starting another. Even with a legal name change, the social security number wouldn't. As Sophie said, fake IDs can be purchased if you know the right people. Ruth Stonewall had leveraged who and what she knew to start over.

Next question. Did she stay in San Francisco or leave the city and perhaps the state? Under that name, there was nothing past the fifteen-month-ago mark. We needed to find her. It would either be a good lead or another dead end, and we needed to know which. I'd gone as far as I could.

Checking in with Marie, she had found the same date barriers as Ruth's. The same lack of information. But something interesting Marie found was that Stevenson possibly was not her original name. It appeared Ruth one, had worked her way through community college, going on to a bachelor's degree, majoring in statistics and financial analysis. Marie tried to back track to high school and got nowhere. Ruth one seemed to have appeared around the age of eighteen or nineteen. Curious and curiouser, the plot thickened. That young she could have been a runaway. She had certainly made her way in the city.

Marie and I interrupted Sophie with the same questions we had regarding the Ruths'. Same result, Sophie said she had scrubbed Ruth #1's social media, not that there was much to find, and no images of her face.

Sophie also hit the date barriers on social media, and the short overlap, although there was even less social media for Ruth #2 than for Ruth #1. Dead ends again. Something had happened, and *poof* she was gone. Nothing, nada, no sign or record. Sophie checked the PD records, nothing in either name.

This time I wasn't discouraged. We made progress and would give this info to Kenzo. He could get his team to investigate places where we couldn't officially go—they had the power of warrants and subpoenas.

This was a good day's work. The fraud case clients who we had taken on was coming along nicely. Erin had been doing the heavy lifting. We had given her a lot of information as a starting point and fed her more as, we or should I say, Sophie and Fiend found it.

Neither Sophie or I felt like indulging in any BDSM play, at home or at the club. The bodies in the park were beginning to get to both of us, and we needed an early night to be ready for a new day.

Chapter Sixteen

The sun shone through a crack in the blinds. The new day dragged me into consciousness. We had gone to bed early, and sleep had evaded me for some time. I still felt tired. The niggle in the back of my mind wouldn't go away. We missed something, and it floated tantalizingly close without actually coming into focus.

Quietly, I slipped out of bed. I didn't want to disturb Sophie. She had been working her computer skills, and that tired her more mentally than physically. Tired is tired, and we needed to be on top of our game. I pottered about the kitchen, but that niggling feeling remained while getting the coffee ritual going.

Breakfast could wait. I didn't feel hungry yet, which in itself was unusual for me. Dressed, with coffee in hand, I left a note for Sophie and had a mug ready for her coffee. I headed off to the office. As I walked, for once oblivious to my city's charm. That thought crystalized into a germ of an idea, which grew into maybe a new stream of information for us to mine.

Opening the office, Marie was already in and busy with the day.

"Hi, just had a brain fart. When Sophie comes in, tell her I have an idea. It will have to wait until I have fleshed it out, so I'm going for a walk."

"Good morning to you, too. Okay. Whatever, boss."

"Oh, and order something for breakfast for everyone.

Feeling that something was about to break, I needed to think the idea through. We, as in no one, had a starting point for all the killings. The field needed to be narrower, and we had already discussed that we had too much data. We had narrowed it down, but not enough. That thing that had been niggling me now leaped to the fore front. Parameters! Sophie and Fiend were always talking about parameters for data. The perp had parameters, too.

The origin date was an important point for the perp. Three weeks was a fixed parameter, one that the perp had set. Something happened at some point to make three weeks critical to the agenda they were following. We didn't know what it represented.

Humans are programmed to follow calendars. It's how we function. In history, it was the seasons. Now, it was down to hourly notes on the phone. Repeating dates is an essential aspect of calendars, birthdays, religions, other anniversaries, and significant events like births, deaths, and marriages.

What if the trigger that set off this killing agenda was the anniversary of a death? I dismissed that a birth or marriage would be the cause for killing five people so far. We start with all the deaths, homicides, suicides, and medical unaccompanied. All of them, and I wanted to include any deaths, even those in hospitals and nursing homes. If there were a three-week gap between the event and the death, that would mean someone was likely under medical care, probably in a medical facility.

Now, to figure out the origin date, move backward.

Take Frankie, the first victim, and her death as the first end date, work back three weeks, and then? The first big anniversary is always a year. That would be our starting point, a significant event that ended in a death three weeks later.

Sophie should be happy to reduce the amount of data by that amount, and I was sure Fiend would be as well. If that didn't work, they would need to go back another year. A second anniversary would be an odd anniversary to use as a starting point unless an additional event caused the trigger.

If that didn't work, they would have to do some computer thing with algorithms or whatever they called them—looking for any death of any description within a three-week window. That was vague as well, I knew, but the chances of a lot of deaths with those criteria had to be slim. Feeling better with what I considered progress, I returned to the office, hoping Sophie had arrived. She was eating whatever Marie had ordered. I was too wound up to eat yet. I would catch up later.

"I think I have found a way to reduce the data."

Sophie jumped at that, "Spill it, I could do with some good news."

Explaining my theory, Sophie got excited and caught up in the moment. She agreed with my approach and started tapping away at her keyboard while calling Fiend. The rest of the day, she and Fiend were back and forth. The fraud case was progressing, and I assisted Erin with some of the physical aspects of the case, including location and how someone could break in without triggering alarms.

Sophie said, "We are done for now. It was a lot of data but an easy dump into the program. Fiend will run it, and the results will be waiting for us when we get in tomorrow. Let's get out of here. That was good thinking, Mas."

"Praise indeed. We will need our rest unless, by some miracle, the data spits out the name and address of the perp."

"Not likely."

"Don't expect it. I do expect it to pop something useful."

Home and feeling a little more relaxed now, we had a third line of inquiry. The killings, Ruth, assumed to be the connection between the victims, and now the search for the point of origin, if the program or algorithm produced what Sophie and Fiend expected it to. I was looking for a name, someone who had died around the time of the first killing a year prior, and there was a three-week gap between the event and the death. There couldn't be that many…I hoped.

****

Sophie was up and around before me and not quietly. Thankfully, she had made coffee, and I could forgive almost anything if I had coffee, good coffee, that is.

"I assume you are eager to get into your program for the results?"

"God, Mas, you are so brilliant. You should be a detective."

"I know I'm brilliant. You just told me."

"I was being sarcastic."

"No, really?"

We both laughed, a lighter laugh than we'd had for some time. We both felt the noose closing in on the perps, keep the momentum going.

The office was quiet when we opened up. Beating Marie in, I opened the office while Sophie cranked up her computer.

Sophie hissed aloud, "Yes, it worked, kinda. We put the algorithm together quickly. It's not perfect, but we have some results, and it's much better than the three hundred and fifty-plus deaths we were working on before."

"And the number is twenty-four, three homicides, six suicides, four believed accidental overdoses, and eleven in hospital."

"That is a much better number. No names attached, I suppose?"

"No, this was pulling the data for deaths on your parameters, but we have a much more manageable number to get through. I'll have Marie pull the death certificates." Sophie paused before continuing with. "I think keeping this in-house would be better, the three of us doing it. If it gets out of hand and we need Fiend, bring him in."

Twenty-four was a fantastic reduction in numbers. If I didn't see the names I was looking for in the death certificates, each would have to be given a thorough review, a deep dive. We each went back to work. Marie pulled the death certificates with help from Sophie, who then started delving into the police files, looking for the reports that matched the death certificates.

I said, "This will still be a lot of work for three people."

No one argued, and we settled to tackle our tasks, all with a burst of renewed energy. Checking death certificates against the police reports of the incident in question—a laborious chore, but one that we were glad to get into. The three homicides were easy. The three-week parameter that popped for the murders was, one, the perp was caught three weeks later. Two, the murder victim was identified three weeks later. Three, the 'accident' victim was deemed to have been murdered after a three-week, completed investigation.

With those three out of the way quickly, we were left to concentrate on everything else. Twenty-one deaths were still a heavy lift. Our discussions of how best to approach the twenty-one deaths to begin with, required we give every one of the deaths the same weight until something gave us pause to change the weight up or down.

Sophie created a spreadsheet for each death and a master where all the information was logged. We all had access to it and could add or change the info. Sophie was the primary keeper of the spreadsheets. The information came in thick and fast as soon as it became clear we needed assistance, and Sophie contacted Fiend. She said he was a little miffed we didn't include him from the beginning.

The process was to skim the info we could, quickly, get on all the deaths, then decide which ones looked the most promising, prioritizing them one by one. From there, one of us would do a deep dive into that single death. We didn't want to miss anything.

While that was happening, the other two, usually Marie and I, would continue gathering info on any deaths, feeding it into the spreadsheets. Perhaps not the most efficient way of doing the work, but once we were done with a particular death, it was done, and we could move on to the next one, which would have added more info and data.

With Fiend on board, he became the keeper of the master and kept it updated. I couldn't understand how he did it. When we put something into a spreadsheet, the master was updated almost immediately.

I asked Sophie, "Does this guy ever sleep?"

Laughing, she said, "I'm not sure, but he has a great work ethic when something interests him, and a great tolerance for long hours."

Still, not knowing what we were looking for, a little like pornography, hard to describe, but you knew it when you saw it.

Kenzo called on the burner. I answered immediately. "Mas, just checking in. Any news on the names we collected?"

"You beat me to it. We came up with four to five names connected to most, but not all the vics."

"Shit, I was hoping for a miracle. The team is still collecting names. We are also checking every license plate entering and exiting the park on the dates of the body drops from a week prior, looking for stolen plates that the perps may have used. A long shot that anything comes from it, but if they use the same plate more than once, it could help."

"Not a bad idea. We do have some good news. Two of the names were businesses, and we discounted those. If you want to chase them, go for it. The individuals got our attention. The first one, Angela Marinelli, and all her connections to the vics are kosher and explained. Now it gets very interesting. Two names, Ruth Stevenson and Ruth Stonewall. What a coincidence, right? Two people called Ruth were involved."

"And?"

"Gimme a minute. Patience. Ruth Stevenson, connected to most of the vics, disappeared—no records of her before the age of eighteen, and nothing past twenty-three or four. Ruth Stonewall overlaps Ruth Stevenson by a few months and has connections to some of the vics. She disappeared approximately a year before the first victim, Frankie, showed up. We believe the two Ruth's are the same person. Ruth one, her social number is good. Ruth two is as fake as a nine-dollar bill. We are following up on those two as if they are one, which connects them to all the victims."

"Great, send me all you have on those two, and I'll get my guys ripping their lives apart."

"Look in your new laptop. Sophie already sent it. Oh, and Ruth one had a KinkInc account, no activity for several years. Ruth two didn't."

"Thank her for me. Anything else?"

"Not right now. I will contact you if anything breaks."

"Ditto, and thanks, Mas."

He was gone. I didn't want to tell him about the new avenue we were investigating, not yet. I wanted to give him something positive rather than another negative if this didn't pan out. Sophie called me.

"This is also weird, Mas."

"What is?"

"I can't find any pictures, photos, or images of either Ruth, nothing, nada. That is weird. Were there any on Ruth's KinkInc account?"

"Nope, at least not a one showing her face. Anything in the DMV records?"

"No, no driving license under either name. She really avoided identifiable documents."

"Neither name shows up in our trove of death certificates?"

"No. Does that mean Ruth is alive and living somewhere out of state?"

"Possible. Everything about her was rooted in San Francisco. Both Ruth's lived here, and Ruth one changed her identity and stayed in the city as Ruth two. Maybe she changed her identity again. That would explain their disappearance."

"Why stay? She was scared of something or someone. Wouldn't it be better to leave?"

"She identified as a Lesbian on KinkInc. Where else would she go with such a large LGBTQ community?"

"Good point, New York would be my choice."

"That is a big jump. Ruth knew people here. Her KinkInc account proved that. Maybe, she felt safer here in that community than somewhere strange."

"All supposition. Finding her would clear that up."

"Kenzo is going to put his team on that."

"Good, we can keep looking at the deaths and matching them to death certificates. Maybe one will give us more info."

Back to working on the deaths and certificates, a slow and laborious task. One by one, we matched a death to a certificate and got a name that made them more real and, in a lot of cases, sadder. Accidents, suicides, and accidental OD are all in the mix. The list got shorter, and the spreadsheets filled with more and more information. Fiend did a fantastic job with the master and all the individual sheets.

The hours passed quickly, and by the end of the day, we had completed five of the twenty-one. None of the results could be connected to the killings or any of the other pieces of the puzzle we had. All three of us were mentally drained. The stress of needing to do this quickly and thoroughly, plus the subject matter, all took its toll. Sophie called it a day.

"I'm taking a page out of Mas's book. We need to be fresh doing this. Let's go to the Lipo lounge and get an early dinner."

I said, "I'm in."

Marie said, "Me too. I'll call Chung, okay?"

I responded, "Of course, Chung is always welcome, part of the family, right?"

Marie smiled and called. He agreed to meet us at the Lipo lounge, with the proviso that we didn't get trashed until he arrived. We didn't, and we all went to a Chinese restaurant, a favorite of Chung's, close by in Chinatown. Early in and early out. The meal was excellent and the company better. Saying our goodbyes, Sophie and I walked home and crashed.

****

The early night did us good. We both woke up refreshed and ready to face a day of more tragedy and sadness in the review of the death certificates. With coffee in hand, we walked to the office. Marie had beaten us in and brought focaccia from Liguria, always the best in the city and always appreciated.

Sophie asked, "What's the occasion?"

Marie responded, "It's today, and that's good enough."

We couldn't argue with her logic because we didn't want to. We all enjoyed the breakfast and hit the work we had before us. Stopping only for regular coffee refills and a delivered lunch. The day followed the same pattern as the previous one. The hours went quickly, and by the end of the day, we had covered six more deaths, and as a repeat of the previous day, nothing we could relate to why we were doing all this. Frustration showed on both Sophie's and Marie's faces.

I said, "This is what detective work is about, lots of disappointment and even more frustration. Detective work is a marathon, not a sprint. We go home, get rested, and carry on tomorrow, and again, until we have something to hang on to, okay?"

They both nodded in agreement. Marie said she was going home and making sure Chung knew she loved him. Sophie said that was a good idea. We locked up and walked home hand in hand.

Both of us had seen death up close and personal. My partner was killed in an accident, and Sophie's sister was murdered. I'd also seen too many mangled bodies as an Inspector in the PD. We needed a release, and I didn't mean a kink one, not this time.

We needed to laugh. We searched for a comedy special and laughed until it hurt. Laughter is good medicine, and we almost overdosed ourselves. Bed beckoned, and we crashed, naked, spooning together.

****

The next day was not so kind to us. We had slept well, but we didn't feel rested. Anxious to start back in with the deaths because the sooner we started, the sooner it would be completed. We still had ten more to go, and going on the previous days' progress, it would probably be at least two days' work. Bleary-eyed and caffeinated, we walked our usual route to the office. Today, we were quiet, each in our own thoughts. I'd seen enough tragedy in the PD to last a lifetime. This was different. This was a concentrated tragedy, one after another.

The accidents, suicides, OD's, accidents you could kinda live with, they were not planned. They happened, and you just had to live with the results, no rhyme or reason. Those who planned and executed suicide, for the most part, were successful. Not all were. The determined ones were successful, and I never understood what could drive someone to take so desperate an action. The OD addicts are all on a short timeline, a mixture of bad dope, infection, assault, and, of course, overdose. Especially overdoses with the new concoctions and much more lethal drugs available at a lower cost. It was depressing, and when this was over, we would all need a vacation to restore our souls.

We all felt the same way. Now was the time to work the data, get what we needed, and close out this depressing project. Erin, working on the fraud case, called needing something from Sophie computer-wise, and me to do some leg work.

Sophie quickly and easily dug out what Erin needed. I followed up on her ask, reviewing the physical location where the alleged fraud took place.

Finding evidence of a carefully forced entry, nothing as obvious as broken windows or damaged locks, but the evidence was there if you knew what to look for, and I did. Taking photos of all the necessary evidence, I sent them to Erin, who would include them in her report to us. We would then close the case with our complete report to the clients.

That only took part of the day. The rest was taken up, continuing our review of the deaths, and due to the Erin distraction, we only completed four. Six left. Do we try for a fifth or leave it as six for the morrow? Unanimously, we decided on six for tomorrow.

****

Another day, another death. This review had gotten to us. Every day we continued, the cases seemed sadder or more tragic. We realized it was us, not the deaths. I pushed for completion today, and we all knew that was a challenge and said nothing. All the finished reviews had yet to produce any of the names I wanted, which was frustrating. I had to think about it.

Without a name that tied into the ones we had to connect to all the victims, we would be back at square one again. Not a place I wanted to be, this review was, assuming we finished everything today, four days closer to another abduction and another body drop. Pushing through, we were vigilant. We couldn't afford to skip any steps. This work had to be one hundred percent accurate to be of any value.

Lunch came, and we ate the delivered food at our desks. The office was eerily quiet, with the exception of tapping keyboards.

Marie paused and said, "I have a name. It's not a hundred percent. Would you guys check it out?"

Quickly, I went to her desk, looking over her shoulder. The name popped off of the screen. Esther Ruth Whitney. The death certificate gave a treasure trove of information, like her fathers and mother's names, including mother's maiden name. Bingo! Stevenson.

We had her. We'd found the real Ruth. Esther Ruth Whitney. The certificate also listed the immediate cause of death, overdose of opioids, and the *'Approximate interval between onset and death.'* Twenty-one days, the three-week gap. *'Manner of death'* suicide. An autopsy had been performed. *'Decedents mailing address'* was listed as Ruth Stonewall's address at Jeremy and Ashton's rental property.

We were tying Esther Ruth Whitney to Ruth Stevenson and Ruth Stonewall. We had a person, and maybe the one who triggered the killings. All her names fit, her age fit, the timeline fit, and the gap between killings fit. It all meshed neatly. Great, this was progress. Now, we had to figure out who was behind the killings.

First, stop by the PD to look up the police report that her attempted suicide would have generated. That would give us more info on her and the circumstances that may have led to her suicide. Hopefully, the person who found her was still in the city. Find them and ask questions they hopefully would be willing to answer to fill in some gaps.

Sophie was excited and passed all this info on to Fiend for him to start digging into the parents. She would be doing the same. The difference in the atmosphere in our office was palpable. A calmness seemed to have descended on us. There was still too much to do for us to relax.

Next was to pass on all our info and data to Kenzo. He could make it look like his team had put it all together. This was our best lead, and we were all convinced that Esther was the point of origin. We could start putting all the data we had into perspective and fill in the pieces of the puzzle. I guaranteed there would still be pieces missing, and as always, it would take teamwork to finish this horror show.

Texting Kenzo on the burner. I told him to check

the new info on the laptop Sophie had given him, and as soon as he could review the material, to get back to me. For us, we were looking for the person who had reported the suicide, Ms. Adrianna Hernandez. The address and phone number were in the police report, a good start if they were still valid. There was only one way to find out. The phone first.

The call went through and straight to voice mail. What we were going to ask was not the sort of thing you do over the phone. Besides, it was harder for the person to say no face-to-face. Sophie checked the DMV and found a driver's license in Adrianna's name and with the same address listed, which is a good sign. Sophie checked Ruth Stevenson's social media, including KinkInc, to see if we could find any links to Adrianna.

A couple of 'friends' looked promising, but with not much to go on, we couldn't be sure. It would be a visit to Adrianna's home address. We didn't know her work schedule. We would need some surveillance to find and confirm it was her. Sophie was trolling social media for signs of Adrianna. She found her, but very little activity and no photos of her face, another media-shy person. I wondered if she had been in a relationship with Ruth and had been cautious about social media because Ruth was.

We would do the surveillance ourselves, adding Oso if he was available for part of the night shift. Oso answered his cell on the first ring.

"Hola Mas, wassup."

"You still free evenings?"

"Depends on which evening, tonight is okay, tomorrow not so much. I can switch up if you needs me."

"No, don't move anything, but tonight would be good. Eight to midnight. Will that give you enough rest for tomorrow?"

"Si, no problem. Senora Tara got a late start tomorrow."

Good news. Oso was still driving Tara Zosa, a former client. After the case she was involved in was closed, she kept Oso on as her driver for multiple reasons. It was a good deal for both of them. I knew Oso from my days in the PD. He had turned his life around, and I was pleased to see it.

Marie would do four to eight, eight to midnight covered, I would take over for Oso at midnight, and Sophie could spell me at six a.m. Yeah, I know, I was a sucker for punishment. Doubting anything would happen between midnight and six, I took the long, boring stint. If Adrianna showed up early all the better. Marie or Oso would call me if Adrianna showed up, and Sophie and I would run over and hopefully get some time with her.

With the plan set, I relaxed, taking in our progress. It was good, but not enough to catch the perps. Sophie said she had some info to share.

"We need a meet." Marie and I huddled around Sophie's desk.

"Okay, Mas. I checked into Ester Ruth's parents, and it's interesting. Her father is a professor at Trinity College, a Christian University in San Francisco, and teaches Evangelical studies. There is the usual blurb on the school, and it's a very, very conservative place from the home page and the mission statement. There's not much on him, just a brief CV; he has spent most of his career at this university, rising from post-grad to associate professor to full professor. Married, spouse not named, three children not named, and that's about it. Comments."

Marie spoke first, "Sounds like a protestant version of the Spanish Inquisition to me."

Sophie laughed, saying, "You might be right; everything points to a narrow version of the Christian dogma. Lots of rules in the online handbook, I would guess they are not LGBTQ friendly."

Marie asked, "Do you think the parents are the perps? Their daughter came out as lesbian, that had to be a mind fuck for them. Her suicide anniversary a trigger for killing the LGBTQ people she knew and worked with?"

Sophie responded with, "Why not."

Trying to be neutral, I said, "Just because someone has a deeply held set of beliefs or faith doesn't mean they were nuts or extreme."

Marie snapped back, "Doesn't mean they aren't extreme and willing to do anything to protect them. Religion has fucked up this planet more than anything. Most wars started with religion, going back to the Old Testament. I don't give a shit what you believe, that's your business, but don't tell me what or who to believe in, that's my business. Chung and I take the Buddhist view, the middle way. We both believe that any extreme is bad, left, right, religious, anything."

Marie never failed to surprise us. I couldn't disagree with her perspective.

Sophie agreed, saying, "Agreed on the religion part. My dad was an early believer in the computer revolution and had a saying about the science vs belief without question argument. *It's better to have questions about answers than answers that can't be questioned.* I always liked that. I have no idea where he got it from. He read a lot of philosophy as well as the science stuff."

"Okay, so we're all agreed. We look into the parents in case they are nuts and killing associates of their daughter."

Sophie and Marie chorused their agreement. Marie will look into the professor and the university. Sophie would follow both parents' electronic footprint. I would pull the DMV records and follow up on that info. We set to work. I was the first to get a result.

"Guys, they own a white minivan. It's the same make as the one we followed from the park, but I'm not sure if it's the same model. Their address from the DMV is in Pacific Heights, the same area where we lost the minivan."

Marie asked, "Do we have them?"

"No, still circumstantial, too many white minivans in the city."

"So, another piece of the puzzle?"

"Maybe we need to confirm it is the minivan and if it is, do they have alibis for the drop dates?"

Sophie said, "This is weird. I can find financials for the father, Weymouth Henry Whitney. Credit cards and bank accounts, but nothing much on the wife, Mary Judith Whitney. There is only one credit card, and the only activity on it is grocery and family stuff, no internet purchases. None. See what I mean. Weird."

Both Marie and I asked, "How did you get that so fast?"

"I hacked the university, very sloppy security, even for an academic facility. I got into Whitney's computer.

It's mostly professor stuff, minimal personal stuff. But I have his credit card and bank statements, and they are not even close to living beyond their means. Bank accounts are in joint names. It seems he keeps Mrs. Whitney on a pretty tight leash."

"Keep looking into them, Marie. Anything?"

"I have an appointment with the university's chancellor tomorrow afternoon for an interview regarding an article I'm writing on influential Christian educators—namely Weymouth Whitney—or a midwest Christian periodical."

"Just be careful. Do you have a back story for cover?"

"Of course. Don't worry. I'll be careful not to tip him or Whitney off."

That was a ballsy move, and it could pay off if she were successful. Marie left to be the first to surveil Adrianna's home address. Oso would spell her at eight, and I would spell him at midnight. I went home to get a nap. Sophie continued her research into the parents. At home, I climbed into bed and went into a fitful doze.

Chapter Seventeen

Sophie had been quiet when she came home. I didn't hear her. My phone alarm went off and jerked me back to reality. My head was fuzzy. I hated taking naps. However, they prepared me for the night's job, which I was sure would be futile. If Adrianna didn't show up by midnight, I doubted she would.

I dressed and went into the kitchen. A sandwich, a fresh pot of coffee, and a note from Sophie awaited me. The note said, *'Enjoy the sandwich, be careful. I love you.'* Followed by a big kiss and hug. What more could a man want? I inhaled the sandwich, enjoyed the coffee, and filled a thermos for the night with the rest—the note I put on the fridge with a Philly magnet.

We hadn't heard from Marie or Oso, so Adrianna had not been home. Early to relieve Oso, I wanted to catch up with him for a chat. Traffic was light at this time of night, and I found a parking spot two vehicles down from Oso. His vehicle had seen better days, a lot better on the outside, but I knew under the hood ran a spotless motor, and as near perfect as could be made, and would probably outrun any pursuit vehicle.

He saw me before I could tap the passenger window. The door lock popped, and I entered.

"Oso, how's it going."

"No complaints, Mas. Miss Tara treats me good, money's cool, and its regular. The nightclub hours are getting better. I'm getting known as reliable, and I can handle anything that comes along without fussing."

"Good to hear, and thanks for doing this for us. We appreciate it."

"Nada man, I owes you, and I pays my debts."

"I told you, you don't owe us anything, and I'm paying you for tonight. No arguments."

"Okay, Mas, you're a strange hombre, but I like you.

He gave me a light punch on the shoulder with one of his ham-sized fists. It hurt, but I wasn't complaining.

"Nothing happening?"

"Nah, quiet as a crypt, ain't seen nothing.

We lapsed into silence for a while. I told Oso his shift was over and to scoot. Getting out of the vehicle, the chilly night air hit me, and I shivered. Quickly, I got in my SUV, turned on the radio, and tuned to a rock station. At this time of night, it played all the old San Francisco bands from the sixties. The DJ was an old San Francisco hand and really knew his stuff, filling in with bits of trivia and local knowledge about the bands.

The time passed, and the coffee disappeared, and now I needed the wide-mouth plastic bottle. I could pee without leaving the vehicle, and my chastity cage easily fit in the bottle without me having an accident. Sophie was constantly in my thoughts, and not because I was always aware of my imprisoned cock. No, Sophie was the one I had been waiting for all my life.

I expected her to hot-foot it back East to Philadelphia when her sister's case had been solved. Thankfully, she had accepted my offer to stay in San Francisco, and it wasn't easy. We were both grieving over a loss and worked at it together. We had become a good team, with work to do for ourselves and each other. Life for both of us was becoming something to look forward to.

Back to reality, a car stopped outside the apartment house. Anticipation rose, disappointment, a man got out and entered the building next door. Shit, one thirty a.m., doubtful she would be coming home any later on a work night. You never knew. I would be keeping my schedule in case she did. Everything we had on Adrianna made us believe she was still at this address. Perhaps she would also be a target for the perp. She was associated with Ruth and maybe even been in a relationship with her, which would undoubtedly put a target on her back.

Time dragged by slowly, and the DJ signed off. A pre-recorded program replaced him. It kinda kept me awake, and these were the worst hours. Your body is at its lowest ebb, and everything is a struggle. The darkness was like a cocoon, and it was dark. At its quietest, San Francisco still had an energy, and with its many faults, I wouldn't want to live anywhere else. Thankfully, the city had gotten under Sophie's skin, and she was beginning to feel at home here. The darkness faded into a weird half-light as the fog enveloped the city and filtered the rising sun.

Sophie passed me in a ride share, and it pulled into where Oso had been. A big smile and a large cup of coffee in each hand. What could be a better start to any day? She entered the SUV, smelling fresh and new, and we kissed hello. The aroma of coffee hit me, and my mouth started to water.

"You are a godsend. A boring night, only one

excitement. A car pulled up outside her place, and the guy got out."

Sophie laughed, saying, "I guess we'll do it again tonight?"

"Good guess, same folks, same schedule."

"Right, then we need to get you home for some sleep. Switch, I'll drive while you caffeinate. We'll pick up breakfast on the way home."

"You sure? I can put in a few hours before I crash."

"Yes, I'm sure. We have stuff to be going on with. You rest. If anything breaks, you'll know. Promise."

Sophie now drove like a local, and that scared me. We picked up breakfast, and Sophie dropped me and it off at home. She continued to the office. Breakfast completed, I stripped off and crashed into a welcome bed.

****

The alarm was not a welcome sound, only it wasn't the alarm, it was my phone. I had forgotten to put it on silent. Groggily, I picked it up, looking at the screen bleary-eyed. Sophie calling.

"Hi, what's up?"

"We have more info. Marie and I would like a conference with you if you're up to it."

"What time is it?

"Two thirteen, precisely."

"Oh shit, I slept longer than I wanted, I forgot to set the alarm, I must be losing it."

"No, Mas, it's called exhausted. Get here when you can. We want your input."

"Sure, give me time to shower and wake up, in that order. See you soon."

The shower was a welcome wake-up. I felt better.

Suddenly, I realized what Sophie had said. They had new information—that lit a fire under my ass. I dressed and was on my way in minutes.

Entering the office, I called, "Okay, what's up?"

We all went into the inner office and gathered around Sophie's desk.

Sophie started, "The parents have a white minivan. The license plate doesn't match any we have on the police list as being in the park, but as we know, those plates were stolen anyway. The parents pulled the plug on Ruth-Ester after being in a coma. She had no brain activity. She wasn't going to recover. That was three weeks after her initial intake."

California has a law on the books that states no brain activity equals legally dead. People can be kept on life support if they are organ donors. The medical staff evaluates the viability of using the deceased's organs for transplant and then pulls the plug.

Marie picked up the narrative, "Ester also had an older sister, Martha, and brother, Luther. I can't find much on the sister. She's moved out of the area but still has a valid California driver's license, and her address is between LA and San Diego. I'm still digging into her. The brother is a different matter."

Sophie took over, "Luther is an ordained minister and associate professor at the same university as Dad. He is a staunch believer and supporter of Christian Nationalism."

I interrupted, "What the hell is Christian Nationalism?"

Sophie continued, "Christian Nationalism, good question. I've been looking into that can of worms. The believers take the bible literally, believe that our government should declare our country a Christian nation, advocate Christian values, not enforce separation of church and state, and allow Christian religious symbols in public places."

"You're kidding, right?"

"Not kidding, they want America to be a theocracy."

That's ridiculous. Our country was founded on religious freedom, religious freedom to worship however you wanted if you wanted. This smacked of fascism, the sort of stunts the Third Reich pulled in Germany.

"You think they are involved in revenge for Ruth's, Ester's, death? She's still Ruth to me. It was how she wanted to be known."

"I don't know, and we must follow the leads wherever they lead."

"True. What else about these Christian nationalists?"

"Usually right-wing politically, some extremely so. Keeping America Christian, even though it never was. You have seen some rhetoric being used now in all political forums."

"Yeah, I try and avoid that crap. America was never intended to be a Christian country. It goes back to what Marie said the other day. Believe what you want. Just don't force it on me. We need to learn more about their attitudes toward the LGBTQ community." Looking at Marie, I asked. "How was your interview at the university?"

"Worth it, for sure. Dr. Weymouth Henry Whitney was a student there, a post-grad, and is now a professor. The Dean was candid, to a degree. Everything was positive. Dr. Whitney was a good teacher and mentor. He had several books published, using post-grad students as research assistants, whom he credited. Seems to go out of his way to be seen as fair."

"I feel a 'but' is coming."

"Kinda, nothing said. I got the feeling that the Dean didn't like him. Some of his comments about very conservative views, without saying it, a fundamentalist is what I would guess. The Dean also said that Dr. Whitney keeps a traditional Christian household, read patriarchal. There is nothing there, at least nothing that would lead me to think he was capable of the killings. I've been working on a transcript of the whole interview. I'll give you a copy as soon as it's done."

"Sounds like we have a Christian Taliban in our midst. Did you say you can't find much on the wife?"

Sophie said, "Yes, very little. It looks like she is kept on a tight leash, very submissive to the head of household."

I asked, "Are we reading more into this than is actually there?"

Sophie looked at Marie and said, "Maybe, but I don't think so. There are some pretty fundamentalist Christian groups out there. There is a Pentecostal Christian group in Appalachia that dances with poisonous snakes to prove that if you believe God will protect you. It's a literal take on a passage in one of the gospels."

"That doesn't make them Christian Nationalists."

"True, Christian Nationalists are more aligned with the Taliban, using religion for their own political ends. The US version of Iran's theocracy."

Marie added, "The son, Luther, would he fit that

mold more than his dad.

Sophie said, "Let's get back to what we do know. Their family finances are sound, and they are certainly doing okay. The mortgage is paid off, probably from the proceeds of his books. The minivan they drive is eight years old. It's a family mobile. He drives a newer Cadillac, four years old and not top-of-the-line. Everything is within their means, nothing suspicious. Go to church every Sunday and attend bible classes during the week."

I jumped on that, "What nights, where, how often, and when do those classes end? If they alibi out, we are still in the dark."

"We are working on that. Marie is in contact with the evangelical church they attend in the Sunset district.

Marie said, "I have to be careful with the questions. I don't want to tip anyone off. I'll be asking as if I want to join them."

I said, "Good move. I will call Father Benny and see if he can give us some more information on the Christian nationalists and what presence they have here in San Francisco."

With all our tasks set, we got back to work. My call to Father Benny was put through, going to voice mail. I left a message for him to call me when he could. I had to confirm with Oso, that he could change his schedule-voice mail. If he couldn't change, it would be a very long night for me. I had to do something, with nothing practical to do on the case. Target practice was a good choice. I picked up my weapon and went to the gun range. One side of the range was empty, asking permission for rapid fire. The owner nodded his okay.

Shooting is therapeutic. Follow the safety process

and procedures. Send the target out. Loading the magazines, weapon's safety on, pointing down range. Loading the weapon, cocking it, safety off, fire. A hole appeared in the target, just right of the center cross. I emptied the magazine in short order, and the holes appeared all over the target's center mass, none as well placed as the first round, but all were kill shots.

Eject the magazine, slide in the new one, repeat. Eject the magazine, reload both, and slide one into the weapon. Follow the process and more holes in the target. Repeat, repeat, the target was shredded, and I was covered in GSR. I worked through two hundred rounds and was satisfied with the results.

Rapid fire is never as accurate as slow and deliberate. Like anything, practice makes permanent, not perfect. That is a lifelong journey. Settling up at the front desk, the owner asked if I had heard about the bodies in the park. I said I had, and he wondered if I had any information about them. I avoided his question and deflected to another subject.

The information was getting out about the bodies, and that was not a good thing, especially with the possibility of another drop coming soon. We would be looking at the missing persons log to try and identify a potential victim, and that was being reactive again.

At least we had a list of Ruth-Ester's friends and contacts, and the perps must also have a list of those contacts to be so specific in picking their targets. Who else had access to her life, family, maybe, but it didn't seem likely from the distance she kept from them. Unless all her belongings were delivered to her parents, another task for Sophie was to check to see if she could find Ruth's computer and if it was still active.

Home, my first job cleaning the weapon, an excellent persistent habit, and this one was ingrained in me as much as breathing. I cleaned the weapon thoroughly, put gun grease where needed, and gun oil in other parts. I reassembled, locked, and stashed it away in our bedroom. Now shower and get ready for tonight's hopefully more successful surveillance.

Out of the shower, I saw a new message. Quickly wiping my hands, I opened the text. Oso, he was available for tonight but only until ten p.m.

"I'll take it." I responded, asking if he could start at seven instead of eight. *"If not, no problem."*

Ding, came the immediate response. *"Seven for sure."*

Great, I'd let Marie know she was done when Oso arrived at seven. The two more hours on my shift would be tedious but not a hardship.

All set, I started dinner for us, pasta, and something tasty to get me through the night. Sophie was late coming home, and she had Marie call, warning me Sophie was working late. Marie went to stake out Adrianna's apartment.

Sophie and I sat and had dinner together.

She asked, "Sure you don't want company tonight?"

"Nah, you do your computer stuff and need a clear head. I can handle the surveillance. I'll call if Adrianna shows."

"You'd better. I need to ask her questions. I want to know more about Ruth."

"Yeah, me, too. There is something off about how she wanted to be as anonymous as possible. I'm guessing it's related to her being gay and her family not readily, if ever, accepting it. Maybe even something deeper."

"This is San Francisco!"

"Yup, and there are intolerant people here as well. You've seen Asian hate demonstrated here. There are bigoted people everywhere."

"Guess so. I never really got into joining anything other than the BDSM/kink community, and even then, I was more circumspect back east."

"Our kink community is more open here, but it's still minority, fringe, and not as accepted as the LGBTQ community. I guess time will tell. Hey, I'd better go. I want to be early. Oso has a hard cut-off. He has to be at his next gig at ten, it's close, but he won't be late."

"Go, make sure you call me…yes?"

"Yes, dear, I'll call."

Sophie smiled while twirling the key to my chastity device she always wore on a chain around her neck. I smiled and left to meet Oso.

Parking was more difficult than the previous night, probably due to the earlier hour, ten p.m. is regarded as early in this city. A spot opened, and I slipped in behind the car, leaving. It was only a block away from Oso, and being early enough, I sat with him, chatting until it was time for him to get to his second job of the night. In preparation, I pulled my SUV up behind Oso and double parked. As he pulled out, I took his spot.

One space closer to Adrianna's apartment than the previous night. With a good view of the apartment and the street, I settled in for a potentially long night. The pedestrian traffic was still quite heavy, and I people-watched as they went by. It's always interesting watching people in San Francisco. The mix of ethnicities and cultures is what makes San Francisco such a great city to live in.

The traffic was heavier, and I had to keep an eye out just in case Adrianna did show up. At 11:10 a car stopped outside her apartment, another false alarm. At 11:27 a cab stopped, and a woman got out. My eyes were riveted. We didn't know what Adrianna Hernandez looked like, only the address. The woman looked Hispanic, to go with the name, and approximately the right age seeing her in the dark. Yes, she went to the apartment door and used a key. Grabbing my phone, I hit speed dial for Sophie's number.

Before she could say anything, I said, "Adrianna's home."

"On my way."

She ended the call, and I watched the apartment. The lights had gone on, blinds drawn, and it looked like she was in for the night. My eyes were glued to the apartment, and I didn't want the surprise of her leaving without me seeing her. Or if she had any visitors, unlikely at this time of night, but you never knew. Time passed slowly waiting for Sophie, it always does when you need it to speed up. A tap on my passenger window…Sophie.

"Got here as fast as I could. Anything going on?"

"Nada, lights went on, blinds drawn, that's it."

"Do you think it's too late to knock on her door?"

"Usually yes, not with the timeline we are on. I figure the next victim will be snatched in the next couple of days, if not already. We don't have time for niceties."

"Okay, let's go."

We crossed the road, our private investigator credentials ready to show Adrianna, assuming it was her. The bell sounded, but nothing moved. I tried it again. This time, I heard sounds of movement, and a shadow crossed the glass door side panels. The door opened, and a questioning voice asked.

"Yes, what do you want?"

Sophie answered, "We are private investigators looking into the death of Ruth Stonewall and the recent deaths in Golden Gate Park. We believe they are related."

"What do you want with me?"

I said, "We are looking for background information about Ruth. She wanted anonymity and changed her name at least twice. We are trying to fill in some gaps, which we hope will give us a lead to the perpetrators."

"Ruth killed herself. It was a suicide."

Her voice carried a lot of pain. Sophie and I recognized that hurt. We knew it intimately.

I asked, "Can we come in? I know it's late, but your information could be valuable."

She hesitated before asking, "How do I know you are, who you say you are?"

We both showed our credentials, but she still hesitated. Then, she made up her mind and said, "Okay, come on in."

The apartment was neat and tidy, feminine in a masculine way if that makes sense. A single person's home. Sparse modern furniture and some original artwork on the walls, with a few photographs of Adrianna and probably some family members scattered about. One photo stood out, not a family member.

Suspecting it was of Ruth, maybe we were right about the relationship between Adrianna and Ruth. That question could wait.

Adrianna said, "Please sit. It's been a while since I talked about Ruth."

We sat and waited. When it comes to interviewing suspects or witnesses' patience is a virtue. She was lost in thought. A frown crossed her forehead. They were not pleasant thoughts, for sure.

She asked, "What do you want to know?"

I said, "Anything you can tell us about her history, family, relationships, anything."

"We were together for about six or seven months before she OD'd. We were planning on moving in together. I wasn't sure if it was an accidental or deliberate OD. She, we weren't drug users per say, we dabbled in some cannabis and very occasionally some X. Alcohol was our drug of choice, and that was in moderation. After she was hospitalized, before her parents came, I accessed her computer. I found some disturbing e-mails from someone called Angel Michael."

"What did they say? Did you know this person?" Sophie asked.

"No idea who he or they were. The e-mails were threatening, saying they had found her again and would always find sinners…that she was a heretic and needed to return to God or she would spend eternity in hell, and they alone could save her. They went on about religious stuff. There were no more e-mails after Ruth was admitted to hospital."

I asked, "Did you keep or copy the e-mails."

"No, I didn't know what to do. By the time I

decided I needed to do something and report the stalking. Ruth's parents had cleared out her apartment. They didn't know we were in a relationship. They assumed I was a friend from work because I said we were meeting for dinner that night. I didn't, don't... want anything to do with them. They are fucking evil."

Sophie jumped in. "What makes you say that?"

"They are all so Christian, high and mighty. Fucking hypocrites is more like." She said it with a voice loaded with venom and anger. "When she came out to them as being gay, actually they accused her of being a homosexual, and she admitted she was. They sent her to a camp or religious place where they 'cure' you of being gay. Assholes, it's torture and abuse. When she turned eighteen, she left home and never returned."

Sophie said, "Conversion therapy...that's illegal."

Before Adrianna could respond, I said, "Only in some states. It's still legal in more than you would think. We had to deal with the results of that crap when I was in the PD, runaways, and kids living on the street. It was better than being at home."

Sophie asked no one in particular, "What is wrong with people?"

Adrianna spoke slowly, "Ruth was a very gentle soul. She was damaged and hurt. She was still willing to give. She was the first to help anyone in the LGBTQ community that needed it, mostly anonymously."

I asked, "Can you tell us more about her? We need to know everything we can."

"I can only tell you what I know, which isn't very much."

I said, "Everything you can about her family."

Sophie added, "Do you remember the login and passwords to her computer?"

"I wrote that stuff down so I wouldn't forget it. Ruth always had me able to access her computer. She was terrible with passwords, and she changed them frequently. She always gave a copy to me as her backup."

Sophie said, "Good habit changing passwords, especially if you are worried about security."

"She was. She was a little paranoid with just cause. She kept me a secret from almost everyone we knew. She started feeling more comfortable, then 'Angel Michael' appeared in her e-mail. That changed everything."

We spent the next hour listening to Adrianna talk about Ruth and their relationship. We asked questions, focusing on Ruth's family. Adrianna only knew what Ruth had told her. She had only met them that once to speak to them. At Ruth's funeral, she kept her distance from them. We had much more information on Ruth's background, and a lot sounded disturbing to both of us.

Adrianna rooted out the last few passwords that Ruth had used on her computer. She had Ruth's IP address. Something Ruth had Adrianna do was take a photograph on her phone of her computer details. Adrianna never asked why and had not deleted anything of Ruth's from her phone.

Our guess that the single photograph was of Ruth was correct, and I asked, "May I take a photo of the photo? Until now, we didn't know what she looked like. None of her social media had her face showing."

"I know, when I asked about that, she would deflect, change the subject, or say she didn't like her photo being taken. I figured it was something in her past and didn't push it."

Sophie said, "Thank you for all this. I know it's hard losing someone you care for. It hurts more than anyone can ever tell you. Just know it does get better eventually. We will let you know if we find out anything."

"Thanks, not sure I want to know. Maybe I will later."

With that, we said good night knowing we had pulled a scab off a partially healed wound. On the way home, we were quiet, each processing our thoughts on the information that Adrianna had given us. I was sure Sophie was also thinking about how to get into Ruth's computer. If it were still active, it would be easy to do. Here's hoping.

We parked outside of the home and would drop off the SUV tomorrow. We walked up the steps, and Sophie asked, "Do you think the parents are the ones doing the killing?"

I had thought about that myself, not coming to a definite conclusion. "Possibly, I'm not sure they have the physicality to manage the body drops or the facility to hold and torture the victims."

"I wondered about that. Maybe they have access to somewhere we don't know about."

"Again, possible, it would have to be somewhere they knew they wouldn't be disturbed. That makes me think the perps own it, or a completely abandoned property, less likely."

As we got ready for bed, Sophie said, "We need a decompression session, just us, for us. Tomorrow would be a good night for Ms. Circe to come to our rescue. What do you think, Mas?"

"I think that Ms. Circe would be welcome." My cock started getting hard at the thought of Sophie's alter ego, Ms. Circe coming out to play. Whatever it was, it would be a good distraction for both of us, and I would hope for a release for me. With that thought forefront in my mind, I crashed into sleep.

Chapter Eighteen

With the prospect of Ms. Circe appearing later that day, Sophie and I were energized. We were up early enough to make breakfast at home. We enjoyed each other's company as the sun rose over the city. We rarely did this on a weekday, showing how much stress we were under. We needed this together time, away from work and out of the kink part of our relationship, just the two of us, connecting on a soul-to-soul level.

It couldn't last, and it didn't. We were in the middle of clearing up when my phone lit up. Kenzo.

"Hi Kenzo, what's up."

"Hi, Mas. I didn't wake you, did I?"

"No, would it bother you if you had?"

Laughing, he said, "No, not really. I'm checking in. We have torn apart the two Ruth's lives, not much to tell. The social security number tracks back to an Ester Whitney, who seems to have disappeared around eighteen. Anything I should be aware of?"

Kenzo knew something he wasn't telling us. Fishing. I guess it was time to come clean."

"We know. We traced Ruth back to Ester RUTH Whitney through death certificates.

"Shit, Mas, and you are telling me this now."

"We needed to be careful and double-check everything before passing it off to you. We have linked Ester to Ruth Stevenson, her mother's maiden name, then to Ruth Stonewall. Her death was three weeks after she OD'd."

"And why are you so sure she is the one that started all this killing."

"The first victim, Frankie, was dropped on the first anniversary of her death. We have been sifting through everything we can find on her and found her partner. We met her last night, and she filled us in on some of Ruth's family background."

"Spill it, Mas. I need to know everything you do and where it came from. This has to follow procedure one hundred percent."

"Chill, we are still piecing this stuff together ourselves. The prime suspects have to be her parents, but I'm not sure that's kosher. Something is missing. Look, let's meet. Can you come to the office? It would be better. We have everything separated and logged by category; what we have done, and how we have done it. Hey, and Kenzo, it's all done right, no crossed lines."

"Got it. Yeah, I can come to you. It may be a while, and I need to make sure no one knows where I am. If something comes up, I'll call on the burner.

"No problem. We are home and will be in the office in thirty minutes, tops."

"Right, see you soon."

Kenzo ended the call. Sophie and I left what we hadn't cleared up for later and went to the office. Driving the SUV to the rented parking spot was easier than expected, and the office was just around the corner. Marie entered as we made the entrance to our building. We told her Kenzo would be visiting.

Opening the office, first things first, I started the coffee. I was on my second cup when Kenzo arrived.

He entered and quickly shut the door behind him. We all looked at him in surprise.

"I may have a tail. I know the brass has someone watching me at the PD. Probably tapping my phone lines to cover their asses if this shitshow goes south."

"Sit down," I said. "We've made progress. It's still not a home run, but we feel we're getting much closer."

For the next forty-five minutes, Kenzo listened intently and asked a ton of good questions. Some we answered. Some we didn't have the answers to, but Sophie had put all our info on the laptop we supplied to him. That was the best and easiest way to get him the information without anyone knowing it.

We also warned him not to push too much in the direction of Ruth's family. We were working on it and had some ideas but needed time to flesh them out. He would get anything we had as soon as we were sure it was good information.

He was skeptical but went along with us. "You've come through so far. Please keep me in the loop earlier. This is going to help and give the team something else to follow. The powers that be still think it's more about sex than religion. Whatever."

He left in a better frame of mind...a good thing. I understood the pressure he was under.

I asked Sophie to look in the PD computers for anything negative regarding Kenzo's handling of the bodies in the park case. We would warn him of any potential danger, anonymously, of course. Sophie complained that it was a sidetrack. She was searching for Ruth's computer and would get to the PD later.

"How's that going?"

Snappily, she said, "I'll let you know when I'm

ready to."

With that, I let her be. I reviewed the notes we had taken on our visit to Adrianna. As I read them, a thought occurred to me. Adrianna had to be in danger. She was Ruth's romantic partner. Others whom Ruth knew, worked with, and interacted with were all in the LGBTQ community and had been targeted for killing. Why not Adrianna? The perps didn't know who she was or about her relationship with Ruth. That was unlikely with the specific targeting so far, or maybe they were saving her as a later victim. If that was true, how many more deaths were we looking at? Too many.

We had to warn Adrianna and tell her what was happening. We only gave her the bare minimum of information when we interviewed her. The possibility was too significant not to provide her with all the information we had and the danger she could be in. She had given us her contact information. I called her.

"Hello, is this Mas?"

"Yes, can we meet for lunch? We need to update you on the situation regarding Ruth's death and the current situation. You deserve to know."

"You sound serious."

"I am. It could be serious for you. I don't want to upset you, but you must know what's happening. Can we meet?"

"Sure. I checked you out when I got to work. It looks like you are who you say you are. You've had some good press."

"Good. When and where?"

"I work close to Japan Town. Do you know the Sushi go-round in the shopping center?"

"Yes, we need somewhere quieter and more

private. There is a restaurant, just the other side of the inside bridge, that would be better. Lunch is on me."

Okay, I know it. Is noon okay?"

"Yes, that's fine, see you soon."

Hanging up the call, I hoped she was not the target for this weekend's body drop. I re-read the notes and made my observations in the margin. It was bothering me. Adrianna should have been a prime target. Perhaps Ruth had protected her by not keeping any reference to her on her computer or phone.

We were convinced that Ruth's computer and phone were the prime source of the perp's information about Ruth's life. If Sophie could find the computer and it was on, she could track it and access it easily with the info Adrianna had provided. That would give us an edge in finding the perps and stopping them. *Don't run before you can walk, Mas. Get Adrianna to safety, and let Sophie do her thing.*

There was no way I was going to be late for meeting Adrianna. I left early. Parking was always tricky in Japan town and was always worth it—one of my favorite ethnic areas of the city. I walked the block and a half to the main shopping center. With time to spare, I wandered around, looking at the various shops and restaurants. Making sure I was waiting for her at the restaurant when she arrived.

Noon came, five past, ten past, and I was beginning to worry and about to call her when she arrived breathless and apologetic.

"Sorry, I'm late. I hate being late. Last minute panic at work."

"That's okay. I was starting to worry something had happened. Let's go in and eat."

We were seated quickly. The restaurant was not yet busy. Once seated, a pot of tea was promptly delivered. I began to explain the situation as we saw it.

"We believe you're in some danger from the people who are doing the killings in the park. You've heard about them?"

"Yes, but what does that have to do with me?"

"You were Ruth's partner. We are sure she is the trigger for the killings. The first body showed up on the anniversary of her OD. Ruth was taken off life support three weeks after you called the paramedics—the next body, three weeks later. The next victim was three weeks after that. Every single victim has had a direct connection to Ruth and has shown up every three weeks since. Where she worked, her landlords, the list goes on."

Adrianna went pale, and her hands shook. A tear appeared and ran down her face. Her voice trembled as she asked.

"What are you saying? That I'm next?"

"We don't know who's next. We do know every victim has been killed in the manner of a saint, a gay saint. All the victims were in the LGBTQ community, just like you are."

"But I don't know anything more than what I told you last night."

"I understand that. I'm here to help you if you will let us. As a precaution, in case you are in danger."

"If what you tell me is true, why isn't more of this in the media."

"The police are trying to keep it as much as possible under wraps. Don't want to start a panic in any community."

"I'm not sure I believe you entirely. What do you want me to do?"

"Is there somewhere you can stay for a few days?"

"Yes, I have friends down on the peninsula. I'm sure they won't mind if I stay with them for a few days."

"Also, vary your routine as much as possible, and never use the same route to and from work. How do you get to work?"

"It varies, bus or trolly mostly."

"Another thing, no nightlife. The victims that we have tracked were snatched at various times of day, but mostly after dark."

Our food arrived, and she picked at hers. I enjoyed mine, I was hungry, and the food was good.

"Call your friends, and make sure it's okay for you to stay. If it's all arranged, I will drive you there today and pick you up in the morning." I knew I would regret that offer, but it was made. "We need to keep you safe until they are caught."

"I can't believe all this is happening. Thank you. Not everyone is so concerned about safety of the gay community."

Laughing, I said, "Sophie and I are in the kink community; we understand to a degree."

"You are? You seem so normal. Sorry, I didn't mean it like that."

"It's okay, it's not what's on the outside, it's what's on the inside that counts. Call your friends. I'll wait."

Adrianna called a friend, but there was no answer, so she left a message. Called the partner and spoke quietly, only giving the bare minimum of details. She smiled and thanked the person. Looking at me, she said, "Good to have friends. We are set. They will pick me up after work and take me back to their place. I'll share details with you so you know where I am."

"What time do you need me to pick you up?"

"Work is flexible unless there is a fire drill. Tomorrow, I need to be in." She broke off and checked her calendar. "You work out the timing to get me into the city by nine-thirty."

Great, not extremely early, although I would still have to leave early to get down to San Bruno and return by nine-thirty. I offered, and it was safer that way. She had picked at her food, finally doing a decent job after I had encouraged her. I paid the check and walked her to my SUV. Driving her back to work, I made her promise to wait for her friends inside until they were outside. She promised. We parted, and after I saw her enter her building, I drove back to the office to update my partners.

Sophie was tucked away behind her array of screens. She said nothing, so I assumed she hadn't found Ruth's computer yet. Marie had a few checks for me to sign, which I did, that kept her happy.

I sat at my desk and began to review everything we had, again. I was concentrating on the newer information. Considering the religious history of Ruth and her family, I wondered if they were the ones responsible for the killings. The parents were probably extreme enough in their beliefs, but were they capable of carrying out the torture and the continuing agenda? I doubted it, but I couldn't dismiss them as suspects, at least not yet.

The parents' alibis for as many of the snatch times,

of which some were pretty broad, would have to be checked and established by Kenzo and his team. They had the manpower to do that quickly and with little fuss. Normal procedure. Unlike us private investigators snooping around, that always aroused suspicion and often resentment.

Marie still had to visit the church for the weekly evening meetings to see how long they ran. She would also take photos of the parents if they showed up. I thought that was this evening and would check with her—a gotcha from behind Sophie's monitors that sounded like good news.

Sophie shouted out. "Ruth's computer is on, and I am in. All the info Adrianna gave us is good. Nothing had been changed since Ruth used it. I am trying to track its location, but it is not as easy as a phone. I'll take a look in her address book and copy it."

That was good news. If and when Sophie got Ruth's address book, it might give us a clue as to who the next target was.

"Shit, shit, shit. It's been shut down again. That was quick. Someone was on her computer, but it's been shut down again. Whoever was in it, using it to get what they were looking for and getting out in such a short time, must know the computer well. At least we know it is still functioning and being used. I'll ask Fiend to monitor it if it comes online again."

I said, "Still useful info. We know it's in use, probably by the perps, and they have to have some computer skills, right?"

Sophie pondered the question before answering, "Yes, some if they had access to Ruth's passwords. That would make it easy for them. Adrianna said Ruth was not good at remembering her passwords, and she probably wrote them down somewhere. Bad idea."

"And they have had a year to go through all her files. Unless the family got rid of her computer, it leads me back to the family as suspects. Have you found out anything more about the brother?"

"Not much to find, married, four kids, wife is a stay-at-home mother. He preaches twice each Sunday, a.m. and p.m. services at a church like the one his parents attend, but it seems it has a smaller congregation. All I can find on his finances is that he is solvent but certainly not wealthy."

"Not with four kids in this city. Do they own their home?"

"Not yet, mortgage. Don't know when they bought it, going through public records for the address."

"Okay, how about we call it a day?"

"Why, Mas, are you eager to get home?"

As she said that, she twirled that key around. Smiling, one of those "I know something you don't" smiles. That, as usual, got me going. A release would be an excellent end to the day, Sophie, or should I say Ms. Circe had blued my balls. I would have to earn my release and be happy to do so. Whatever she wanted was alright by me.

"Not at all. We can't do anything else here today, and Marie has her church thing, so I thought an early night would be good."

"But Mas, what makes you think it will be an early night."

She was teasing me, playing with my mind. A mind fuck, and she was excellent at those. She kept me on edge, and I loved it.

"Nothing at all, dear."

"Well, let's go and see what the night brings."

My cock was brutal in its cage, pre-cum was going to mark my underwear, and I was anxious for whatever was to come, pun intended.

As we walked out of the building, Sophie said she would prefer to eat out tonight, as it would save clearing up, and we could get straight to the desert. She chose a restaurant close to home, where we were known. Seated with drinks delivered, Sophie absent-mindedly undid a button on her shirt. A view of the top of her cleavage appeared. I knew what she was doing, and I loved it. Tease and denial.

We ordered our favorite dishes, and another button was released. More cleavage was exposed, and the edge of her bra. Her comment that it was hot in the restaurant was an excuse, and I agreed she was *hot*. The food arrived, and Sophie was the only person I had ever seen who could make eating spaghetti look sexy. Sophie swirled the fork, lifting it with just enough pasta and sauce. She leaned over to take the fork full of pasta, her shirt opening even more as her lips closed over the pasta.

This was doing nothing to relax me or my caged dick. Food is an underrated erotic adventure, and Sophie was using it to her full advantage. Leaning back, she smiled, her shirt closing up a little. My eyes had dropped to her shirt as it closed, which caused her to open one more button. More teasing gave me glimpses of what lay beneath. Winding me up to keep me on edge was working like a dream.

Leaning forward for another mouthful of pasta, her shirt opened tantalizingly, showing me more of her bra, a confection of sheer and lace. Her nipples had hardened and were like beacons in the fabric, directing me to the cleavage. Turned on was an understatement. I couldn't wait for the meal to end and get us home for dessert.

Sophie didn't bother to rebutton her shirt, and that caused some heads to turn as we left the restaurant. I chuckled to myself, thinking if they only knew. We made it home in record time, and as soon as we had closed the door behind us. Her lips attached to mine in a deep, lingering kiss. Responding only with my lips, I knew better than to grab her, so I gently enveloped her in a gentle hug.

Breaking away breathlessly, she said, "It's time you were appropriately attired. Strip, I left you something this morning for tonight, and I will summon you when I'm ready."

"As you wish, Ms. Circe."

I undressed quickly and carefully folded my clothes, leaving them in a neat pile. Still erect in the cage, I waited to be summoned. For service to Sophie's alter ego, Ms. Circe, in any way she desired. Ms. Circe had not asked me if I consented to anything she would have me do. I knew it would be something we had discussed and engaged in prior occasions.

She had left me the usual wrist and ankle cuffs, with the addition of thigh cuffs and no posture collar. The wrist and ankle cuffs took me no time to attach. I've had plenty of practice, and the thigh cuffs took only a little longer, partly because they were joined together by a short chain that hobbled my stride. All locked in place, I was ready for her.

Waiting has never been one of my strengths, and

Ms. Circe knew it and played on it. Waiting, wondering what she had in mind, it played on my mind, mind games. Anxious feelings began to rise. Why was she taking so long? My stomach had butterflies, which was normal for me in this situation, and tonight, there were lots of them.

"Mas." I heard my name called. Her voice went through me like a jolt of electricity, even though I was waiting to hear her summons. "I need my desert. Come to me."

I didn't need a second invitation, as I hurried to the bedroom as fast as my joined legs would let me. The locks on my cuffs rattled with each step, and announced my arrival. The bedroom was softly lit with dimmed lights and fragrant candles. Sophie was standing on one side of the bed, backlit. I could see she was wearing something diaphanous. The outline of her body was clearly shown in silhouette. Whatever she wore or didn't, I never tired of looking at her. There was always something new to discover about her body. A freckle here, a tiny scar there, a crease I hadn't noticed before. I loved this woman more than I ever imagined I could love anyone, which sometimes scared me.

"Mas, where are you?"

"Here, Ms. Circe, at your service."

"I certainly hope you're at my service. It's what I expect, and you know I prefer to reward than punish, but sometimes you need a reminder of who is in charge."

"No reminders required. I always know who's in charge, you, Ms. Circe."

"Well, we shall see how good you are tonight. Please mount the bed and lay on your back in the center."

Following her instructions quickly, I settled in the center of the bed, waiting for the next instruction. I had an idea what it would be, and I was right.

"Please extend your arms out to the corners of the bed."

Reaching out to the upper corners, Ms. Circe swiftly clipped my cuffs to chains bolted to the base of the bed. My arms could move a little, not enough to reach the clips. I was fixed until Ms. Circe released me.

"Now, please spread your legs as far as you can."

The thigh cuffs joined by a chain restricted the spread I could achieve. Ms. Circe adjusted a spreader bar to the correct length and fixed it to the ankle cuffs. She then clipped the center of the spreader bar to a chain attached to the base of the bed. My legs were stretched and fixed, less mobile than my arms.

Ms. Circe was not finished with me. I could not move enough to see what she was doing, but I felt her attach a clip to the outside ring of the right thigh cuff, which she repeated on the left. Now, I was not able to move my legs inward or outward. Finally finished, I was at her mercy. Reveling in the feeling of helplessness and knowing I was someone else's responsibility; the feeling was freeing. My body responded by relaxing, almost melting into the bed. She would direct me to her needs, and I would fulfill them.

"Mas, what happens next will determine how the evening ends." Waiting for her to begin, she was taking her time, observing me, an object for her pleasure. "You keep yourself in good shape, and the scars make interesting commentary on your past."

She mounted the bed, kneeling beside me, naked.

She had disposed of her peignoir. Now I could see her to her waist. Her hair was pulled back into a high ponytail, and she had no makeup. She smiled at me, looking at her. Her breasts were rising a little faster than usual, nipples hard in anticipation, buttons in a crinkled pool of aureole. She jiggled her tits because she could, knowing what effect it would have on me. The result was already in place; my dick was hard in the cage, my flesh was oozing out of the slots in the cage, and I was ready to explode.

She rose, straddled my stomach, and bent forward so our lips met. Hungrily, she kissed me, and I responded. How I wanted to be in her. The key to the cock cage, the one she wore around her neck, landed on my chest. For such a light key, it felt like a ton of weight. Feeling my cock throb in the cage, and the cage moved with every beat of my heart, this was such sweet torture. Rising on her arms, her tits tantalizingly close, I tried to reach out with my open mouth. Ms. Circe pulled away, chuckling.

"Not yet, Mas, you need to earn your pleasures."

No response was needed. I knew my place.

"Hmmm, do I blindfold you and let your imagination run amok, or let you see, and the vision sink in? Such a dilemma."

She was playing with me, having her fun, knowing it would turn me on and keep me on edge until she was ready to deny me or give me a release.

Slowly, she moved up my torso, a blindfold in hand, twirling it until it flew off her hand.

"Tonight, you get to see, enjoy."

She was easing herself over my outstretched arms and shoulders. She lifted herself over me. I looked up, her pussy over my face. Seeing the underside of her tits, nipples standing to attention, her head thrown back, an arousing perspective.

Lowering herself slowly, very slowly, down onto my waiting face, teasing me and herself in the process. Barely touching me, she stopped, open-mouthed my tongue reached out to her. At first touch, she moaned and sank completely on me.

Her fragrance enveloped me as I started to lap at her labia, deliberately avoiding her clit. I had been in this position enough times to know how to play her for her maximum pleasure. Taking my time, I used my tongue as a probe. I tested and teased her, responding to her movements on me and her breathing as a guide.

My eyes were open, and the view up her body was entrancing, urging me on as Ms. Circe's tits jiggled and her legs clamped down on me. She relaxed her legs, and I changed my tongue from soft, broad strokes to firm and used it on specific points, changing frequently from hard to soft and back again. Her responses were becoming more intense, and her breathing ragged. Moans and hisses escaped her as I now intermittently worked her clit. She started to ride my face back and forth, my face lubed with her juices. Her scent was driving me to distraction as she slipped up and down my face. Playing first with one breast, then the other, alternating and pulling on her nipples.

Fixed as I was on the bed, the only part of me that moved was my tongue pleasuring her. My captured cock throbbed and bounced with my increasing heartbeat. Without a doubt, I could do this all night, and I loved doing it. Ms. Circe needed the release of her orgasm, and I would be the instrument of it.

Working her body, I began to guide her to that place she could not control. Slowly, I intensified my actions in specific order so she could build on my ministrations. Consciously, she may not have known what was happening, but her body did and followed me. She was letting go of the here and now, floating into just feeling what was happening, letting everything go.

Her motion on my face became more aggressive and erratic, her breathing hissing and gulping, broken up by moans of pleasure. Ms. Circe was approaching the point of no return, balancing her there for what seemed an age. I pushed her over the orgasm precipice. Her legs gripped my head as if to crush my skull, and she went rigid, not breathing. This tension could not last, and in an explosion of her juices, she gushed into my mouth, releasing her orgasm. Ms. Circe shuddered as she squirted into me again, mistiming her contraction. I almost choked, barely closing my throat in time, then swallowing her emission.

As her orgasm receded, she became limp, sliding down my body, laying her head on my chest. Listening as her breathing quietly returned to a normal gentle in and out, she was empty of any tension, still floating. I remained quiet and as still as I could. Only her head moved as my chest rose and fell with my breathing.

A sense of all is well with the world enveloped me. Ms. Circe had been taken to nirvana, and I had been the instrument of that journey. I loved this woman in all her facets, and I would do anything in my power to please her and protect her.

Sophie stirred like a big cat, stretching out. She was almost purring as she said, "Mas, that was another excellent orgasm for Ms. Circe to remember. We go to places I never imagined existed."

"My pleasure."

"Our pleasure, Mas, and we will continue tonight."

Slowly easing herself off of me, she disappeared, leaving me bound and fixed. All I could do was listen to her move about our home. She was quiet. I couldn't determine what she was up to. She returned to me and showed me a key on a chain dangling from one hand, ring pliers in the other. Immediately recognizing them both, my heart leapt, maybe I would get a release as well. She laughed as she saw my reaction to the keys.

"Yes, Mas, it's the key, and I will use it."

Kneeling on the bed beside me, she removed the piercing ring attaching my penis to the chastity cage. Once done, she unlocked the cage itself. She had to tug it off my full cock. Not knowing what she had planned excited me and made me anxious at the same time. All I knew was I wanted and needed a release. My dick stood to attention, and Ms. Circe chuckled as she saw the effect she had on me.

"As good as your tongue is, and it is the best. I want you inside me, filling me."

I couldn't believe my ears. This was paradise to me, and I couldn't wait for her to begin. She would be in control as usual, and I didn't care.

"A word of warning, Mas, if you come before me, I will punish you."

That was a certainty, the punishment. It had happened before, and I didn't want a repeat. I was not afraid, but her punishments weren't fun, at least for me.

She had put all the pieces to the cage to one side and sat astride my thighs. Smiling, she moved up my body, lifting herself over my jutting member, stiff and throbbing. Holding my dick in one hand, she guided me to her nether lips and opened them with her other hand. Rubbing the head of my dick against her slick lips, she teased me before sinking just enough to envelope the head. Her heat was like a fire on my skin. Moving off of me, she repeated the action, and I wanted to scream "take me".

She took me, sliding down the length of my cock in one smooth motion. My cock was wrapped in a warm flesh cocoon. It felt like coming home. I groaned. Ms. Circe was motionless, feeling my size in her, me feeling her muscles exploring me. This was paradise, and we…she hadn't started to move. I tried to thrust up into her, fixed as I was. I had little range of motion, and what I did have galvanized her into action.

Slowly rising on me, sliding down in excruciating slowness, up and down, feeling us joined physically by my dick and her pussy, mentally and emotionally wholly joined. We were not two, we were one.

Leaning forward, she started to ride me, smooth, long strokes on me, never quite coming off me, taking my length, using me for her pleasure, giving me pleasure. Her tits swung close to my face, out of tantalizing reach, nipples so close, never to reach my waiting lips. Seeing Ms. Circes' expressions change from frowns to smiles fluctuate as she worked me inside her. She was horney and slick, and it felt so good to be inside her; all I needed to do was not come before her, and seeing her naked on me was pushing my limits. The intoxication of seeing and feeling her mounted in me. I was not sure I could hold out and not orgasm before her.

Lowering her torso almost onto me, her nipples

grazed my chest, and they felt like they were carving grooves in my flesh. Every back and forth raised my arousal a notch. I knew I would soon be unable to stop the gush of an orgasm, even that anxiety did nothing to lessen my arousal. My cock was as hard as fit to burst, and I wanted this feeling to last forever.

Ms. Circe was rapidly grinding on my rigid penis, her motions becoming less coordinated and her breathing becoming more intermittent. She was gulping in the air as if she were drowning. She was close to orgasm, as was I. She was making noises I had never heard from her, guttural from her soul sounds.

Without warning, she exploded in an animalistic orgy of shuddering limbs and sounds of complete abandon. She continued to move on me with a strength she had never shown. As she rammed onto me for the third stroke, I couldn't restrain myself any longer and shot my seed deep into her. Raising my hips as far as I could, I squirted into her a second time, a third, and I was spent.

She collapsed down onto me, breathing heavily and still shuddering slightly; her movements dissipated into a relaxed heaviness on my chest. Silence, all I could hear was the sound of us breathing. Those sounds melded into one, and without conscious effort, our breathing matched each other, gently rhythmic. I lost all sense of time.

Stirring slowly, Ms. Circe rose and dreamily said, "I love you, Mas, in every way. I never want to lose you. You have made me a better person."

My only answer was, "I love you in every way I know."

Sophie was back and released me from the bonds

that held me. Stiff from being in one position, I work the stiffness out under the shower's hot water. We showered together, soaping each other, caressing and cleaning us. This intimacy was the high point of the night for me. Dried and in bed, we nestled against each other before sleep took us.

Sophie sleepily mentioned, "You did not ask for permission to come. That omission will be addressed."

I didn't care. Whatever the punishment, it was worth it, and I was asleep in seconds.

Chapter Nineteen

I woke up feeling refreshed for the first time in a long time. Ready to go. Check with Kenzo if he has anything new to add to the pile of data we had. Marie would be reporting in on her religious adventure of the previous night. I hoped she would have some definite info to give Ruth's parents an alibi or put them in the frame as the perps.

Coffee on, the morning ritual began. Coffee mugs, two, sugar in one, milk in both, coffee poured. I put one on Sophie's bedside table. Stroking her bare shoulder, she came around slowly and stretched out. The aroma of the coffee would do the rest.

Omelets, boiled eggs, or poached, choices choices. Boiled eggs and toast, then out the door. I had the feeling something was about to break and hoped it wasn't another missing person report tied to this case. My phone dinged, text. I looked at it, Adrianna.

"Mr. Hammett, no need to pick me up today. My friends will drop me at work door to door. Thank you for caring."

I would follow up with her later and confirm it was safe for her to go that route. I would have some recommendations for alternatives.

Sophie came into the kitchen asking, "Mas last night was just what we needed. I can't believe how you accommodate my kinks. I don't understand how it can get any better, but it always does."

"They are my kinks as well. Two sides of the same coin, remember."

"I have never felt this way with any man before you. It still scares me sometimes, but I wouldn't want to be anywhere else but here with you."

"I feel the same. I find it hard to put into words other than I love you."

We hugged and kissed. Sophie broke away, suddenly realizing I was still unlocked from the previous night. She said, "We didn't lock up my property last night. Get to it, Mas, you know the rules."

"Yes, ma'am, right away."

"Oh, and I won't forget last night's omission."

She said it with a laugh, and the mood was light. I went into the bathroom to put on the chastity cage before my dick got too hard to stuff into the metal cage. It felt odd not to have it on after all this time. Sophie had left the cage key and the ring with the pliers to attach my cock to the end of the cage. Done and returned to her.

Breakfast over, we left for the office. Walking briskly in the chill morning, we had a good time. Marie had beaten us in.

"I was just about to call you guys. An interesting evening, to say the least, and coffee is ready."

Mugs filled; Marie had our full attention.

"Well, I got there early to eyeball the people as they arrived. They all looked so normal, boring but normal. The host was welcoming and explained a lot of stuff about the Church and the programs they offered. I let her ramble, listening for anything that could be used for background. By the end of her spiel, it sounded like a cult to me."

Both Sophie and I said, "And"

"Give me a break. Doing reports like this is not my thing."

"Okay, continue, please," I said.

"Okay, this was a bible study class. About thirty people showed up, mostly couples and a few older singles. I was one of the few younger people. The host asked one of the couples to say a beginning prayer. They were older, and later, I found out they were Ruth's parents. The wife just stood there while he said the prayer. He also led the meeting. The meeting began with the entire group as one, and we broke up later into groups of five or six. He would come around and talk to the group, giving commentary or guidance on the scripture.

The passages he talked about were from Revelation, pretty nasty stuff, with death and destruction, like some horror movie. The group was all for this, believing they had already been saved and would soon be meeting Jesus.

What was really creepy was that they thought they were the only ones saved. They want our country converted to a Christian nation, with religion guiding the politics and all government. They didn't say it outright in the meeting, but from comments I heard from many of the attendees, they think all other religions were either false or sinful, and that would include some Christian denominations. I wanted to get the hell out of there. They're nuts and not good nuts."

Marie stopped, done reporting. It was a lot of information to take in, but to me, it confirmed the religious aspect of the murders.

I asked Marie, "Were you able to ask about the Professor and his wife's attendance at these meetings?"

"Yes, the host confirmed they attended all the mid-week bible study classes because he is the study leader. The bad news is that the classes finish early enough to probably give them time to do the body drops. So that part doesn't help."

"Right." I began to think about the snatches. Sophie beat me to it.

"They couldn't have taken at least two of the victims. They were in a bible study with plenty of witnesses."

"Possibly, the timing would have been tight but doable if they had assistance, which is even less likely. They probably didn't do the snatches. I think the parents are responsible for the murders, at least in the origin. Someone else in the family is a better bet for carrying out the killings."

Marie and Sophie said together, "The brother?"

"You two are scary together. I think he needs a closer look. Make sure he doesn't know we are looking at him."

Sophie said, "He won't know a thing. I'll get Fiend on him, who is still looking at all our data, as a double check to see if he can poke holes in our theories."

I added, "Or confirm them."

"True." Sophie continued, "Have you heard from Kenzo lately?"

"No, he's my next call. I wanted to hear from Marie first."

Marie heard me and said, "Remind me not to volunteer for anything in the future. They're scary people. Didn't have anything in common with the Jesus

I knew as a kid."

I said, "I believe you are correct. They are scary."

Indeed, I believed they were dangerous to our country. I wanted to know more. We are not a theocracy, and hopefully never will be. Now I needed to call Kenzo, if only to catch up. There was no answer. No problem, knowing he would get back to me when he could.

This would be a good time to chat with Father Benny about this Christian nationalist stuff. He seemed to keep his finger on the religious pulse, and it wouldn't hurt to get info from a religious inside source, and he hadn't gotten back to me, yet.

Adrianna was safe for the time being. We couldn't rely on her not being a target. However, Ruth had been careful in shielding her. Time was running out to find and protect the next victim, whoever that would be.

My call to Father Benny was put through to voice mail. I was not having much luck today, and that feeling of something going to break began to fade. This was frustrating, and I had nothing productive to do until I heard back from any of my calls. Sophie still had computer stuff to do. Marie had the office to run. I needed something-anything to occupy me.

Saved by the bell, my cell burst to life, Father Benny calling back. "Hi, Benny. How are you?"

"Good. Is there any progress on your case?"

"Yes and no. Two steps forward, one back. We believe we have identified the trigger for the murders. Her first name is Ester Ruth. That's all I can tell you right now.

"Interesting."

"How so?"

"She is named after the only two books in the bible named for women."

"What?"

"Ester and Ruth are two books in the biblical canon. That's not a coincidence. Although there are others mentioned in the Apocrypha."

"Excuse my ignorance. What's an Apocrypha?

He laughed gently, without mocking, he said, "They are writings of a dubious nature, not verified and outside of the accepted canon. They were not considered divinely inspired but regarded as worthy of study by the faithful.

"Great, I'm not sure that helps, but I need to pick your brains on some aspects of this case. Do you have a few minutes?"

"Sure, anything I can do, please ask."

"What do you know about the Christian Nationalists?"

"You picked a can of worms there. They are extremists and, in my opinion, do not follow the teachings of Jesus as he taught them, which is probably a sin on my part for judging them. What do you want to know?"

"Anything you can tell me."

"They are small, compared to the mainstream Church, but effectively lobby. They want to turn our country into a theocracy, a Christian version of Iran, if you will. If they succeed, they will be as dangerous to the world as Iran is."

"How do you identify them?"

"Look at the politicians. The more secularly and religiously extreme they are, the more likely they are supported and funded by extreme religious groups."

"So, is there a difference between fundamentalists and nationalists?"

"Huge differences. Within the Catholic Church, some folks would like mass to be performed only in Latin, fundamentalist, not nationalist. The Amish are fundamentalists but are not nationalists. As soon as you mix politics and religion, you have a disastrous stew. Separation of Church and state is critical to our country's survival."

"I agree, but please explain your reasons."

"Our country was founded on religious freedom. If one sect or religion gets to be the only one aligned with the secular government, it becomes so powerful everyone else is at risk of persecution."

"Like some of the Middle Eastern countries?"

"Exactly. There, the secular government answers to religious leaders in many cases. Iran is slightly different. Anyone can practice their religion if they obey the country's rules. There are Jewish, Christian, and Zoroastrian communities in Iran. Again, it's the hard-line extremists that screw it up for everyone. I fear that would happen here if we became a theocracy. Even I would be in danger as a Catholic."

"Back to the Christian nationalists, how are they funded? Lobbying costs money?"

"Groundswell, many small donations, and of course big donations from wealthy believers, dark money, you name it. They have, in some cases, aligned with white supremacists."

"How does that work?"

He laughed with a palpable sadness, "Easy, the enemy of my enemy is my friend. They also have some charismatic preachers running ministries as a loose network."

"Like a Christian Al Qaeda, that's a bit cynical, isn't it."

"Probably, but the reality is they're not opposed to violence and want to combine religious fervor with political ends by any means. Our country is in social trouble. You see it every day in medical, housing, addictions, extremes of politics on both sides. The part about "We the people" seems to have been forgotten. Sorry, it's just been a couple of bad days.

"Anything I can do?"

"Thank you, Mas, but no, this is on me. Actually, yes, solve your case and save the future victims."

"Trust me, Benny, we are doing our best."

"Then I will continue to pray for you and your colleagues—blessings on you, Mas.

Benny clicked off the call. He had given me food for thought, but I needed something tangible or useful on the case. I was still hanging on the theory it was religious and personal. If it wasn't Ruth's parents, the next in line was her brother, and that was for Sophie and Fiend to investigate.

Where the hell was Kenzo? That sinking feeling that something had happened hit me, and it wasn't a good something. So much for my feeling that we were going to get a break. Kenzo would call when he could, and I wasn't going to bug him if he was in the middle of a shit storm.

Sophie was in computer mode, and Marie was dealing with office stuff. I told Marie I was going for a walk, and she nodded and waved bye.

Thinking through the case, what hadn't we looked at in depth? We had covered pretty much everything we had. Fiend had reviewed all our data and, so far, hadn't come up with anything we hadn't. Kenzo's team did a thorough search of Ruth's life and all the murder victims and their connection to Ruth. Think about the case. Was there anything we could follow up on that we hadn't, or could at least work on some more?

I went through every item I could think of, and then it struck me. The minivan Ruth's parents owned; why such an old vehicle when the other was much newer? Did they buy it new or used, and where from in either case? Wait a minute, colleges use all sorts of vans for student transport, including minivans. Fleet sales and the most common color for them is white. What color vans did SF Christian University use? I would bet on white. The professor and his son Luther would have access to the college's vehicles.

Getting back to the office, I pulled up the college website and reviewed all the photographs I could find, and yup, there they were, a neat row of white mini and passenger vans. Only the larger passenger vans had the college logo on them. The minivans were blank-anonymous, just another white minivan.

"Ha, Sophie, I need you."

"What is it? I'm busy."

"Important, I want your input."

"It better be good."

I explained what I was thinking and how it could be the break we were looking for; there had to be forensics in one or more of those minivans. The lack of evidence linking the family directly to the vans was an issue for Kenzo, but I would run it by him anyway.

"That, Mas, is why I love you. Great thinking. The only problem is Kenzo probably doesn't have enough probable cause for a search warrant."

I answered, "We don't need a search warrant. Whatever we find, we get tested, then compare the results to anything Kenzo has DNA-wise or anything else. We can be confidential informants or whatever it takes for him to get a warrant. Let's be careful so we don't trigger a cleaning frenzy on the vans.

"You mean we break in, middle of the night job, and hope we don't get caught."

"Sounds about right."

"Run it past Kenzo first and make sure he has plausible deniability if it goes sideways for us.

"We'll cover his ass, no worries," I said, smiling.

"Okay, now leave me alone to work on the family with Fiend."

Now, I had a plan of sorts, well, the start of one. First, I had to recon the college and the areas where the vans were parked overnight. Security shouldn't be a problem, but better safe than sorry. It would be checked out. Then, another thought hit me. Maybe the vans had built-in GPS. If they did, we could pull the data, and if it showed the vans in the park at the time of the body drops, that would be a digital tie into whatever physical evidence we found in the vans.

The problem was, if Kenzo couldn't provide reliable evidence to a judge for the warrants, anything we supplied him would be considered the fruit of a poison tree and no use in court. Kenzo, was retuning my call.

"Hi, anything new?" I asked.

"We think we have another snatch, two on the missing person's board. One looks more promising than the other. One is probably a runner from an abusive relationship. The other, I think, is a probable snatch, and the next drop is this weekend. The timeline works. Fuck it, Mas, we gotta nail these bastards. I'm not sure how long I've got. Time is running out for me on this investigation.

"Can we meet, usual place?"

Excitedly, he asked, "Do you have something?"

"Nor exactly. We have an idea, and I want to let you know what we are doing and why. Also, to give you a heads up for plausible deniability."

"Ah shit Mas, do I want to know?"

"Yes, can we meet?"

"Sure, give me thirty minutes, an early lunch on you."

"No problem."

Hanging up the call, I felt for Kenzo, pressure from the brass, the press, and making Kenzo the scapegoat. Not if we could help it. The plan to raid the minivans at the college, sketchy as it was, would be done—anything to assist Kenzo in closing this slaughter of innocents, legal or otherwise.

Marie looked up as I went past her. Kenzo was all I said, and I left. The drive to Watanabe's was the usual crawl, and I was still there before him. Wanatabe bowed a greeting and nodded in the negative.

He came over and said, "Mr. Hammett, please use our storeroom this time. The upstairs will be occupied for some time. I have set up a small table for you."

I assumed the room we usually used was occupied by people playing Go.

"How did you know I was coming?"

"Otake San called in an order, saying he was meeting you. Is that alright?"

"That's fine and thank you." Wanatabe was his formal self, using Kenzo's surname

"Anything to help Otake San."

He showed me to a small storeroom with a small table set up with two chairs. It was cramped but big enough for our purposes. I sat and waited for Kenzo.

As Kenzo arrived, Wanatabe brought our usual pot of tea and pot stickers. It was good timing.

"Sorry, I'm late. What can you tell me, Mas."

"Sit, eat. We think the perps use the college minivans, where Ruth's father and brother teach. We will visit and collect samples from each van and have them tested at a private laboratory. You can guess which one. Don't say anything. It would be best if you had plausible deniability. If we come up with anything, you can use it under a confidential informant cover to get the warrants for official searches and hopefully get the GPS history of the vans."

"Mas, thanks. You know I can't get involved with any of that. That's pretty close to the fruit of a poison tree. It could get the entire case tossed out of court."

"Not if we do it properly. We aren't so tied to legal stuff as you are."

He was silent, pondering what I had said. I stayed quiet, not wanting to interrupt his train of thought.

"Mas, if one of you sign up for a class that takes away trespass, at least for one of you. You have a right to be on the campus, and if the vans are open. Great, if not, that could be a problem. If you open all the vehicles, it would appear they were all left unlocked. Still risky."

"We have to follow every lead we have all the way."

"Agreed, but I can't be part of this. Don't tell me when, okay?

"Done. What about the missing persons who reported them?"

"One has to be a snatch. She fits the profile and was involved with Ruth a while back. That relationship's been confirmed by her current partner."

"Another person connected to Ruth. She has to be the one. What's her name?"

"Bridget Belmondo."

"Sounds French. Any other background?"

"Yes, kinda, she's Haitian. Her parents came here decades ago before the earthquake hit. We are following up on everything we can find. We don't know where she was snatched, only that it was two nights ago and reported yesterday. We are scrubbing her computer history and phone and digging into anything we can find on her. Her partner has been constructive, and her involvement is not suspected. She also found a couple of old photos of Bridget and Ruth together. Anything we get, I'll put on the laptop."

"Good. Will advise on anything we get."

We chatted about anything but the case as we ate. Kenzo seemed to relax a little, and his shoulders dropped as we concentrated on the snacks Wanatabe brought. Kenzo needed the break and a break in the case. We separated, and I made my way back to the office to prepare for our mission. I liked the idea one of us should enroll in a class. Well done, Marie. I was laughing to myself at what I expected her response to the idea.

The office was quiet when I returned. Marie nodded when I came in, and Sophie was behind her screens. Sitting at my desk, I wanted to get my thoughts in order before I disturbed the two women. Thought through, I had the skeleton of the plan. Now was the time to get input from the two people who would have to work it out with me.

"Guys, I need your input on the plan for the college mission."

Sophie said, "What? I'm busy."

"And we will be busier very soon. We need to make sure this is right, or as right as it can be."

"Okay, good point. Is Marie joining us?"

"Yup, and she will now have a bigger part to play."

Marie heard me and said, "What have you gotten me into now? Not more religious shit?"

"Not this time." Laughing, I added, "You are going to college."

"What are you talking about?"

Good question. Our original plan had gaps. After my conversation with Kenzo, his idea of one of us enrolling or registering for a class made a lot of sense, but I needed to get both their buy-in and general input to make the plan workable and as safe for us as possible. We didn't want to get caught for multiple reasons, mainly not to raise suspicions in the perps if they were using the college vans, and I was sure they were.

I laid out the plan and asked Marie if she would be willing to enroll-register for any class that would get us access to the campus-of course, she said yes and bitched.

"Yes, I'll do it. You owe me big time. I fucking hated school. College was even worse, full of idiots who didn't know their ass from their elbow, and thinking the world owed them, didn't have a clue about the real world."

"What brought that on," asked Sophie.

Marie was quiet for a minute before continuing.

"This is San Francisco, lots of people with lots of money, who don't have to work or struggle, wondering where the next meal is coming from. My family was the two working parents bringing up kids. We never went without, but there was nothing spare, ever. Vacations were a day at the beach. If we were lucky, we would go down to Half Moon Bay and harvest shellfish. We were happy because me and my brother didn't know any better, at least until I went to college."

"I didn't know you had a brother?'

"He joined the Navy, died in a training accident, and I'm not going there."

Both Sophie and I said we were sorry for her loss, and we were all silent. Marie had never talked much about herself or her family.

Marie continued, "Anyway, I'll sign up as long as I don't have to attend any classes. It's only to get access to the campus, right?"

I couldn't resist trying to lighten the mood, "Well, it would be a shame to waste the opportunity to improve oneself by taking a few classes."

"Fuck you, Mas, you're being an asshole."

Sophie joined in, saying, "Yes, Mas, sometimes you're an asshole, and this is one of those times. No, Marie, you don't have to attend any classes. You are smart enough already."

Laughing, I said, "Okay, I give up. I was kidding! Back to business, Marie, get on the college enrollment as soon as possible. Kenzo has identified another person, connected to Ruth, who is missing, believed kidnapped." Both Marie and Sophie let out sounds of dismay. "I figure we can expect a body drop this weekend. We need access to the campus to go over the vans for forensics and then keep an eye on the vans from Friday night on. If they are using the college vans, we may be able to catch them in the act over the weekend. I will bring in Oso. Tara doesn't keep him on for the weekends.

Sophie said, "Teams of two, you and Marie, me and Oso. Yes?"

That was a good idea. The body drops were done by a duo, from what we had seen when we almost had them. This combination gave us two good teams. I knew Marie could drive really well, and I could handle myself in practically any situation. Sophie had picked up all the bad driving habits of the locals, so there was no problem.

Oso would follow Sophie's instructions to the letter, plus he could handle himself against any individual who wasn't extensively trained. Growing up on the streets gave him an excellent grounding in fighting dirty-read survival. A stint in prison honed those skills. Yet he was a good man for all the rough times, poor start, and some awful decisions.

I had no objection. Still, I wondered why Sophie chose Oso and not me. I would trust Oso with the life of the woman I loved. No question. Perhaps it had more to do with Marie. I knew Marie better than Marie knew Oso, and Sophie knew Oso was reliable. I would be happy if we all got through this safely. Not that I expected anything particularly threatening toward us to happen. You never knew, and we would be prepared. Sophie and I would be armed legally, and we hopefully had surprise on our side.

Oso answered on the first ring and, after I had explained what we needed, said he was all in. That item was taken care of, and I checked in with Marie. She had signed up online for some classes. She would have to go in later to get her photo taken for the college ID and sign the necessary docs to make it all official. She was done and done. Now, all we had to do was wait until nightfall for our forensic mission.

Chapter Twenty

Time dragged slowly. I hated waiting, but you can't hurry nightfall. The sun would drop behind the incoming fog when it did, and not before. Tonight, it looked like it would be a night with a thick fog. Good.

Marie went off to do her college stuff. Sophie was chatting a lot with Fiend. It seemed about the data he was still crunching through, and he had come up with some questions for Sophie. I went home and prepared a simple dinner and changed into all black for the night. I checked my weapon and Sophie's. Good to go. My lock pick gun was in its case. I put it with my warm jacket, hat, and forensic sample bags. I was ready to go, and I would recheck everything when Sophie had changed and was ready to venture out on our mission.

Sophie came home in a rush, saying she was sorry she was late, but Fiend had come up with a few questions she couldn't answer, and they had discussed them at length.

I asked, "And the result is."

"More fucking questions. Fiend has crunched all the data we gave him, and he agrees that the perps must be related to Ruth."

"I hear a 'but' coming."

"Yes, the parents have alibi's, which Marie confirmed, for the kidnapping of some of the victims, not all. It also doesn't mean they are not involved somewhere along the line. Fiend also agrees that the son Luther is the most likely to be the one, along with his wife, which is where we hit a snag. He looked into her, not that there was much to find, even less than her mother-in-law, except that she works with multiple Christian charities and does a lot of outreach in the evenings with youth, addicts, and the homeless. That is a double-edged sword. She is out and sometimes solo, so she has the opportunity to meet up with Luther, and no one would know. However, she is often with others in teams of two or more, so she doesn't have the opportunity to disappear without someone noticing, and both can occur on the same night. Fiend doesn't think she is involved with the kidnappings but can't be sure about the body drops. He will continue to dig, not that he holds out much hope. She is almost off the grid."

"Then how does he know about the charities?"

"They are organized, and each charity organization keeps digital records of who signs in on any given night and the area in which they work. They do it for safety, to track the people they work with, and 'to save' as they put it. It also helps them raise money when they can show what work they do and the results."

"Of course, money had to come into it somewhere," I said cynically.

Sophie smiled and said, "Dinner first, then I'll get ready for tonight. It looks like it's going to be a damp one. Oh, Marie is all registered with the college and will meet us there to show us around her new campus."

"Fine, dinner is ready. We will need to go over all our equipment as well."

"Good idea. Did you check my gun?"

"Yup, good to go."

"Thank you. I'll check it myself if you don't mind."

"Big Boots has taught you well."

That focused us on the night's mission. Doing illegal things, even for the right reason, was still illegal, and in this case, could tip off the people we were trying to catch. Anyone who says they don't have any anxiety before a mission is either lying or a psychopath.

We ate in silence, and as soon as we had finished, Sophie left to get changed, which took her no time. Like me, she was in all black. She made the black outfit chic and much better looking than mine. She checked her weapon and slipped it into the holster in the small of her back. I had already done the same with mine. Our jackets against the damp night air would hide the weapons. We were ready with my key gun in my pocket and Sophie putting more sample bags in her purse.

Marie called as we were walking to my SUV. She was already on campus and investigating the layout. Good thinking. We arranged to meet at the far end of the furthest parking lot and review the information Marie had found on the location. Internet searches and maps are very useful but differ from on-site details.

The drive over was slow. The fog and the heavy traffic slowed everything down, and we were not in a rush. The later we arrived, the better. Fewer students about and less chance of security doing a thorough patrol. No one likes the fog, the cold, and damp gets in your bones. People think, oh, San Francisco. It's California, and it must be warm. Nope, not San Francisco. The temperature drops fast, like a stone in a pond, when the sun goes down and the fog rolls in.

Entering the campus, we followed Marie's directions, seeing a few students walking and huddled against the damp, and no security patrols. Marie was precisely where she said she would be. We exchanged subdued greetings, and she gave us all the information she'd gathered.

"Guys, all the vans are parked in one spot around the back of that building." She indicated a low building across the parking lot. "It's a one-way road and not well-lit. All the vans are parked next to one another, minivans first, then the bigger passenger vans. That area has better lighting, but I didn't see any cameras. The bigger vans also block the minivans to a degree. Is that all good?"

"Excellent, couldn't have done it better myself," I said.

We moved off quickly as if going for a stroll. We melted into the fog and carefully walked around to the end of the building. Nothing, no sounds close, only the mournful sound of fog horns in the bay. The fog seemed less dense, and we found the minivans. Locked. No surprise. The Key gun took care of the lock on the driver's side, and from there, I opened all the doors.

Sophie started on the center section of the minivan, Marie the trunk area, and I stayed with the front. We worked quickly, not bothering with fingerprints, probably too many to identify, and Luther and his father would have access to the vans if needed.

Samples were taken from the floor. Marie had brought a small battery vacuum. We should have thought of that, which was good for her. Another reason she was a partner. Everything we took was carefully bagged and labeled, with the vehicle's license plate as a common identifier. I took a photo of the VIN to match the license plate, just in case someone swapped the plates with another van. You can't be too careful.

Photos of the front and back license plates were taken. They were not great images in the fog, but they were clear enough. The rear plate looked as if it had been removed and replaced more than once from the scratches.

Next vehicle, same process. We moved quickly without rushing anything. We were looking for anything that would tie any of the vans to any of the victims, a long shot. The vans would have been cleaned and used several times over since the murders began, but it was the best option we had.

Repeat with the following vehicle, number three, with the same process, carefully record everything we did and took. It was stressful, but the work went smoothly—a car engine in the fog, then an eerie, sick yellow glow of headlights coming up the road. Quickly, we closed the back hatch of the van we were working in and hid in front of the vans, each of us in front of a different van. The car slowed down but did not stop, and soon, the red glow of the taillights disappeared. We collectively breathed a sigh of relief and went back to work.

One thing the fog had masked. The college had five minivans, but only four were parked. Shit, shit, shit. I would bet the fifth van was being used to transport the next victim to or from somewhere in the city. Wherever it was, the location had to be isolated to mask the victim's torture. There had to be a connection if it was property held by Ruth's family or the college. Everything in San Francisco was close—houses on top of one another, a commercial holding was a better bet, and colleges had investments and assets all over the place. Sophie would need to get on that one.

I asked, "Sophie, investigate any assets held by Ruth's family and the college. One of them has to be where they are holding Bridget, and maybe we can get to her before they kill her."

"Got it. Hold these sample bags. Only the top two need the vehicle's plate."

She handed me a bunch of sealed sample bags. I photographed the license plate and wrote the number on the two bags.

Only one more van to go. This one proved no more difficult than the previous three. I concentrated on the front, Marie worked the backspace, and Sophie was back examining the central area. We wrapped up quickly and rechecked all the vans, making sure I had re-locked them. The sample bags were stashed between Sophie and Marie's purses.

Back in the parking lot, a security car was waiting for us. He was looking at our vehicles.

Marie took the lead, saying, "Hi, officer. I was showing my employers around. I am starting classes soon and wanted to show them where I was going. This is so exciting-even if the weather is crappy, I'm finally getting to go to college."

He looked taken aback by her enthusiasm, smiled, and asked, "May I see your ID." He took a good look at her brand-new photo ID.

Marie asked, "Is there a problem."

He responded, "No problem, miss. I'm just checking to make sure everything is alright. It's a nasty night, and I didn't recognize the cars. Have a good night all.

He left, and we all breathed a sigh of relief. We went our separate ways after we had put all the samples in the SUV, Marie to home, Sophie and me to our house, to sort out all the sample bags we had taken on the night's work. We crashed once we had done that, even though it was still early. The stress of the case, the night's mission, and the probability of another body drop in the next two or three days weighed heavily on us. The lab we were going to use opened early. The processing would cost us, especially as I would insist on a rush on everything, and I would be getting flack for that request from Cathy, the lab manager.

Up early after a crappy night, I inhaled a cup of yesterday's leftover coffee and put the coffee on for a fresh pot. I re-examined all the sample bags and the notes we had taped to each one to help the lab with their analysis of the contents. We would also forward all our results to Kenzo for comparison when they could obtain their own. There could be some awkward questions regarding where we obtained the samples. I would have to smooth talk the lab manger. I knew her, and hopefully, when I explained what and why we were doing it this way, she would be okay with it.

With itchy feet, I loaded the SUV with our forensic contraband and headed out too early. Better than not doing anything. Parked in a prime spot in front of the lab, I waited. The lab manager, Cathy, was early, and she saw me waiting. She tapped on my window.

"Mas, what the hell are you up to now? Don't tell me. I'm not going to like it, am I?"

Laughing, I said, "Probably not. Are you early enough for me to buy you breakfast?"

She smiled and said, "Sure, but you better not try to bribe me."

"What me? Never, but I need you to listen to me."

"Oh, shit, I knew it, I'm really not going to like this."

"If it's too much, you tell me, and I'll go elsewhere."

"Bullshit, you know this is the best private lab in the city."

"That's why I'm here."

She climbed in, and we drove on her directions to a local Taqueria. I was ready to kill a breakfast burrito. There are a lot of good Mexican cafes in San Francisco. We walked in, and she was greeted as only regulars are. We took a corner booth, and strong coffee with bitter chocolate was delivered as soon as we sat down—her choice for breakfast. A menu was placed only in front of me. A big menu and my mouth started watering. I settled for a breakfast burrito with a side of pickled jalapenos. She was quiet and enjoyed watching me look through the menu.

Once my order was placed, Cathy asked, "So, Mas, what sort of trouble are you in now?"

"Not me, the city." I paused. "You have heard about the bodies showing up in the park?"

"Christ Mas, you aren't caught up in that mess, are you?"

"Yes, we are assisting Kenzo, unofficially, of course. We have some samples that need forensic testing to compare to what the PD have discovered in their searches of the crime scenes."

"And these samples were not officially obtained." It was a statement, not a question.

"Not even close," I told her, fully disclosing how we obtained them. "If they are what we think they are, we can do a workaround claiming confidential informant status."

"That's risky, Mas, and could come back to bite you."

"I know, but there will be another body dropped this weekend if we can't find her. That's worth the risk. We have theories and ideas on who is responsible, but no proof yet."

"How many will this make if it happens?"

"Six, and we believe there is another person at risk."

"Get me the samples. I'll put a rush on it. You owe me big time for this, and you will be billed at full rate."

"Bill the office. Kenzo is on the hook for the investigation, and we owe him. Even if we didn't, it's the right thing to do. These perps are really fucked up. You've heard of the way they have been killed?"

"Of course, you can't keep secrets like that in this town. Don't forget I used to work for the ME."

"Sorry."

"When can you get the samples to me?"

"They are in the car, all labeled and with notes on them and chain of evidence signatures that may not hold up, but the contents will if they're what we think they are."

"Fingerprints?"

"Didn't bother, too many others to eliminate, and the perps would have legitimate access to where they would be found. I didn't want to risk the time to download the van's GPS. If we've got what we think we've got, Kenzo can get a warrant for everything."

"Good, that helps. Enjoy your breakfast, and let's get to it."

We ate quickly, and I dropped her and the samples off at the lab.

I couldn't resist, "Cathy, talk soon."

"Fuck off, Mas, and let me do the work. Don't call me."

Laughing, I drove back to the office. Marie had arrived and got the office going. She said Sophie messaged her saying she was talking to Fiend, rehashing something, and would be in later.

Next, call to Kenzo to inform him of the successful mission on the vans. Saying one van was missing when we visited them. Let him know we would be staking out the vanpool on Sat night and Sunday if needed. No answer. I left him a cryptic message. He would get back to me when he did.

The perps had to know the park would be under surveillance. Were they going to risk another body drop? Good question. If they thought they were on a mission from God, they would risk it. I expected them to risk it. I hoped Kenzo had enough manpower to cover all the entrances and exits. They were asking to get caught, and the number of bodies they had dropped was getting a lot of media coverage, mostly wrong, still emphasizing the gay, kink, and fetish aspects of the victims. The police hadn't caught them, and pressure on them to do just that was mounting. It was a mess.

Sophie arrived with a smile. Marie and I both asked. "Why the smile?"

"Because I've come up with some info that will help." She waited before saying, "There are some properties that the professor owns and some the college owns registered under another business name."

"Where are they?" I asked.

"Patience, grasshopper, I am getting to that. The college properties are all above board, either managed by them or a property management company, and better yet, none are in a location that would lend itself to holding a prisoner for torture.

The professor has two properties, one a rental duplex, not a suitable location. The last one is listed in a company name with the professor and family as registered officers. It's not rented, and I can't find any business tax records for the last couple of years. The professor pays property taxes on time, which is low for this city. The best part is that it's in the Hunters Point industrial area. His property is bound on one side with a road. The other side is a vacant industrial manufacturing building with thick walls. Behind, nothing but a wetland area. That has to be where they are taking and keeping the victims."

"Great work. I'll get this to Kenzo ASAP.

Marie said, "Maybe they will be in time to save Bridget."

"Maybe, but I doubt it," I said as I speed-dialed Kenzo's number. He answered.

"Mas, give me some good news. We are still reviewing everything we have. I've been slipping in suggestions from your info. The brass don't want to hear it. They are forcing the team to keep looking into all the kink connections."

"Get a team down to Hunters Point. Sophie is sending the address to the laptop. We think it's where they are holding the victims. It's owned by the professor but has no tenants, and it's industrial. Keep it a small team and very quiet."

"Great, thanks, I'll go myself. I can always call back up if needed."

"Keep us in the loop."

"Got the address, thank Sophie. I will do it. Gotta run."

He was gone. I hoped he was in time to save Bridget, but I had doubts.

Sophie asked, "Tonight is Friday. What if they drop the body tonight.?"

"Out of pattern," I said, "but a possibility. They have always been one step ahead. They must expect the police to have staked out the park for Saturday into Sunday."

Marie spoke up, "Let's start our watch tonight. I'm up for it."

Sophie and I agreed as one. I called Oso. He was working until midnight. That worked for us. Sophie would pick him up at the end of his shift at the club where he worked most evenings. Marie would pick me up at the office at ten p.m. not that I expected anything to happen before two a.m. or even later. Better an hour early than a minute late.

We planned to be armed and with two-person teams. One would be using dash cams and video if needed. The plan was for the two teams to patrol the park, consistently using phones so we didn't overlap too much, which meant we could cover more of the park. Now the hard part-waiting.

Pottering about doing a lot of nothing to pass the time, I was about to leave the office when Kenzo called.

"And?"

"You were right, it's the place. No one there, and

267

plenty of stuff to keep forensics busy for a while. A lot of blood. With the volume, it has to be from several victims, some fresh. A torture chamber looks like something out of a medieval horror painting. Some bags of redimix concrete. These perps are sick bastards. The question is, when did they move Bridget? And when do they plan to dump her."

"We think they may move up the drop time. Sophie and I are patrolling the park in two teams tonight."

"Two teams, who?"

"Me and Marie, Sophie and Oso."

"Why do you think it's tonight?"

"They are smart and expect the PD to cover the park tomorrow as per the usual drop time. Bringing the time forward beats your coverage."

"Good point. I will activate the entrance and exit cameras tonight. The park is too big to cover effectively, even knowing what we are looking for."

"Agreed, if we can catch them in the act, it'll be a miracle. I figure you would log every minivan on entry and tail them."

"That's the plan. I may not be able to bring it forward. A lot of organization and shift changes to get the bodies we needed for Saturday night."

"At least the cameras will be a help. Will you have someone monitoring them?"

"Yes, they will be monitored live."

"Give us a heads up if you get anything?"

"Of course, as long as they don't fall asleep watching those screens, they get the info to me." He laughed. We both knew how boring stakeouts were, and watching a monitor screen at night was even worse.

He said, "I'll get you all the info on the Hunters

Point place when I get it."

To prepare for tonight, I went home and cooked up a bucket of pasta with a simple sauce of olives and tomatoes. The protein, fresh shrimp I picked up on the way home. Cooking is a meditation, and it relaxed me, like being submissive did, just differently. Food was ready for when Sophie came home, and then I checked over our weapons and made sure they were loaded with hollow points. With that done, I showered and dressed casually. I didn't need all black tonight.

Sophie arrived early, followed my example, showered, and asked, "Did you check the weapons?"

"Of course, both. You'll want to check yours."

"I want. BB drummed it into me. Good habit."

I smiled, saying, "No complaint here."

After Sophie had showered, we sat and ate in silence, each with our thoughts. Being sure Bridget was already dead or would be in a few hours, I lost my appetite. Sophie asked what was up, I told her, and she pushed her plate away. It was still too early to meet Marie at the office. I kissed Sophie, told her to be careful, and left for the office anyway.

Chapter Twenty-One

The cool evening air had a chill that made my walk easy and refreshing. My mood had shifted from melancholy to frustrated anger. No one deserved what these perps were doing to other humans, and it seemed that the Police and, by extension, the FBI profilers were fixated on the gay-kink-sex aspect of the killings, which probably made for better media coverage than religion.

I opened up; the office seemed desolate without my partners. I booted up my computer for no reason than I had time to kill. There was nothing from Cathy at the lab. We were at least another day out, if not longer, in hearing from her. There were a lot of samples. Nothing from Kenzo, not a surprise. He would be wrapped up at the professor's property crime scene. If nothing else, it would give Kenzo an excuse to question him and the family members about the property and their involvement with it. I heard the door open, and Marie called out.

"Hello Mas?"

"Yes, I got here early. You're early too. How come?"

"Probably the same reason you are. I want to get this started. I brought some coffee and snacks."

"At least one of us is thinking, thank you."

"It was Chung's idea. Are you sure you want me to drive?"

"Sure, it's your vehicle. You know it better than me. Besides, I'm the armed one and know what we're looking for. You concentrate on driving. I'll concentrate on watching."

"Got it. Do you think we will get them?"

"Yes, if not tonight, they will be got at some point, hopefully sooner than later.

"Ok, let's hit the road. By the time we get to the park, it'll be dark."

"Yes, Ma'am." I thought Sophie was rubbing off on Marie a little too well.

We walked to the rented parking space. Marie used it to park her old Jeep, one of the old ones built like a tank and still running perfectly. We climbed in, and Marie took off like the local driver she was. Weaving in and out of traffic, a cab driver couldn't have done it better. Even with her driving skills, it was dark when we began to cruise Golden Gate Park. There was still a good amount of traffic using the park, and people were leaving after a day of fun and relaxation. The Park Museum and facilities had all closed, and the workers were part of the exodus.

We drove around getting a feel for the roads and the park in general as the traffic diminished. Locals used the park roads as a cut-through to avoid the bordering East-West roads of Lincoln Way and Fulton Street, using the North-South artery of the Presidio bypass to get to Route 1. None of this would affect our mission. We were not looking for a transitory person. We were looking for a killer dropping a body, and that, going on past performance, could be anywhere in the park.

It would be a miracle if we caught them in the act.

Best case scenario, the police got a suspicious van on their monitoring system. One of us gets the message, and we manage to find and follow them until the police can pull them over on whatever pretext they could come up with.

Marie cruised the park, driving steadily. I had a map of the park on my lap and directed her around some of the less traveled roads and areas. I figured they would use either JFK Drive or MLK Jr. Drive to get into the park and then use one of the smaller, less traveled roads to do the drop. If we were right and they brought the day forward-this was so frustrating. The conversation was minimal. Neither of us had much to say, and we concentrated on the job at hand.

Midnight rolled around, and nothing suspicious had occurred. My phone went off. Sophie.

"Mas, I just picked up Oso, and we should be in the park in about twenty. Anything?"

"Nothing so far. We started early and have a good feel for the park. We are going to weave up and down the minor roads. If you concentrate on the park perimeter roads, I think that will be the most efficient way to use us."

"Makes sense. Oso is nodding in agreement. He's driving."

"Keep your phone open, just in case we get lucky."

"Got it. But it will be Oso's phone."

"Let's make this work. I figure the drop will be between two and four a.m., and the park rangers will be at their lowest physical ebb. But I wouldn't bet on it with these perps."

"Agreed, let's just hope we can get them."

"Hey Sophie, you and Oso be careful, right?"

"Got it, Mas, we're good."

The phone call remained open and silent. We could hear the traffic noise decrease as they closed in on the park. At least we were moving and had company. I pitied the poor bastard who was stuck in front of the police monitors covering the cameras at the park entrances. Nothing was happening, and even though it was too early for my drop time estimate, I wondered if we had it wrong.

Nothing, it was now one-thirty, and nothing from the police, and we hadn't seen anything suspicious. We were approaching the time I expected something to happen. Kenzo, here we go.

"Hi, Kenzo. Do you have a suspicious vehicle?"

"No, a body."

"What the fuck, how and where?"

"A box was dropped off in front of the DeYoung Museum on Hagiwara Tea Garden Drive. The park ranger just called it in. He will wait until I get there. Wait until I get there to show up."

"Nothing on the police cameras?"

"Nothing. The officer monitoring the screens didn't leave and swears he didn't doze off. I believe him. They had to get in the park a different way. Some areas don't have a curb. They could drive over the edge onto the bone-dry dirt. That can easily take the weight of a van."

"Can you get someone over to the college and see if all the vans are there? If not, which one is out? Shit, I am getting tired of always being one step behind. Is it Bridget?"

"Already on the van. I don't know body-wise. I expect it is. I'll call as soon as I am on site, fifteen minutes max."

This was getting old. Too many people had died, and we were not stopping them. From day one, we knew they would continue until they were stopped, and we hadn't done our job yet. I switched back to Sophie and told her what had happened and where to meet me when I gave her the okay.

Marie said, "What else can we do to end this shitshow?"

I replied, "Honestly, I don't know. I am hoping something pops from the forensic samples we took from the vans. If not, I don't know. Everything is circumstantial."

"God dammit, Mas, you are too good an investigator to let them escape."

"Thanks for the vote of confidence. I've got to admit these guys are good. We have to be ready for when they make a mistake and recognize it.

"You will be. I believe in you and Sophie. Let's get to where Kenzo said the body is. I'll take it slowly, so he gets there first."

While Marie drove like she was in a funeral procession, I started to think about what else we could do to get the perps cold. We had lots of circumstantial evidence but nothing to take to a prosecutor and get the case going. Whatever it was, it had to be bulletproof, and the germ of an idea was starting to form, nothing to make sense yet. I knew it would grow if I let it. Returning to the current issue and body. Marie parked in front of the California Academy of Sciences, opposite the De Young. All we had to do was walk across the plaza, and it was easy to get to Kenzo without impeding the police investigation.

The front of the DeYoung was lit with flashing red

and blue lights, washed out with the acid yellow of the portable flood lights. We could see the mass of bodies surrounding a single point. The crime scene unit was bustling about like ants.

Marie decided to stay in the vehicle. I started to stroll over when I saw Kenzo arrive and talk to the officer in charge of the scene. Kenzo was still talking to the office when I arrived. He turned to me, saying.

"Another fucking shit show. No one saw anything, and guess what? The security cameras don't go quite as far as the drop site. I wonder if they were aware of that."

"They were. I guarantee they researched the drop site ages ago. This site is just another drop for them. Can I see the body?"

"Yeah, I don't know the saint on this one, so I have no idea what it means."

"Can I take a photo to get it to Father Benny?"

"Sure, go ahead.

Taking the photograph, the face looked sadly peaceful. As I walked back toward Kenzo, I heard him exclaim.

"Oh, shit, here comes trouble. Mas, you'd better get lost. The brass have arrived to stick their oar in."

"Got it. You'll hear from me ASAP on anything we find. Good luck."

"Try a goddamn miracle."

I left him to face the senior officers and returned to Marie—her first question.

"Was it Bridget?"

"I don't think there is much doubt, but Kenzo will confirm. Let's go home." I called Sophie, "Meet you at home," I said.

I called Father Benny while Marie drove to drop me off. He answered just before going to voice mail.

Sleepily, he asked, "Mas, another one?"

"Yes. I have photographs, and I would like your opinion. Not a pretty sight."

"God have mercy. Send it over. What do you need?"

"Identification, on who it's supposed to represent.

Sending the photos took no time, and Benny responded promptly.

"She is the Black Madonna of Czestochowa, from Poland. It's a long story. The short version is that she is also famous in Haiti, where she is known as Erzulie Dantor. She is a mix of Christian icon and Haitian voodoo. Erzulie Dantor is recognized as a patron saint of lesbians. She fiercely loves and defends women and children, especially lesbians. There is much more to the story. I believe that is who your latest victim represents."

"Sorry for waking you, Benny. You have been very helpful, I think."

"Mas, if you need anything from me, please don't hesitate, day or night."

"Got it, Benny. Thanks again."

"Blessings on you and your associates."

He hung up. That made sense. A previous lover of Ester Ruth was killed as a lesbian protector. Well, our perps were making a statement saying no one could protect the '*sinners*' from them, proving it by killing a representation of the protector. They had some seriously fucked up theology.

Marie was silent on the ride to my home. Sophie had beaten me home after dropping off Oso. She was waiting for me.

"Do you have anything?"

I showed her the photograph of Bridget. Her body had been jammed into a wooden box with only her head showing, and her head had been framed with an open front box. The inside of the box was painted gold, contrasting with her dark skin. The two slashes on her right cheek had bled, leading me to believe they had been done perimortem. It would be interesting to find out how she was killed, indeed not as violently as some of the previous victims had been-small mercy.

"She looks sadly peaceful," she said.

"I agree. It seems less violence was used on this one. She's still dead, though."

"Yes, she is. Let's go to bed, Mas. I'm tired and want to start fresh tomorrow."

"Good idea."

We went to bed, holding each other like our life depended on it. Sophie was soon breathing deeply and evenly. Tired as I was, I didn't fall asleep. My mind was churning over everything that had been done and was being done. The perps, how they performed, and how they kept evading being definitively identified and captured. One fact kept coming to the surface. Why hadn't they identified Adrianna, Ruth's last partner, or were they keeping her for later persecution?

My idea was forming out of the fog, just like the city revealed itself from the fog that enveloped the city almost daily. It was still nebulous but getting more defined. A lot more work needed to be done before I could, or would present it to Sophie and Marie, or especially Kenzo.

Chapter Twenty-Two

I must have finally drifted into sleep. I woke with a start. My phone went off like a fire alarm. Groggily, I answered.

"Mas Hammett, how may I help you?"

"Wake up, Mas, it's Cathy. Get your ass down to the lab ASAP. I will have coffee."

The line went dead, and I was fully awake. Shit, she must have something, and something good. To be in the lab that early on a Saturday, especially this early, I looked at my phone. It was already nine am . I groaned. I was getting too old for these late nights-make that early mornings. I dressed quickly. Sophie was stirring.

I kissed her and said, "I'll call you as soon as I have something concrete."

All I got was, "Uh huh."

The quickest way to the lab was through the city, and on a Saturday morning, the traffic at this time was light, and I made good time. Cathy was waiting for me at the main entrance. The lab was usually closed on the weekend, but Cathy had once again gone above and beyond.

"Took your time getting here, didn't you? Here's your coffee."

"Jesus, Cathy, we had a late night and got beat again; another body dropped."

"I know, I heard it on the police scanner. Another reason I came in early was to check the results of tests we were running."

"What do you have for us?"

"Easy first, the concrete dust in the second van matches the concrete used for the locations in the park, to hold the cross, and to weigh the drum in the stake murder. It will also match most of the concrete sold in the big box stores, but it's part of the big picture. Next, there were small wood splinters that matched the wood used in what remained of the burned stake, commonly available wood. The splinters were found in vans number two and four, still circumstantial. The rust in the fourth van matched the rust from the stake drum exactly. I would swear that drum was in van number four." She stopped to take a breath.

This information was good, but nothing definitive, circumstantial at best. We needed something to nail these bastards. Cathy continued.

"You guys did a great job of collecting samples. You found blood, small amounts, more than enough to test. Someone had done a reasonably good job of cleaning up, but not perfectly. You have enough samples to get blood type and DNA results. We matched all five victims' blood DNA, skin cell samples, and hair. "

"Yes! God, Cathy, I could kiss you. Thank you. This is what we needed to move forward."

"Wait a minute, Mas, this is all useless, all collected illegally, doesn't mean shit. Unless the police can get a warrant. Anyway, let me finish. Some IDs were identified by hair and skin cells, but there was no blood. All I can say is they match the information and forensic results you provided via the police department reports. I worked with the ME, so if what we have matches her findings, we are certain they are accurate. What you do with those results is your problem. Please be careful, Mas. Your actions could blow up in your face."

"Can you pinpoint which vans they used for the snatches and which for the body dumps?"

"Not really. What I can say for sure is that the the victims were in the four vans you collected samples from at some point."

Van number five, the one missing when we did our collecting, will probably have some evidence if they used that van. Shit, in a good way, that is a van we didn't touch. Me thinks a confidential informant is about to drop a dime to Kenzo."

"Like I said, be very careful. You will get my full reports waiting for you on Monday morning. I hope the cost is worth it, Mas."

"I know, and we appreciate you going the extra mile. Bill me at the office under something innocuous. Would you prefer cash?

"No, just send payment when you get the invoice. You gotta be above board just in case anything comes back to us at the lab."

"Okay, whatever you want. Look forward to the reports on Monday."

"Bye, Mas, let me get on with it."

Cathy showed me out, and I heard the locks click behind me. We had more info and now proof that the professor and his family were the perpetrators. I wasn't sure which members were guilty if not all of them. My money was on Luther, the son, and the professor with coerced assistance from the wives, which made more sense and covered the professor and his wife with an alibi for most of the snatches. Kenzo needed this info, and then he could decide what to do with it and how to proceed. My call went to voice mail, so I left a message.

Not in a hurry, I made my way back home. Sophie was in the kitchen and looked gorgeous in a ruffled, just-got-up way. I loved this woman. I hugged Sophie from behind, nuzzling her neck. I restrained myself from caressing her boobs. There were consequences for that uninvited action.

"Where were you? I missed you," she said.

"At the lab." My comment got her attention in a hurry.

"And the results are?"

"The victims were in the four vans we got into at some point. Definite proof, blood, skin cells, hair, and other circumstantial evidence. Different vans at different times to do the snatches and then to the park to do the body dumps. Cathy couldn't say when each van was used or for what and wouldn't guess."

"She confirmed we have forensic evidence on some the victims in those vans?"

"Yes. I figure there is probably evidence in van five as well. In fact, it wouldn't surprise me if that was the van used this week to snatch and move Bridget."

"So, what do we do now?"

"We wait for Kenzo to call, tell him the good news, and then go from there. We will have the written reports from Cathy on Monday."

"You're not telling me everything. Spill it, Mas."

"No, and not yet. I have an idea, but it is nebulous

right now. As soon as I have it sorted in my own mind, I will present it to you, you and Marie."

"Okay, I'll wait, but not too long."

"Deal." I said, laughing at her intimated threat."

The fact that Kenzo hadn't returned my call yet was starting to bother me; he must be in something critical, especially for a Saturday. I had to be patient and wait for him to get back to me.

With nothing to do but wait, Sophie and I went to the local market to do our weekly food shopping and other chores. The exciting part of the private investigator life you never see on TV or in books. Yes, even private investigators went to the bathroom and had to do chores to keep the home and business running.

We walked to the market, taking our time, stopping to look at things that caught our eye or were on sale. A deal never hurt. We had completed about half our list when my phone went off. Kenzo.

"Hi Kenzo, is everything okay?"

"Not even close, but I am on this case until the end. The brass had me in for a meeting this morning. That's why I'm late calling you. They made it very clear this case is on my team until it's completed successfully, or I am the scapegoat when it all goes pear-shaped. Fuck them. I just want to catch the perps."

"Well, we might just be able to assist with the former. We got the lab results from our mission in the vans. The victims were in four of those vans at one point or another. Some results are circumstantial, such as the concrete and wood splinters we found. But blood and hairs were recovered, matching the results of your ME's reports on DNA. The Professor and his family are the perps, no question."

"Are you kidding me? Are you sure of the results?"

"Do you want to question Cathy and her lab techs' results?"

"Not a chance. Cathy would rip me a new one. Great work."

"Yeah, but none of it is kosher. We didn't have a search warrant."

"Don't worry about that. Your idea of using a CI cover is a good one and legal for the most part. With all the information we have about the victims, their connection to Ruth, and then to her family, the industrial site they own. It increases the case I can sell to a judge for warrants on their home and the college. Two of them work there, and the college has white vans, which we know have been used for the body drops, etc. I'll make it work."

"As soon as we get the hard copy reports, we will send copies to you. We can close the net on this real soon with any luck."

"Thanks, Mas, Sophie, and Marie. This would have been a worse shit show without you."

"We aren't done yet, so don't count your chickens."

"I know, we got them. We have to prove it beyond any doubt. I get it."

He hung up, and there was a niggle in the back of my mind, one of those bad news feelings. I knew we weren't done with this case, not yet. I mentioned the feeling to Sophie.

"What is it, Mas? Why that feeling now? We are getting close?"

"If I knew that, I would have an answer. Something is not right. Why leave Adrianna as the last one if they knew about her? She should be the first target."

"Maybe, like she said, they were careful, Ruth and her."

"Or they were leaving her to last."

"You mean, the professor always knew about her and saved her for the last victim."

"I'm not sure she will be the last victim. There are a lot of martyred saints, and Ruth knew more people than have been killed so far. They won't stop until they're stopped."

"Agreed, so what do we do now? You were working on something ready to spill?"

"No, not yet soon, I promise. I am going for a walk when we get home and drop off our shopping."

"Want company?"

"Thanks, not this time. I need to think, and your gorgeous self will distract me."

"Thank you, kind sir. That is called deflection, and I might need some deflection tonight. Think about that."

Laughing, I said, "Cruel and unusual punishment."

"Not until tonight," she said with a smile.

Holding hands, we made our way back home. We put everything away, and I left for my thought walk. I had to get everything right. I was about to put someone I loved in grave danger. If anything went wrong, it would be fatal and on me.

The plan would have to be enticing and foolproof to trap these perps. They had been too clever, and so far too careful to be caught in the act. The snatches were researched, planned, and executed exceptionally well. Maybe the way would be to pressure them into a rushed action, one they hadn't had the opportunity to research and plan for as they usually would. To make them do that, it would have to be something they couldn't resist. Something or someone that mattered to them more than their plan. Take them out of their comfort zone.

This idea was nuts, entrapment if it worked, and right now, there are too many moving parts to be considered a sane idea. I would need the buy-in from a lot of people, and my talent for persuasion would be tested.

To set a trap, you need bait. The only bait I could think of that would lure the perps was Adrianna, at least her name, if not her person. I couldn't ask her to be bait. I could ask Marie and Sophie to volunteer. Marie, for preference, looked more Hispanic than the blonde Sophie, who would work if Marie rejected the plan.

We would need to get the message to the perps, via a third party, that Adrianna was leaving the city and state for good, with no forwarding address. It's pure fiction on our part, but it should get their attention, with a concise timeline for them to act on mistakes made and perps caught. Easy in theory, more difficult in practice.

The first thing on the agenda is to get Marie chipped, as Sophie and I were. That action, which Sophie had insisted on, proved critical in the Bodies on the Bridge case. Marie was now a partner, and what was good for Sophie and me was good for Marie.

Next, to design the trap. The best traps were simple and believable. Complicated left too much to go wrong. The information had to come from a credible source, the police, a journalist's report, social media, or all of the above. The perps may not know their torture chamber was compromised. Their awareness and suspicions would be raised if they did. I was betting on them being mission-oriented, mission above all else. Nothing had stopped them so far, but they'd had the advantage of long-term planning and executing their plans.

That I hoped would make them overconfident. The only negative they had suffered had been the discovery of their torture property, and they could easily explain that away *'they didn't know it was being used, it was unoccupied'* plausible deniability. It did add to all the other circumstantial evidence that our best bet was to catch them in the act, the kidnapping, not the killing part, and the most significant risk.

All I had to do was come up with who, what, when, and where, and the safety of the bait. First, we had to make sure Adrianna was safe and out of the way. The best place to set the trap would be Adrianna's apartment, so her buy-in was critical. We would explain what we were doing. It was for her safety, and she had to stay hidden until this was all over.

I rethought my idea about asking Marie. She had been seen at the church and the college campus, so she was out. That left Sophie using a dark wig as a disguise, and we didn't need to fool all the people all the time, just the perps for a very short time. I would build in a shitload of safety factors with Kenzo's assistance and police department support. I would hide in the apartment. There was no way I was going to let anything happen to Sophie.

Making my way home, I needed to talk this through with Sophie. Sophie was pottering about our home. I interrupted, and my tone of voice caught her attention.

"What's up? Have you heard anything?"

No, but I have an idea and want-need your input."

"Okay, spill it."

Spending the next ten minutes laying out the plan as far as I had developed it. Sophie listened silently, concentrating on what I was saying until the end.

"Phew, that's a stretch, making them break the pattern. I'm in Mas, you knew I would be."

"Yeah, but only if we can guarantee your safety. We need to plan better than the perps have, and they have planned very well. Now that I have your buy-in, please poke holes in the plan. We need to make it better. I will contact Adrianna and put the proposal to her."

"No, Mas, we will do it together. Our first contact with her was together, and this is more important. Non negotiable."

"Yes, Ma'am, got it. I will set up a meeting."

Adrianna answered on the first ring, "Do you have something?"

"Yes and no. Can we meet with you? We have a proposition we think you will find interesting?"

"Sure, not much going on today if you come to San Bruno."

"Deal, what time is good for you?"

"Any, just call me when you are on your way."

Okay, be with you in the next hour or so, and thank you."

Sophie heard me and looked at me quizzically.

"We have an appointment with Adrianna today in San Bruno. Let's get to her ASAP."

We grabbed our bags, including a set of client docs, and left to pick up the SUV. Being Saturday, the traffic was heavy but flowed, and we made it down the peninsula to San Bruno in good time. Sophie called Adrianna, letting her know we were on our way and giving her an ETA.

Adrianna and the couple in whose home she was sheltering met us at the door. They gave us suspicious looks and hovered close to Adrianna, who thanked them and said we were okay.

She said, "They're very protective of me. I told them some of the issues."

"Good. We have a proposition for you to assist in getting the perps."

"What sort of proposition?"

Sophie jumped in, saying, "We would like to borrow your apartment. We are going to bait them into trying to kidnap me in your place. It's basically a trap. I will be you until we catch them in the act. You will be safe here, out of the way."

She looked pensive, then asked, "And you will be playing me!"

"I will," said Sophie before I could say anything.

Adrianna laughed out loud and said, "You look as Hispanic as I do Asian. Not at all."

"I don't have to be perfect, just enough to bait them into making a mistake."

"If they're as smart as you say they are, you won't fool them for a second."

I could see her mind working, and I said, "Not a chance in hell are we putting you in jeopardy. These perps have already killed six people connected to Ruth, and they are not going to stop until they are stopped. So no, you will not be the bait."

"Mas, you don't have a choice. If I decide to move home, you can't stop me. Then what? We work together and get the people that killed my partner. I loved Ruth, we were good together. It was easy being with her. From day one, it felt right, not perfect, just right."

Sophie asked, "You don't realize how dangerous this could be. It could be fatal."

"You were willing to put yourself in that position."

I answered that statement, "We are professionals and will take precautions. You can't or not in the allotted time."

"Then you need to devise a plan that includes and protects me. I am doing this. End of story."

She looked determined, and her voice carried a conviction. I figured arguing with her would be futile. Shit, this was a complication we didn't need, and now we were stuck with it. We had to make the most of it.

"Okay, Sophie and I will come up with a plan. We will include you when we have something. Nothing will be finalized until we have run it past you and get your buy-in. Once we have a plan, we have to stick to it one hundred percent. if not, you will probably end up tortured to death." That comment got her attention. She paled and nodded in understanding. I hoped she took it to heart, and we could actually protect her.

Adrianna said, "I guess I'm trusting you with my life."

"Yes," both Sophie and I said at the same time. That eased the tension a little.

Sophie and I will contact you when we have something worth talking about. We promise it won't be a long wait. We also would like to make you our client. No charge to you, but it would cover some legalities, confidentiality, etc."

She looked puzzled, shrugged her shoulders, and agreed. We spent the next thirty minutes reviewing the contract, explaining what it covered and how it protected her and us.

She smiled a wan smile, saying, "At least now I feel like I am doing something. I have been in limbo, going through the motions since she died. It's really been that long." Tears appeared in the corners of her eyes. Her friends called out, asking if everything was okay. She responded firmly, "Yes."

We said our goodbyes, with promises of meeting soon, and reminded her to call us, regardless of the time, if she was concerned about anything.

The trip back home was full of conversation regarding a plan to bait the perps into attacking Adrianna. Everything we came up with was shot down by the other. There is too much risk to Adrianna, impractical to cover, and many different reasons. What we needed was something simple and practical. The old KISS principle—*keep it simple, stupid*—that was what we had to do.

The one plus is that Sophie and I would be a team in protecting Adrianna, not just me protecting Sophie as Adrianna. The only victim taken in daylight was Ashton, the realtor, and that was well-planned. Putting pressure on the perps, so they didn't have time to plan thoroughly and take risks they didn't have to in previous snatches. That was our advantage if we played it right.

Breaking it down, daylight was safer for Adrianna. If we could make it even safer, that would funnel the perps' efforts to a night snatch. A call to Tara Zosa, who we had worked with and for. She was employing

Oso as a driver, and I wanted to borrow him to ferry Adrianna to and from work, she owed us, and with this story I was sure she would help.

While Adrianna was at work, have an off-duty police officer escort her during the day and at lunch. When Oso dropped her off, back at her apartment, it looked like she was the most vulnerable. Sophie and I would be inside waiting for her, and it would appear she was alone and easy prey. That was the trap, simple as long as it worked. I would run this by Sophie to see if she could poke holes in it or develop something better. I called out to Sophie. I explained the plan, and she responded.

"I like it in principle. It's simple and doable. If you can get Tara's buy-in and Oso's agreement, hire an off-duty officer for the duration. A lot of 'ifs'. I can't think of anything better right now. Once we agree on a plan that's it. No changes."

"Exactly, once we have a plan, that's it. We are committed to it. We have to be flexible enough to adapt to circumstances around the basics. You know there will be surprises."

We both laughed at that, knowing that however good a plan was, there was always something to mess with it. We would make sure it was as perfect as possible. At least we were both on the same page.

My first call was to Adrianna, and she was subdued. She had started to grieve for Ruth, and the seriousness of her situation had finally sunk in. She agreed to everything I proposed, even the lunchtime chaperone.

"Are you always this compliant?"

"No, usually I push back on everything. I am out of

my depth with all of this, and I want the bastards who killed my Ruth."

She sobbed into the phone before collecting herself and asking if there was anything else she could do. I suggested finding a therapist, and it would help. She laughed a bitter laugh.

"The best therapy will be seeing the bastards face justice of any sort."

"We'll be in touch before the announcement of your leaving the state. The only person you tell about this, and only if you have to, is your boss. Got it?"

"Got it, and thank you for doing this."

"They must be stopped, and this is our best option. Sophie will pick you up tomorrow and take care of the only thing we need to. Be careful."

Hanging up the call, I hoped I was right, and this was the best option. The next call would be Oso. I already knew what his answer would be, but I had to ask. I figured Oso would still be home after his late-night adventures, and he was.

Sleepily he answered, "Hola, who dis."

"Oso, it's Mas."

"Hola amigo, wass up."

"We need your driving skills for a short while. I will clear it with Tara to make sure it is okay, but I wanted your buy-in as well."

"What you need, Mas, you got."

"Hold on, Oso, I am not going to screw up your job with Tara. If she says no, it's no, okay."

"She's good people, Mas. She will be okay with it. Besides, she owes you as well."

"I am not playing that card with either of you. If Tara allows our ask, we will pay you as well."

"What's the job?"

"We need you to drive a client from her home to work and back again at the end of the workday."

"Sounds too easy, what's the catch?"

"She is a target involved with the bodies in the park."

"You in that one, man, they's some sick pendejos. I'm in."

"I thought you would be. I had to ask, and it's all on what Tara says, okay?"

"Sure, Mas, I talk to her as well."

"Wait until I have spoken to her. That way, it will be sorted before you need to say anything."

"Whatever you says Mas. I'm good. Say hi to Miss Sophie an take good care of her, man."

"Take that one as done. Talk soon, adios amigo."

I ended the call and wondered how far he could have gone without some bad decisions. There was no point in calling Tara on a weekend. That call would be my first call on Monday. I would have to be patient on Sunday and not drive Sophie crazy. That could have consequences when her alter ego, Ms. Circe, appeared. I updated Sophie and settled as best I could to wait until Monday.

Chapter Twenty-Three

Sunday dragged on like a bad party you couldn't leave. I kept as busy as I could without driving Sophie completely nuts. I cleaned and sorted stuff that didn't need it, pottering about just to make time go by. We now had a plan and would have to make it work.

After a restless night where I tossed and turned, which thankfully didn't disturb Sophie, I got up early, weary, and ready to get the week underway. First things first, coffee. With that in process, I started to think about how to approach Tara, although we were now on better terms after a very rocky start. She could still be frosty toward me.

Tara was known to be an early starter. I waited until eight-thirty before calling her office. I didn't want to push my luck by calling her cell uninvited.

Her assistant Kristen answered the call on the first ring. "Mas, I recognized your number. Hi, how are you?"

"That's a little scary for a Monday morning." I said with a chuckle, "Up to my neck in it. How is Tara?

"Crazy busy, oh, and I am now a junior partner in the company."

"Congrats, good for you, and well deserved. Look, we need a favor."

"Of course. Why else would you be calling. Kidding Mas. What do you need."

"You have heard about the bodies in the park?"

"Yes, oh shit, are you involved in that mess? Is it another Zodiac?"

"Yes, we are, and no, very different to the Zodiac. We are going to try to trap the perps. To do it safely, we need to borrow Oso to pick up and drop off the person we are protecting and who we believe will be the next target." She didn't need to know the plan.

"When do you need Oso?"

"Not sure, it will be soon and probably only for a short time."

"I'm sure Tara will agree in these circumstances. She also has some Asia trips planned, and one is coming up soon. It would make it easier if your timing coincided with her trip. I'll talk to her today unless you want to, directly?"

"Ah no, you breaking the ice will be better." She laughed at that, remembering the rocky start I had with Tara.

"Okay, Mas, I'm sure she will want to speak with you anyway."

"Sooner than later would be good if she does."

"Bye, Mas. Please say hi to Sophie for me."

"Will do, and thank you."

That got the ball rolling. The next call would be Kenzo, and this call would be more difficult. Trapping the perps was a risky project, and as a police officer, he would be in a difficult position if it went right or wrong. We would need him and his team's resources to nail everything down, make it all legal, and put the bastards away forever. I called the burner, and Kenzo also answered on the first ring, a good sign.

"We need to meet as early as you can. We have a

plan, and we need your input and kinda blessing."

"Ah, come on, Mas, what shit are you stirring up now?"

"That is why we need to talk face to face. We can get the perps. Just listen. If you can't or won't be a part of that, that's fine. We'll have to work out something that works for all of us."

"Works for all of us! Fuck it, Mas, you know the position I'm in, and what's this, all of us. It's me who'll get burned if I can't close this case and make it airtight."

"Don't you think we know that? It's me, Mas, we got your back. Just meet and listen. You can walk away after you hear me out if you need to."

"No promises, usual place?"

"Where are you now?"

"Embarcadero, stadium end."

"Can we make it Blue bottle coffee in the Ferry Building, twenty minutes?"

"Yeah, I can do that. Coffee is on you."

"Great, see you in twenty."

Kenzo was a friend, and I felt terrible for him. He was between a rock and a hard place. He had used the police resources the best way he was allowed. His hands tied by both the police department and the FBI Profilers theory.

Getting to the Ferry Building in twenty minutes would be a stretch for me, but I would make it somehow. This was too important to all involved and the city. Late, by three minutes. Kenzo was leaning up against the wall opposite the coffee store. He looked exhausted, his shoulders sagged, and his head dropped to his chest. His face was drawn and thinner than I could ever remember.

He started as I said, "Hey, you okay?"

"Sorry, I was miles away. Just going over everything again, see if I missed anything."

"You can't miss what you don't have. Your hands were tied from day one. We are more flexible, and we can end this together. Coffee first, then you can shoot holes in our plan. Have you eaten anything today?"

"No, not very hungry—coffee's fine."

"Bullshit, you gotta eat. We'll pick up something."

We ordered our coffee and were silent while we waited for the drip coffees to do their thing. It takes time, and there is always a line waiting. We took our drinks outside. The air was a little chilly as it was still early. We sat sipping the excellent brew, and I slowly explained how we came to the conclusions we did and the plan to trap the perps. We knew that there were at least two perps and possibly more.

Kenzo sat in silence, listening intently, with no interruptions. When I had finished, we were both quiet. Kenzo was thinking about what I had said.

"Mas, I agree with your conclusions about what has happened and that the whole thing is driven by religious revenge. I am not sure about moving forward. You are taking a hell of a risk with Adrianna."

"I know, at first, we were going to use Marie, but she would be recognized. She's been in two of the perp's locations, so it would be Sophie. When we put the plan to Adrianna, she laughed at using Sophie as a Hispanic decoy. She volunteered and put us in a difficult position. Use her, or she was going to move back into her apartment unprotected. No way we could allow that. Not a kosher way of doing things."

"You got that right. Adrianna put you in a difficult position. I can see why you planned the way you did. Not a bad plan if it works."

"We can handle inside-of-the-apartment action, which is where we expect it to happen. What we need is outside assistance, police assistance, to be exact. If the perps manage to get Adrianna outside of the house, we need your guys to stop them in their tracks."

"Great, now I will have to come up with an excuse to have my team surveilling a potential victim instead of following up on pointless, useless leads going nowhere."

"You're in?"

"I hate to say it. Mas, as whacky as you are, this makes sense, and it's the best option I've heard so far. For all our resources, if you aren't looking in the right place, you aren't gonna get the right answer. I'm fucked if I don't solve this, so what's one more risk. One thing, I want in on all the planning, timelines, everything, okay?"

"No problem. When we have everything firmed up, we'll review it with you before we implement the plan. Good enough?"

"Yes, as long as you give me a decent lead time to get my part in place. I will have to pick my officers carefully. Some are not, shall we say, reliably in my corner."

"Plants reporting up the chain?"

"Pretty sure on two, possibly one more. I'm not taking any chances."

"Let's go get breakfast near the office, okay?"

"Why not? I'll just check-in. I don't have any meetings until later on Monday. The brass wants updates. They roll in when they roll in." He said in a jaded tone of voice.

Walking back to our office, I called Sophie and said to meet us at Mama's, a local breakfast place. Even with the usual long lines, we were so regular they usually found a spot for us, much to the dismay of the non-regulars.

Sophie had beaten us to Mama's and was seated at a table for two, with three chairs crammed right next to the main door. It was not ideal, but we would take it. Kenzo sat opposite Sophie, and I sat squeezed between the table and the door. We ordered, and Sophie jumped right in, asking.

"So Kenzo, what do you think of the plan?"

"Honestly, it's nuts, but I can't think of anything better, and I'll take whatever I can get to stop these perps."

She smiled, "Well, thank you for the vote of confidence."

"Don't get me wrong. I appreciate what you guys have already done. My hands are tied by the department, and I'll do whatever I can to assist you execute the plan. Adrianna is crazy, putting herself in jeopardy like this. Make sure you take care of her."

I said, "That's the plan. No way they will expect us to be waiting for them inside the apartment."

"Agreed, but don't underestimate these guys. They have been very disciplined in all their efforts so far."

Sophie added, "That's why we want to take them out of their comfort zone."

Kenzo sighed, "That could make them more dangerous and unpredictable."

"Which is why we need your assistance," I added

in the silence after Kenzo's statement.

The food arrived, and we ate without comment. Kenzo polished off his in-record time and sat back sated, commenting.

"I needed that more than I thought. Thanks for making me eat. Oh shit, I gotta run. Thanks again, both of you. Keep me in the loop-yes?"

We both said yes in unison, and he was gone. We looked at each other and started to talk at the same time. Stopping, I told Sophie to go ahead.

"This is starting to get real. We need to finish this quickly."

"Couldn't have put it better myself. I'll contact Adrianna and bring her up to date. Colleen will be on the list to out Adrianna as leaving the city. I'm sure she will be able to make it seem real. Probably on social media, print would mean bringing in her editor."

We left and walked back to our office. Marie was busy with her stuff and said, "Mas, checks to sign. I have been thinking a lot of this stuff would be done more efficiently online, quicker and easier, and I wouldn't have to bother you for signatures."

Before I could say anything, Sophie jumped in and said, "Go for it. You're a partner. Figure out what needs to be done, and we'll authorize it."

Of course, I had to have my two cents, "Don't I get a say in this?"

Together, Sophie and Marie said, "No."

So much for respect for the boss. Which I really wasn't. The way we had set up the partnership, and I was more than okay with it. I went into the inner office to call Adrianna. Before I could dial, my phone went off. It was Tara Zosa calling me.

"Hi Tara, thanks for calling."

"Hi Mas, from the little that Kristen told me, I don't have a choice. Looks like you have got yourself in the poop again." She laughed genuinely, "Of course, you can have Oso, and I will pick up the tab for his salary."

"You sure? That's very generous of you and appreciated."

"No problem, Mas. I will make sure Oso takes good care of whomever it is. Some mornings, I might be in the car, depending on the calendar. Would that be a problem, meaning would that put me in danger?"

"No, in fact, that would be an added deterrent to the potential kidnappers. They are only after our client. They have been meticulous in how they took the previous victims, with little or no forensics. I don't think they would risk snatching her in broad daylight, riding with Oso, and if you were also with them, that would be another negative."

"Good to know. You heard that Kristen is now a partner? I will have our new admin, Grace, send over my schedule, and please keep it confidential."

"Yes, I did hear about Kristen, and smart move on your part. No question on confidential."

"I know. I do have some good ideas every now and then." At least she said it with a lightness that would not have been there in our past interactions.

"No one will get your schedule from us."

"If I didn't trust you, you would not be getting it. Keep me in the loop. I have to go. Good luck, Mas."

She was gone. That piece was in place. Now, call to Adrianna, then Collen, the journalist, followed up by a call to Big Boots, an SFPD motorcycle officer and well-known and respected member of the Kink community. He would find some off-duty Police officers to chaperone Adrianna at lunch. We were getting there.

Adrianna picked up on the first ring and sounded cautious. She should be.

"Hey, it's coming together. We have a ride from your apartment to work and back taken care of. The driver's name is Oso, and he will look after you, door to door. I would trust him with Sophie's life.

"Thank you. You will let me know as soon as possible when I can move back to my home?"

"Oh yeah, we want this over as much as you do. We'll be in touch when we have everything sorted, and it should be soon."

"Mas, thank you for doing this. I mean protecting me."

"It's what we do."

That done. Next Colleen. This call would be to set up a face-to-face. As expected, my call went to voice mail. I left a cryptic message. Big Boots was next, and again, my call went to voice mail. I left the details of what I needed and guaranteed he would return my call with answers, not more questions. Working with competent people is always a pleasure.

Calls were made, and there was nothing to do but wait for the results. Target practice would be a good distraction. I yelled out to Sophie and Marie where I was going and my approximate timeline. Sophie called back. She had a self-defense class later that morning. Check.

The walk home was a good time to think about the plan and look for weaknesses, issues, and potential flaws. I couldn't find any from our end. No plan is perfect, and if it's too rigid, it's got a good chance of failing. The opposition won't play by our rules, so we must be flexible and adjust to the inevitable challenges.

The shooting range was busy for the time of day, so there was no rapid fire. Two hundred rounds and the targets became shredded. The time was well spent, and I felt better and more relaxed. The trip home was uneventful. I checked my phone for messages and texts. Nada. The first thing to do was clean my weapon. I stripped it down and gave it a thorough cleaning. With my weapon secured, my GSR-covered clothes went into the laundry bin, and I went to the shower. The hot water felt cleansing, and I was ready to get back to the office.

On the way back to the office, I checked again. No messages, damn it, where was everybody? They would get back to me when they got back to me. The office was quiet. Marie was busy, and Sophie was at her self-defense class.

Keeping busy, I reviewed the forensic reports from Cathy and her lab. They read well, thorough and concise. The police lab would have plenty to do when the CI information filtered through Kenzo, and he obtained the warrants to examine all the vans. The police department forensics team would have more time and unlimited access to find more evidence of the crimes.

Marie called out, "Collen on one."

I grabbed the landline, "Hello, Collen. Thanks for getting back to me."

"Hi yourself, Mas, what do you need?" She said it with a chuckle.

"Oh, not much, your ear for now. You decide if

you want to help after."

"Uh oh, what have you gotten yourself into now?"

"Off the record for now. You get the exclusive if it all works out. You didn't do too badly the last time, right?"

"You got that right. My book about the whole corruption story is coming out in the fall. Thanks again for that. What do you need?"

"We are trying to trap the perps responsible for the bodies dumped in the park."

"No shit. How do you get mixed up in all these weird cases?"

"Natural talent. It all starts innocently enough, then it goes sideways in a hurry, and by then, it's too late to duck and run. We need your help."

I let that hang. After a brief pause, Colleen bit and cautiously asked, "What exactly do you need?"

Explaining as much as I had to about our plan, she read between the lines and asked, "Trust me, Mas, tell me everything. Then it will be easier for me to assist. You know you can trust me. I have proven that. Give you my word."

"Okay, deal. Someone's life is in the balance here. This one has to be tight."

"You have my word."

The next twenty minutes were spent giving Colleen the entire plan. She had comments and suggestions, and all were good and on point.

"Mas, this is crazy. I can't fault your thinking or planning. Except." Here it comes, I thought. "We need to get this into the print press as well."

"That means going through your newsroom editor. I don't like that!"

"It will be fine, after the "Bodies on the Bridge" story. I have a certain leeway, and he trusts me more or less. I can pitch this to him without too much detail, and the payoff of stopping a serial killer exclusive."

"You sure you can pull that off."

"Yup. You are good at what you do, and so am I. You wouldn't be talking to me if I wasn't."

"True. We're good. You write it up. It will be happening soon. I'll give you the final details when it's go time."

"Agreed. Talk soon, Mas."

She was gone. Another piece was in place. Now for Big Boots to get back to me. That should be the end of planning and on to execution. Marie left a message on my desk while I was talking to Colleen to call the name and number of a potential new client. I called and arranged a meeting for later that day. I left a note for Sophie via e-mail. If it wasn't on her computer, it didn't exist.

Sophie came in looking worse for wear, sweaty and disheveled. I asked, "Good class?"

"Bastard put me through the wringer today. I ache in places I didn't know I had places."

"Want to quit?"

"Don't be stupid, Mas, these classes are awesome. It's about the physical effects and the power to control. Them and yourself."

That magic word again 'control.' Right from day one of our meeting, control was the watchword. Her need to control and my need to relinquish it, we made a good team.

I updated her on the conversation with Colleen and the upcoming client meeting, later. She said she would go home and change for that meeting. It was a good day, except for the non-response from Big Boots. If he didn't get back to me by midday tomorrow, I would start to worry.

The client meeting sucked, and something was off. So, we closed out the meeting without committing to take them on as clients. As soon as we left, we both decided not to take the case. Our antenna, gut feeling, whatever you want to call it, was definitely saying something was not kosher and to leave it for someone else. We were both on the same page on that one.

Even though it was relatively early, Sophie said, "Let's stop off for a quick drink, then an early night?"

"Good idea." I agreed.

The bar was local to our place. We knew the bar person and chatted with her, being slow this early. We strolled in the cool evening with no rush to get home, and when we did, it was straight to bed.

Chapter Twenty-Four

The morning arrived with my phone going off. Damn, I had forgotten to set the alarm.

I answered, "Mas Hammett."

Before I could say anything further, Big Boots started, "Hey, Mas. Sorry I didn't get back to you before. I've had all sorts of issues. Not your problem. So, tell me, how many bodies do ya need, what for, and for how long?"

He patiently listened to my list of wants and needs, telling me it would take a couple of days to sort out a schedule, and that he would get back to me as soon as he arranged it.

He closed out, saying, "See ya, Mas, back to the shit show."

His was the last piece we needed. I was confident we could pull this off. Sophie had woken and was out of bed and in the kitchen, clattering about making breakfast. Huevos rancheros, which translates to ranchers' eggs, is an excellent hearty Mexican breakfast.

As we ate, Sophie said, "I am seeing Adrianna this morning and will knock off a couple of things on our 'to-do' list."

No issues from me. I was going to go over to Adrianna's apartment, check it out, and make plans to defend Adrianna's home. When she went over later,

Sophie would install the wireless cameras for the best coverage.

We parted company. Sophie to meet Adrianna and me going to the apartment. There were three entrances to her apartment—the front door, the back door, and lastly through the garage. The apartment above Adrianna's only had two, the side and back. We had to concentrate on the three we could control—locks, cameras, and vigilance.

The one that worried me the most was the garage, which was on a remote that could easily be hacked. That one needed a review. Maybe make it so inviting they would use it and prepare for them to enter that way. They had used the garage when taking Jeremy Hale, the realtor. Why not use that knowledge against them without assuming it would be the only entry point they would consider?

The apartment was nicely laid out and open, with good sight lines from the front door to the back door. Two bedrooms and a single bathroom were off to one side. The apartment should be a defendable location. Kenzo's police officers in unmarked vehicles stationed outside, close, but not on top of the location in front and the access alley out back. We should have everything covered. Even if the perps got in, they would still have to go through Sophie and me to get Adrianna and get back out through the police officers.

However perfect a plan in theory, there was always the unknown and the unexpected to wreck it. The plan I would propose didn't have any obvious holes. Sophie would find something to improve on. Then, with her input, give it to Kenzo to rip apart. With his okay, explain it to Adrianna. After all, it was her life we were putting in jeopardy.

The plan was a good compromise between rigid and flexible, and I would get Sophie's opinion as soon as I returned to the office. Before returning, I checked the alley at the back and walked up and down the street out front. It was a quiet section of the street during the day, busier at night with several restaurants and a bar close by, and the busier, the better I liked it.

The drive back to the office was uneventful and gave me more time to consider how we would prep Adrianna. I wanted her in a place between confident and anxious.

Sophie was already back, after dropping Adrianna at her office. We reviewed everything we had in place and what was left to do. I ran my observations regarding Adrianna's apartment past Sophie.

She listened without interruption. After I had finished, she said, "Nicely done. I can't think of anything I would change. My only comment is that I would like to visit the apartment to check out the camera placement, not that I don't trust you. We need to make sure they are as well positioned and innocuous as possible."

"No offense taken. Do you think we are ready to run this past Kenzo?"

"Mas, we are as ready as we are going to get with planning. Now, we need to implement this plan before the perps choose the next vic. Set up a meeting with Kenzo."

"On it. How did it go with Adrianna this morning?"

"Good, she is a trooper, just a little sore. She liked our thoroughness and all the precautions."

"Good. All we need now is for Big Boots to come through with the security detail and then give Colleen the 'Go' signal. When can we move our stuff into Adrianna's apartment?"

"Anytime we like. It will be like camping out." She said it with a laugh.

A laugh to hide the tension we both felt. We were taking a huge risk. The perps were dangerous, and I didn't think they would hesitate to take us out if we got in their way. We would have to be on top of our game.

Kenzo didn't answer the burner, so I left a message for a meet. The timeline was now on him. While I waited for him to return my call, I started making a list of materials I wanted to take to the apartment. It wasn't a long list, and everything on it was necessary.

Kenzo called as I was reviewing my list.

"Mas, how's the planning going."

"Good, almost complete. Big Boots is organizing the protection detail for the days. Sophie and I will be moving into Adrianna's apartment ASAP. Everything is in place for Colleen to put the info about Adrianna's supposed departure from San Francisco. We only need to give her the okay to go, and it runs in the paper, hard copy, online and social media. All that's left is your part, getting the PD surveillance and protection coverage for outside sorted."

"Working on that, I am picking the teams carefully. Only my original team, those I trust, I don't want any of the officers foisted on me anywhere near this. However, I may not have a choice. I'll keep you in the loop. Tell you right now. The brass are not happy with this plan. If anything goes wrong, I'm done."

"Hey, Kenzo, that's why we are doing this. Stop

the perps and protect your ass. It's a twofer, you can't have one without the other. Trust us."

"Trust's not the issue, it's the fucking politics."

"Let us know when you have your teams sorted. I'll keep you in the loop when anything happens or changes. This is going to work."

"I hope so, and not just for my career. You will hear as soon as all is set on my end. Thanks, Mas."

He hung up the call and mixed emotions washed over me starting with anger at how Kenzo was being treated by the PD, as well as frustration we hadn't caught the perps, and sadness for what the victims and their families were going through had turned this into an absolute shit show.

Sitting at my desk and lost in thought, I didn't hear Sophie call out to me.

More insistently, Sophie said, "Earth to Mas."

"Eh, sorry, I was miles away."

"I know. I want to go over to the apartment today and install the cameras. The sooner that's done, the less we have to do later."

"Good idea. I will put the equipment together today and pick up anything we don't have, and it shouldn't be a long list."

Marie had overheard this last part of the conversation and said, "If you need me to get anything, happy to gofer it." Quietly, she added, "Wouldn't it be a good idea for me to be with you in the apartment? I mean, three people are better than two, right?"

Together, Sophie and I said, "No."

I continued before Sophie could say anything, "This could be dangerous. Sophie has been training, probably not enough for this, and you haven't at all. If I could do this on my own, I would. Two people are the best number to defend this apartment. If there are any surprises, we should be able to handle them. Thanks for the offer. If we thought we needed you, we would have asked. Trust us. You are our partner. Right, Sophie."

"Yes, and I concur. One hundred percent."

Marie looked mollified and said, "If you need me, I will be on the end of a phone, any time day or night, got it? I love you guys."

Oh shit, this was getting maudlin. I said, "Let's go and get lunch."

Sophie and Marie chorused agreement. We locked up the office and left for an early lunch. A rare event that we were all available for lunch at the same time; it felt good. Our local go-to eatery offered a California fusion menu. It was always fresh and interesting.

Seated and drinks served, we chatted about everything but work. Sophie and I asked Marie how she and Chung were doing now they had agreed to buy Simon's place.

Marie's eyes lit up like beacons, and off she went on a tirade of happy things that were going on. Redecorating, modernizing some stuff, keeping the good old traditional stuff, and generally making it into their home. Hearing about good things happening to someone we cared for was good medicine for all of us. We couldn't wait to see Marie having good things happen to her, and we'd discover what Italian Chinese babies looked like. I'd put money on them being very cute.

Lunch was served and didn't disappoint. We were comfortable enough with each other that we picked off each other's plates, three for the price of one. We charged it to the office as an office lunch meeting, and all three employees of the business were in attendance. My phone went off, and I didn't want to break the relaxed feeling of the lunch. Shit, it was Big Boots.

"Hi, good news."

"Mas, I only give you good news." He laughed before saying, "Excellent news. When I reached out to prospective officers and explained what you needed and why, you got all you need." He paused for effect. "At no charge." He waited for my response.

"Are you shitting me? Why."

"Several reasons. They want the perps caught. Not catching them is a bad look for the entire PD, and they want to assist. They also know the shit storm Kenzo is going through. Many know of him, some by reputation, and some have reported to him. They also know, to quote several, '*Kenzo is fucked with the brass and media if he doesn't get a result.*' They are all in.

That was a turn-up for the books, unexpected and appreciated. I would make sure Kenzo heard about this assist. I would make him feel good, if nothing else, to know he had support from the rank and file.

"Please let them know it's appreciated. Get me the list, and I will give them all the info about the protection detail. Once it kicks off, which will be soon, it shouldn't last very long. That is our expectation. We're going to rattle the cage."

"Great, remember that old saying. 'Be careful what you wish for. You might just get it'. These perps are dangerous. You guys take care, and Mas, make sure you look after Sophie."

"I hear you, the client first, Sophie second. You got my word on that."

His voice carried a note of concern, and I meant what I said. Click, he was gone. The mood had been broken, and it was back to business. All three of us were somber on the way back to the office.

As we walked, I explained what Big Boots had said about the protection team. Both of them were surprised and pleased at the support that Kenzo was getting. This case was all coming together. We settled back at our respective desks.

Sophie fidgeted around her desk, unlike her. I asked, "Okay, what's up?"

"Something you said when Marie asked if we needed her."

"What specifically?"

"I had been training but probably hadn't enough for this job."

"True. This one is different from McGarrigan's place. They were professionals. These perps are motivated by religious fervor, not professional, making them dangerously unpredictable. I am more concerned with this one."

"Now you are worrying me, Mas."

"If I didn't think you could handle it, I wouldn't have put you in this situation. Make sure you listen to me, okay."

"Mas, in these situations, you are the boss. I know that. However hard it is for me to give up control. I'll be okay, promise." She said it with a wan smile.

"Okay, let's get all the stuff together."

I went to one of our supply cupboards and pulled out all the equipment on my list that we stored here. Body armor for both of us, flashlights, spare batteries for everything that needed them. Our weapons were at home, and we would pick them up with extra magazines and boxes of ammunition when we were ready to move.

As I was checking everything over again and checking it off my list. My phone dinged. Big Boots delivered the list of officers for the day shift. Looking it over, I recognized only a couple of names. However, if Big Boots was happy with them, so was I. An e-mail from Kenzo popped into my inbox as I was about to talk to Sophie. Quickly, I opened it. He had his teams organized and ready to go. All the pieces were now prepared and ready to be put into play.

First, I called all the officers on Big Boot's list and either spoke to them or left messages. Next, I texted Kenzo and thanked him for the support. Done. Then called Colleen the journalist, giving her the go-ahead to publish the fictional story of Adrianna leaving San Francisco and her reasons for doing so, making sure her relationship with Ruth was clear. That should bait the trap.

Everything was go, and we would move into Adrianna's apartment today. The story would hit tomorrow, and we had to be established in the apartment. The perps would put the apartment under surveillance, and Kenzo's team would do counter-surveillance. A surge of adrenaline ran through me. It was time for the end game.

Packing all our equipment into the SUV, Sophie and I went home to get the rest of the necessary items. We made short work of picking up the items and packing our change of clothes. We would stop on the way over to pick up food for the duration. Frozen meals and snacks, we wanted to be as invisible as possible to the outside world. There would only be food delivery when Adrianna was home.

Adrianna had given Sophie a spare key when they had met earlier, so that was an easy one and a remote for the garage. Marie met us at our home. She would drive us over and return the SUV to its usual spot. No one would know there was anyone other than Adrianna in the apartment.

The drive over was slow and tedious. Sophie had brought the cameras with us. She hadn't had time to get over and install them, with the plan in the execution phase. I texted the two officers who would have the first shift guarding Adrianna tomorrow with quick affirmative responses.

I used the remote to open the garage as Marie approached the address. Marie drove directly into the garage, and I quickly closed the door behind us. Thankfully, Adrianna didn't own a vehicle. No one to see us enter and no nosey neighbors to wonder what was happening. Then she helped Sophie and I unload and take our stuff into the apartment's second bedroom.

Marie asked, "Do you guys need anything else?"

"I don't think so." Replied Sophie, I nodded in agreement.

"If you think of anything, I'm on it, whatever the time, right."

I said, "We get it, now go. We'll be fine."

We did a group hug, and breaking away, she left us. Sophie took the cameras and agreed with all my suggestions for location and position except one, and she was right. The camera installation took two hours. Sophie made sure they were functioning on her laptop.

That done, I loaded our weapons with hollow point

ammunition. The spare magazines always had hollow points in them. If we could take these perps alive, fine, but keeping Adrianna alive was our prime concern. The perps, dead or alive, would be done, the case would be closed, Kenzo would be a hero and out of the shit.

The blinds were drawn and the apartment was gloomy in the half-light. Nothing we could do about that, so we rested on the bed until Adrianna came home. We dozed. The night was going to be our time to be awake and ready. Sophie heard Adrianna coming in the front door before I did. We made ourselves known even though she expected us to be here. It was still an invasion. We chatted for a while, and I suggested she go out but stay local. She asked why.

"Adrianna, tonight is your last night of freedom. When the story hits tomorrow, you will be in danger until the people responsible for all this carnage are stopped."

She looked down and said, "I hadn't thought of that. I will be my own prisoner."

Sophie said, "We are here, and sure, it will be over soon."

Adrianna smiled, saying, "One way or another, right?

She turned and went into her bedroom, closing the door behind her. We could hear her sobs through the door. Making ourselves busy with nothing, I started dinner with a large frozen lasagna, which should keep us going for a few days. Adrianna could order food in, etc.

When she came out, she looked better and more relaxed.

I asked, "You okay?"

She replied, "Better, now it's hit home. This is real."

Sophie asked, "Any regrets about your decision to be the target?"

"Nope, none, I still miss Ruth, it's just scary."

"If you weren't scared, I would be very worried," I said. Continuing with, "Now comes the boring part."

Adrianna said, "The waiting." It was a statement, not a question.

Sophie and I said together, "Yes."

That caused Adrianna to giggle and say, "You two are a cute couple. How did you meet and get involved in the PI business? You are so different from each other?"

That was a segway I could get behind. Telling our story would take her mind off what was inevitably coming. We all pottered about getting the table laid and glasses for wine. For Sophie and me, it was our last night for alcohol until this was over.

Adrianna made a large salad, and I checked the lasagna, and it was almost ready. As we worked, Sophie and I regaled Adrianna with our story. We did not sugarcoat anything. We did play down the kink aspect of our relationship. She didn't need those details.

Dinner was over, and Adrianna and I cleared up while Sophie monitored the cameras. A double check on the functionality in the darkness. She said they were okay. The front door light was on a motion sensor, and the ambient light from all the nearby buildings gave enough light for the cameras, especially in the front.

We were all tired, and stress played a big part in that feeling, particularly for Adrianna. We all said good night. Sophie and I checked all the doors and went to bed. Sleep did not come quickly to me. I was running every scenario I could think of. I had the feeling that we had missed something. I couldn't put my finger on it, and no use pushing. That would delay it. Tomorrow was another day, and I would figure it out.

Chapter Twenty-Five

The alarm went off, Sophie reacted immediately, and I came around more slowly. It was early, and there were sounds from the kitchen. Adrianna was an early riser.

Bleary-eyed, I entered the kitchen, asking, "How come you are up so early?"

"Busy day, and the least I could do is make you breakfast. Coffee in the pot."

"Now we're talking. Thank you."

Thankfully, she had good coffee, and it was welcome. I took a mug into the bedroom for Sophie.

She kissed me in appreciation and asked, "Why so early?"

"Adrianna has a busy day and is making us breakfast."

"Nice, anything from anyone?"

"Gimme a break. I brought you coffee, which I thought was the most important thing!"

"Good point. Now please go check your incoming for anything." She said it goodheartedly.

"Yes, Ma'am," I responded with a smile.

Oso confirmed that he was on his way and would be arriving on schedule. The first day-shift officer confirmed he would be waiting at Adrianna's office. He would stay until after lunch and hand over to the afternoon officer, who would then remain until Oso picked her up to bring her home. The night shift would be Sophie and me inside, and two teams of two from Kenzo's task force. Then, it would repeat until we caught the perps, assuming they took the bait.

Breakfast was excellent and simple—veggie omelets with a side of bacon and toasted sourdough bread with local honey. We were ready for it, and the food disappeared quickly.

Sophie called out, "Adrianna, your chariot is here. You can trust Oso. Mas has known him for years."

"Great, why Oso? That's bear in Spanish."

Sophie laughed, saying, "Wait till you see him."

With that, the doorbell rang, and I opened it. Oso filled the doorway.

"Hola Mas, Miss Sophie."

Adrianna said, "Holy shit, he's huge." Sophie and I laughed, and I formally introduced Oso to Adrianna.

Oso kinda blushed and said, "You be safe wid me, Miss."

"Sorry Oso, I wasn't expecting someone so…big. We Hispanics aren't known for size. Pleased to meet you."

"Likewise. Miss, we better get going. I got yo number, and I'll be waitin for you to bring you home. If somethin olds me up, I'll call, and don't come out unless you sees me, I'll escort you to the car. Okay?"

"Yes, got it. Thank you for doing this."

"Tink nothing of it, Mas and me goes way back. He's good people." As an afterthought, he added, "So's Miss Sophie."

Adrianna picked up her bags, and as they left, Oso gave me the morning paper. We observed Oso scanning the street for anything suspicious. Adrianna got in the back of the car, Oso got behind the wheel and moved smoothly into the early morning traffic.

The apartment became silent, an oppressive silence. We looked at each other. Sophie shrugged and sat at the kitchen table, no doubt accessing her monster computer remotely. I opened my laptop and looked for any updates. There was nothing new from anyone.

The paper Oso had left caught my attention. I wanted to see and read Colleen's story. Colleen had neatly tied her article to the ongoing saga of the gruesome murders in the park. The police thought the LGBTQ community was the target of the killings. She brought in Adrianna's name in connection to the LGBTQ community and a couple of the victims. Noting that Adrianna would be leaving the city very soon, saying she felt unsafe. Cleverly, Colleen had included several other people who felt the same regarding their safety. Nicely done. She delivered all the information we needed to be exposed without being overt or obvious.

Now the waiting game, Sophie had more than enough to keep her busy. Me, not so much. I would be getting reports from the watching officers periodically, morning, noon, and night, with a lot of time in between. The waiting was the worst aspect of any plan.

An e-mail from Kenzo. He had managed to get a judge to sign off on a search warrant for the college vans. He was holding the warrant, hoping the perps took the bait and tried to go after Adrianna. Then he would have cause to really rip their lives apart. Everything we were doing was high risk. We knew it, and we accepted it.

Hours passed slowly and boringly. I napped for a

couple of hours, preparing for the night, although I didn't expect any action against Adrianna the first night. Tomorrow would be the earliest they could mount any action if they saw Colleen's article today. I agreed with the profiling done by the PD and FBI that the perps would be following the media coverage and would see the article either in hard copy or in the media somewhere. Night two was probably out as well. The perps would have to find Adrianna's address, which is not a stretch for these guys, then surveillance and plan their attack. Night three and onward would bring the most danger.

Sophie and I had discussed the perps, trying to figure out how many perps there were—landing on two primaries with the possibility of a third. Our thoughts went to the father, Weymouth Whitney, the son Luther Whitney as the primaries, and Weymouth's subjugated wife as the third person.

All in the family, no outsiders, tight, all with motive and means. We felt that all three would be involved in the action against Adrianna. The men would snatch Adrianna, and Weymouth's wife doing the driving. She was a competent driver in her actions after doing the body dump in the park.

As expected, Adrianna made it home without incident. The evening was quiet, and all the officers reported in with nothing untoward to report, the quiet before the storm. Adrianna crashed early, and so did Sophie. I was left alone with my thoughts in the glow of the night lights.

Sophie relieved me at one a.m. I lay on the bed fully clothed and my weapon ready on the bedside table.

****

My head and mouth felt like cotton wool when I woke to dishes clattering. Coffee. I needed Coffee. Sitting up, I noticed a mug of coffee next to my weapon. How I loved Sophie. Drinking as I entered the kitchen, I was welcomed with.

"Morning, sleepy head," Sophie said, and Adrianna just smiled and kept working the pans on the stove.

Oso showed up on the dot. Adrianna disappeared with him. Officers reported in. Same as the day before, nothing and more nothing. Sophie crashed, and I woke her in the afternoon. The day dragged on.

Eventually, Adrianna came home from work, escorted to the door by Oso. Kenzo's counter-surveillance team reported nothing suspicious going on with the perps. That, to me, was suspicious, but I could do nothing about it. The officers on duty at the apartment reported nothing suspicious. Sophie took the early shift and me the late one. I couldn't second guess myself. Night three would be the real test.

****

Breakfast was the same routine, except I was the one who took Sophie the wake-up coffee, for which I received a thank-you kiss. The day was same as the day before—nada, zilch, nothing. The time was beginning to wear on me, same with Sophie. We were wound and ready to act if and when needed. This night was the one I expected something to happen, wanting it to, although that would mean an attack on Adrianna.

Hour by hour, the day dragged by. Adrianna arrived home at the same time she had the previous two days. There was nothing from Kenzo on the suspected perps. Weymouth kept the same schedule. Home, college, home. Luther had the same routine. Home, college, home, then bible class at the church where he preached, back home. Mary, Weymouth's wife, home, store, home. That was it, nothing else, no visitors, not even a delivery.

Kenzo's team stationed at the apartment had nothing suspicious to report. This was starting to bother me. They had to have done some surveillance on Adrianna to make a snatch plan. They were too clever to wing a kidnapping. We were missing something that niggle at the back of my mind hadn't revealed itself, but it wouldn't go away.

"Sophie, something is bothering me. The perps have done nothing out of routine. Why? They have to research to plan a snatch and have always done so meticulously. Even out of their comfort zone and the short timeline, they need information to plan. These perps, doing God's work, don't want to be caught."

"I see your point, but we can do nothing except be prepared. Which we are. They have to come to us. That gives us the advantage. We know they will come. Just a matter of when."

"Tonight, would realistically be the first time they could try anything. The first night was the day they found out about Adrianna leaving, and the second night would have been planning and research. They don't know when Adrianna is leaving town. They can't leave it too long, or they could miss their chance at getting her."

"Agreed about tonight. Maybe they are working out each family member's part in the snatch and how to implement their plan."

"Fuck! Sophie, you are a genius."

She looked at me like I had two heads and said, "Thanks, I think, what is it?"

"Family. You said family, and we haven't considered two other family members. Luther's wife is in the family and probably subjugated to Luther, like her mother-in-law to Weymouth. Where is the sister? All we know about her is she's not at her home. We may have more people involved in this than we anticipated. I gotta call Kenzo."

"I think we both need to do the night shift together, taking turns to monitor the cameras while the other naps out here."

"Good idea," I said as I dialed Kenzo.

"Mas, what's going on?"

"Can you put an urgent trace on Sarah, Luther's wife, and Martha Whitney? I think the family that prays together kills together. I was figuring on two, maybe three perps, favoring three. Now, it could be as many as five."

"Shit, Mas, are you sure. This idea is way off the reservation. None of the profiles have considered this. I've never heard of a family of serial killers."

"Manson family."

"Oh, come on, Mas, they weren't a family."

"They acted as one and believed they were family. With this family, it's some crazy perverted Christian mythology."

"Okay, I will run all the checks I can. There won't be much I can do until tomorrow. I will ask the locals to check on Martha and find out where she is. Stay safe, Mas."

"Working on that one." He hung up, and I told Sophie, "We put on the body armor tonight. I don't like these possible developments. Three perps is one thing. Five is very different."

We kept all this from Adrianna, who again went to bed early. No sense worrying her unnecessarily. As soon as she was in her bedroom, Sophie and I put on the body armor and set up for the night. Two hours on, two off, repeat. It was draining, in other words, the mental aspect of not knowing if anything was going to happen, then the physical, which had a different effect on us.

Nothing, on edge, nothing. Efficiently, we switched off every two hours without incident all night.

Chapter Twenty-Six

The dawn crept through a crack in the blinds and announced a new day, and we welcomed it. We started breakfast, well coffee and then food. Adrianna was surprised that we were both up. We brushed it off as no big deal. Breakfast was done and cleared up. A day we would use to catch up on sleep and prepare for another night of little or no sleep.

Oso picked up his charge and was gone. Reports came in with nothing to report from any sector, our private officers, or Kenzo's teams on outside duty. My epiphany of last night worried me. I hoped Kenzo and his task force would come up with something we could hang our hat on.

Praemonitus praemunitus, the only Latin I knew, *forewarned is forearmed*. We now expected five assailants, not three, a big difference, and we would prepare for that event, but it would be more on Kenzo and his teams to back us up and seal the apartment to make sure no one escaped. I would discuss that issue with him after I had more time to think it through. Sleep was the priority for both of us, and we took it.

****

I had put my phone on silent; I woke up to several missed calls and texts. I scanned them to prioritize the order in which I would answer. Kenzo had left texts and voice mails, and he was first.

There is nothing about Sarah or Martha. Sarah was clean, nothing on her, no records of any sort, and was now under surveillance. Martha was the same, except no one the local PD contacted knew where she was. She hadn't been seen in her local haunts, which meant libraries, churches, and church functions. In fact, no one was sure when they had last seen her.

I would put money on her being in San Francisco, which was the missing piece in the family puzzle. What I couldn't get my head around was the probability the whole family was involved in a revenge murder spree. Ruth's death, due to religious bigotry and her family stalking her, pushed her to suicide—so much for love thy neighbor and forgiveness.

Kenzo answered on the first ring. He agreed to double up the teams for the coming night. The surveillance and counter-surveillance teams had yet to come up with anything. There were no positive sightings of the sister Martha. The only photograph Kenzo had been able to obtain was years old. She could have changed her appearance and probably had.

Marie had called us regarding office 'stuff.' Just an excuse to make sure we were okay. We called her back together on speaker. Took care of the office 'stuff'. That was a good break away from the case.

All the officer reports were nothing to report. Only the lunchtime officer had anything close to suspicious. Another woman from Adrianna's office had her bag snatched as she left the main entrance. The officer was not distracted by the event. He kept focus on Adrianna, and there was nothing to report.

If anything, I was more convinced we were right, and tonight would be another test of our endurance.

Unless something unforeseen occurred, and it always seemed 'something' did occur. We covered all the bases as best we could. Kenzo's additional teams would be on station at nine p.m. He could not get them there earlier, but that had to be okay, because we couldn't do anything about it. We didn't expect an attempt on Adrianna until the early a.m., which made tactical sense.

Adrianna arrived home on schedule with Oso escorting her to the door and waiting until she was safely inside.

She seemed more relaxed than in previous days. She dropped her bag and purse on the dining room table and said, "Oso is a sweetheart. I can see why he likes you. He told me some of his story. He didn't want to. I bugged him, and it made the ride go quicker."

"He's a good man. Good as his word."

"He has a lot of time for you, Mas; he told me how you helped him. What he told me makes me feel more comfortable with you guys."

"Well, I hope we can live up to the hype," I said it with a laugh I didn't feel.

"I'm going to get changed and order takeout. Do you and Sophie want anything?"

We chorused we were fine, still working through the frozen delights we had brought with us. While Adrianna was changing, Sophie and I put on our body armor and covered them with sweatshirts. There was no sense in waiting. We always had our weapons with us when Adrianna was in the apartment. Sophie pulled a couple of frozen entrees out of the freezer and cranked up the oven. At the same time, I monitored the cameras. All was quiet.

The fog was starting to roll in. It would be one of those damp in-your-bones nights. We weren't planning on going anywhere.

Adrianna placed her order and said, "It's going to be thirty to forty-five minutes minimum for delivery."

Sophie asked, "Who did you order from?"

"A local Indian restaurant. Why? Did you change your mind about ordering?"

"No, I want to check the delivery before I open the door. Did you order through a service or directly with the restaurant?"

"Directly, they have their own delivery guys."

I asked, "Do you know all their delivery people?"

Adrianna started to look concerned, saying, "It's just takeout, and I don't know if I have seen all the guys they use. It's been someone different each time I have ordered."

I continued, "Always a guy?"

"Yes-no, once it was a girl, all the other times a guy, and I don't order that often."

Sophie said, "That's fine. We are making sure we cover all the bases."

"I know, being escorted and guarded constantly is a weird feeling."

"With any luck, it will all be over real soon," I said.

Adrianna picked up the remote and put the TV on. Sophie took over monitoring the cameras as I checked on dinner. I poured Adrianna a glass of wine and water for Sophie and me. The timing worked out. Her delivery would be here when our dinner was ready, and we were ready for food.

Sophie called out, "Mas, here quick."

Catching the urgency in her voice, I asked, "What is it?"

"Nothing, a white minivan pulled into the drive. It reversed out and went in the other direction."

"False alarm," I said. "Better to question, and it be nothing than the alternative."

The evening turned to night. Eerily dark with the drifting fog, churning thinner to thicker, making watching the cameras more difficult. The passing car lights were acid yellow and hazy. The fog made it difficult even to see the vehicles. Being inside and warm, a cocoon against the night.

We were sure the fog would delay Adrianna's dinner, and ours was almost ready. Adrianna said for us to go ahead and eat. We dished ours onto plates and sat at the dining room table, keeping one eye on the cameras as we ate. We were about halfway through when Sophie noticed a shadow approaching the front of the apartment. They were carrying something, dinner?

The doorbell rang, and as it did, I heard a noise at the back door.

Sophie called out, "Don't open the door." It was too late. She opened the door, and it burst wide open. Adrianna flew backwards. Sophie was on her feet, moving toward the door and going for her weapon. She was hit from the side. Two voices shouting.

All this happened in an instant. I was drawing my weapon when I felt something tag my back. Turning, I saw a woman pointing what looked like a gun at me. She had a surprised look on her face and pulled the trigger again. My leg exploded in pain, and I stumbled and put my hands out to break my fall, losing my weapon in the process. The pain stopped as suddenly as it had started.

My mind was still functioning. The tag on my back was the first shot with a Taser, and the prongs hadn't penetrated the body armor. The second shot hit my leg, causing me to fall. One of the prongs must have fallen out. A Taser only works when both prongs are in contact with the body. The woman was on me and picked up my weapon.

Sophie had reacted to the person who blindsided her and was fighting tooth and nail. She hadn't managed to draw her weapon and was using all she had been taught in self-defense class, but she couldn't handle two people.

As I started to get up, we heard a scream. It had to be Adrianna. Everything froze for a second. Another person entered the apartment and went directly after Adrianna. Sophie had forced one of the attackers back away from her. The other still had one hand on her. Looking back at the woman who had tased me, she was pointing my gun at Sophie. I yelled to Sophie and jumped in front of the woman as she pulled the trigger. My chest felt like I had been hit with a sledgehammer, and I went down. My head buzzed, and my breathing hurt. I heard more shots and a scream, followed by more shouting.

Getting up, I was hit, more like shoved, losing my balance. I went back down. When I stood up, I saw the woman who had aimed at Sophie on her back. She'd been hit twice. Once in the chest and once in the abdomen. Glazed eyes? I knew she was gone. Where was Sophie? I called out, but there was no answer—the room stank of cordite. Going toward the front door, I saw Sophie slowly getting up off the floor.

"Are you okay?"

"Yes, I'm alright, we just got fucked. They got Adrianna and rushed her down to the garage."

"Yes, we did, but we are not done yet. The PD officers must have stopped them. Where the hell are they?"

Sophie leaned back against the wall and started to sob. Tears welled up and started to roll down her cheeks. Quietly, she asked, "Is she dead?"

"Yes."

"You saved me, Mas. She pointed the gun right at me. I don't even remember drawing my weapon or firing. If you hadn't got in the way, my god, Mas, are you alright? She shot you."

She flung herself at me and hugged me. That hurt, and I didn't care. She was sobbing on my shoulder. I saw red and blue lights approaching through the open front door. Breaking apart, Sophie slumped back against the wall. I left my weapon on the floor near the body, who I assumed was Ruth's sister, Martha. The open back door slammed against the wall, and the two officers stationed in the back alley entered with weapons drawn.

The entire event was over in seconds, from door opening to gone. Where the fuck were the officers watching the front. The two officers who had come in the back door took over. One went out front to direct the incoming PD, and the other called dispatch for the ME's wagon and to notify Kenzo of the situation.

I had to think, and fast. How had they done this so quickly and efficiently. I had to slow my thoughts down. One approached the front door; another came through the garage. Why hadn't we heard or seen that?

Distracted by the TV, the soundproof door to the garage, and the events happening at the front door. The back door had been locked, and I'd checked that. Picked? We hadn't seen anyone approach, concentrating on the front. Shit, some hotshot PI's we were, and Adrianna was paying for it.

The arriving police officers cordoned off the area. Waiting for the Inspectors to arrive. Kenzo and the rest of the team were on the way. The officers knew who we were and gave us some latitude. I went down to the garage. The door was still open, and tire marks were on the floor, wide like a minivan. The minivan that pulled in earlier must have dropped one of the team close by. They opened the garage when instructed, and the minivan pulled straight in. We hadn't heard it open due to the fire door and the sound of the TV. These perps were good. They had planned quickly and well, and we had the element of surprise. Numbers count.

The forensics team arrived and started processing the scene. They scraped Sophie's nails for DNA samples and tested her for GSR, which was positive. They took her weapon. The EMTs looked Sophie over, and there were scratches and contusions, but nothing serious. The first inspector took her statement, and the second inspector took mine.

Kenzo arrived in minutes, anger and frustration written all over his face before we could say anything.

He said, "I'll fucking kill him. Son of a bitch disregarded my instructions and pulled the car out front off station, 'to go get something to eat he said.' He wasn't even on the roster. He pulled rank and told the junior officer he would take his shift."

"Fuck, which explains why they had a clean

getaway."

Kenzo added, "We just killed Adrianna. Someone is going to pay for this, and it ain't going to be me.

Quietly, Sophie said, "We are good if we can get out of here and bring your team with us."

Blankly, he looked at us, "What do you mean, she's gone."

Smiling, Sophie said, "We had a GPS tracker implanted in her. We have them in us, just in case. It's how Mas found Tara and me when we were taken."

That seemed to jolt him into action, "Great, do your thing. Can you do it from here?"

"Already done, I pulled it up while we waited for you. We don't trust anyone but you."

As she finished speaking, two officers walked in. One looked very uncomfortable, the other feigning concern. He was the one responsible for pulling the front protection team. Kenzo asked the younger officer who gave the order to leave their station. He said the senior officer.

Kenzo turned to him and asked, "Why were you on this detail? You were not assigned."

He gave some lame excuse about offering the officer he replaced time with his family. Bullshit, he was watching Kenzo's team, and that was the only reason he switched. Before anyone saw me move, I cold clocked the bastard. He went down and hit the floor out cold. The other officers in the room just stood and waited to see what Kenzo would do as the on-site senior officer.

"Oh dear, he seems to have tripped over his own lies. Get this piece of shit out of here and to an EMT."

All the officers on Kenzo's team laughed, and the

young officer who had been teamed with him volunteered to take the garbage out. That brought more laughter. That inspector would have a hard time explaining his actions when the inquiry got to him.

Kenzo organized the officers into those staying and those accompanying us to follow the GPS tracker. I got my backup weapon from my bag in the bedroom and was ready to go. Sophie had been tracking the signal to keep her mind off the night's events and secure Adrianna. Kenzo barked orders, and we left Sophie and me in Kenzo's car, four officers following in two PD SUVs.

Kenzo asked, "Where to Sophie?"

"They are heading south toward the peninsula. We can make up time on them if you use your lights."

The blue and reds went on, and the car picked up speed. An idea hit me. They couldn't be that crazy, could they? Whatever plan the perps had, we had messed with it and taken one of them out. Fall back to what you knew and knew worked.

Asking, "Sophie, are they heading toward torture property?"

"Mas, you are brilliant. Yes, it's the right direction. We can't intercept or catch them."

I said, "Kenzo, lights and sirens, hoof it, and screw the fog."

"Got it. Hold on, this is going to be a bumpy ride."

He wasn't kidding. I had good nerves for fast driving, but being the passenger was a whole different experience. As we approached every intersection, Kenzo had the front and left side. I had front and right side. I watched and called clear at every intersection, my side, at least as much as I could see. Traffic regulations didn't apply right now.

Thankfully, the idiot drivers were not out. We made good time, with Kenzo only making one hard swerve. Approaching the industrial area, the lights and sirens stopped. There was no point in advertising our arrival.

Engine cut and coasting the last hundred yards toward the building holding Adrianna. Only minutes behind them, they had driven carefully, especially in the fog. It's not a good idea to be stopped by the PD with a kidnap victim. The other PD SUVs drifted in behind Kenzo. Immediately emptied, they all had body armor on as standard. Two had shotguns, the other two pistols.

I asked Sophie, "Are you good to go? You can stay here if you want."

Sophie's pale, grave face looked at me before responding, "I'm good, Mas, promise."

I reminded her, "Stay behind me. Got it?"

"Got it."

Kenzo gave Sophie a thumbs-up and a smile.

We huddled Kenzo, and one of the other officers had been inside when the torture chamber had been searched. Kenzo directed the officers, and he instructed all of us on the building layout. One officer took charge of the other three, moving around to the rear of the building and leaving two at the side entrance. Staying in contact with wireless comms, we would be with Kenzo. We didn't have the comms and would rely on Kenzo for information and instructions.

I checked the van hood…warm, and I nodded to Kenzo, who motioned us forward. Would they have locked the front entrance behind them? I doubted it. But we carefully checked it…no resistance. Quietly, we opened the door and heard raised voices but not what was said. Stealthily moving into the reception area, we followed the sounds of the voices.

First, Kenzo and me, weapons drawn, and lastly, Sophie. The building opened up into a large open space. We scanned the area. Adrianna was seated in the center, bound to a chair, her head dropped to her chest, unconscious or drugged. A steel trolly was next to her, with what looked like tools laid out.

We could see the side door across the open space. We couldn't tell if it was locked but assumed it was. Other parts of the building obscured the back door.

All four people whose voices we heard knelt in a circle, holding hands, heads back, praying for the strength to do god's work. The bile started to rise in my throat. We had to end this now. I gently tapped Kenzo's shoulder and drew a finger across my throat. He nodded and spoke quietly into his comms, telling the others to breach on the first sound of his voice. He heard the affirmative from both pairs.

He held up his left hand, thumb, and two fingers and counted down. One, two, three.

Kenzo yelled, "Police, stay where you are. Stay on your knees."

A boom went off, the side door opened, and the two officers entered, covering that side of the room. There was another boom from the back of the building, and the two officers entered the room from another door.

The people kneeling had heads on swivels. The sounds from different directions kept them turning, taken completely by surprise and off balance. On their knees, they were at a disadvantage. The shock was replaced by anger. We had closed in on the group, surrounding them. Luther jumped up and charged at the officers who entered via the side door. He didn't have a weapon, and one officer tased him, and the other cuffed him. As they got him to his feet, his wife Sarah got up and moved toward her husband.

"Stop," Kenzo shouted.

She stopped. I guess used to obeying a male voice. She was cuffed without resistance. Weymouth and Martha had not moved. They had both started to pray again. Even when handcuffed and pulled to their feet, they seemed oblivious to what was occurring around them. I began to doubt they would stand trial. Being mentally incompetent to stand trial would be my guess.

Sophie had gone to Adrianna and cut her bonds with one of the tools on the trolley. She had been drugged and was semi-conscious. Sophie comforted her by telling her the medics were on their way, wrapping a blanket she found around her shoulders and asking her what she remembered, who she was, and so on, trying to get her mind working. I looked around and found a small bag with syringes and a bottle of clear liquid with a label I didn't recognize.

Kenzo said, "It's an animal tranquilizer, newer on the street, seeing more of it. How's Adrianna?"

Sophie said, "She's still pretty much out of it. She doesn't seem to have been injured, except for some scrapes and bruises. They didn't have time to start their torture routine. Thank God for prayer."

We all looked at her and started to laugh—a needed release of tension. We had the perps of six horrific murders and the kidnapping of Adrianna. They were done, and they would never hurt anyone again.

The medics arrived along with the rest of Kenzo's team and forensics, who shooed everyone away so they could get to work. Kenzo's Captain arrived, and soon after, the Police Chief. Good news travels fast. I called Colleen to make sure she was ahead of the media frenzy.

The capture of the perps with a victim in hand, along with the information from Kenzo's *'confidential informant'* regarding the college vans and the forensics that would be collected from the college vans, previously from the torture site, and tonight. It was now open season on the professor and his family. Kenzo's part would continue until he tied up all the loose ends and a slam dunk case for the District Attorney.

Kenzo was a hero, and the police chief told the reporters who had found the scene that he had always had complete confidence in Lt. Otake's ability to solve the case and apprehend the perpetrators of these horrific crimes. Bullshit, he was just as ready to throw Kenzo under the bus if this had all gone sideways, and it could have, even with Sophie and I doing our part. We didn't want recognition. That was for Kenzo. He deserved it, and we owed him.

All I wanted to do now was go home, drink too much, and sleep next to the woman I loved. I called Marie and asked her to pick us up on the corner of a street a couple of blocks away. We slipped away, waving at Kenzo and holding my hand to my head like a phone. He nodded and went back to conversing with his team.

The fog was thinner on this side of San Francisco, but the air was still cold. We shivered as we walked the two blocks up and two blocks over. Marie must have driven like a bat out of hell to get there as we reached the corner. She parked in the middle of the road, jumped out, and ran to us, arms open.

"Thank God, you guys are alright, you are alright, yes?"

I answered, "Yes, we are alright, and Sophie saved my life tonight."

Marie screeched, "What?"

Sophie said, "It's more like he saved mine. We'll tell you about it later."

"Not a chance. I need to know my partners are okay. What happened."

I started, "Take us home, and we'll tell you on the way."

"Get in, get in." Marie hurried us into her car and took off.

We told her the story from start to finish. She said nothing while we took turns telling our parts. I could see her grip the steering wheel tighter at some points. We completed the story with our call to her. We stopped talking, a dead silence in the car.

Marie said, "I should have insisted on coming with you. An extra person could have changed everything. I'm sorry."

Sophie called Marie out on that comment, "No, it wouldn't have made any difference, and it would have put you in jeopardy. We all have to stick to what we do well, and you organize and support and do a lot of things Mas sucks at, and I'm not good at."

I joined in, "Marie, you are the partner we need. We made you a partner for a reason. Like picking us up in the fog, no questions asked, at least not until you got us."

That comment broke the tension, and we all laughed. I was going to talk to Sophie tomorrow about the shooting and insist she get counseling. She would need it. In the PD, it was compulsory after any officer-involved shooting, and it was valuable. I figured she would fight it, I would insist, Big Boots would back me up, Kenzo as well.

Marie dropped us off at home and promised breakfast in the office whenever we showed up, threatening us not to be early. Sophie stripped off as soon as she was in the door and went into the shower. I Picked up after her and took my backup weapon, cleaning it thoroughly and securely storing it. She was already in bed when I finished with the weapon. I took a quick shower and quietly joined her, thinking she was asleep. She wasn't, she backed into me, and we spooned.

All she said was, "I love you, Mas."

Chapter Twenty-Seven

Where was she? I was awake in an instant. Her side of the bed was empty and cold. I jumped out of bed, grabbed a robe, and called out, but there was no answer. Shit, where was she? Coffee had been made and hot. She was on the deck, curled up in her robe on the two-seater, looking out over our city. She didn't hear me open the slider.

I asked, "You okay?"

She jumped at my voice, "Sorry, I was miles away. Not really. I can't get the image of that woman dropping. I killed her, Mas."

She started to sob, her reaction to the reality of taking a life. If you are a normal person, there will be a reaction. I sat down beside her and put my arm around her.

She dropped her head on my shoulder, asking, "Will I ever be okay with this?"

"That's why you will be getting counseling, no arguments. Big Boots and Kenzo will agree with me. If you want, I will go with you."

"How did you cope with your first time?"

"Hard. It was a clean shoot. It was him or me. Counselling was-is compulsory, and it helped. Each time is different, and thankfully, I haven't had too many."

"I'll go. Do you know anyone?"

"Yes, and she's good. I'll call today. We will have to make full statements to Kenzo's team, and they have to be one hundred percent accurate. We have to make Kenzo's job as easy as possible, so the DA has the best case going into court."

"Okay. Thank you, Mas. You saved my life last night. I can't thank you enough or enough times."

Quietly, I said, "It's what we do for those we love."

"Does your chest hurt?"

"Just sore with a nasty bruise. Had worse. Let's get dressed and get to the office before Marie sends out a search team."

She smiled. I knew she would be alright, given time. We took our time getting dressed. I, of course, took my time looking at her as she dressed, Sophie oblivious to my observing her. We walked holding hands, each lost in our thoughts. I could guess what Sophie was thinking.

I was going over everything that had happened and how to make my statement to the Inspectors in clear, unambiguous words. I knew it would be weeks, if not months, before everything was sorted, and the trial, if there was one, could be a year or more out. My priority was Sophie.

Marie, as promised, had coffee waiting for us, and breakfast on its way. We sat and talked about nothing in particular and how the process of Marie buying my deceased partner's house was proceeding smoothly and would close in a couple of weeks.

Halfway through breakfast, Kenzo arrived. He looked like shit. Still in the same clothes as last night, not even been home to change. Marie got him a mug of coffee and a plate. We all shared our breakfasts with him. He hadn't said a word so far. He just looked exhausted.

Finally, he looked at us and said, "Thank you, all of you. I think without your help, I would be out of a career, and worse, killers would still be out there."

Sophie said, "We owed you, and we always pay our debts. Besides, like Mas says, we like you."

I said, "You would have solved it sooner or later; you're too good to fail on a case like this."

Kenzo shrugged his shoulder, saying, "Thanks for the vote of confidence; I'm not so sure. The PD focused on the gay-sex-kink aspect of the crimes. Mas, you got it right early with the religious part."

I said, "We had a different perspective, and profiling is not an exact science."

"True. At first, I thought you were in denial about the kink aspect, being in the community. You are too good an investigator to be blinded like that, and that also applies to Sophie. Anyway, I wanted to drop by to say thank you. You can take your time coming in to make official statements. It's back to just my team; all the others are back with their units, except Ryan." We looked blank. "Right, the officer who tripped and broke his jaw. If he's lucky, he will be doing traffic stops for the rest of his career."

We laughed at that. Kenzo got up to leave, thanking us for sharing our breakfast, his last words.

"Sophie, get some counseling. It helps. See ya."

Sophie's face went blank as she said, "I promised Mas I would, thank you."

He was gone, and we went back to sitting around. Before long, the phone started ringing off the hook. Marie fielded the calls, and we only took the ones we wanted. One of them was Big Boots. No, he didn't want me, just Sophie. I don't know what he said, but she smiled and looked at me.

Sophie said, "Mas said you would say that, and I promised him and Kenzo. You taught me well, BB, really well."

I could see tears well up in her eyes. Everything was still fresh, raw. She passed me the phone.

"Hi, BB."

"Well, you kept up your end. Kenzo told me what you did. Thanks, man. I'm just glad you're both okay. I don't have so many real friends that I can lose any."

That came as a surprise. BB was Mr. Congenial, and he knew everybody, and everybody knew him. You get to know who your real friends are over time if you are lucky.

"It's what you do when you love someone. No hesitation, BB. I would do it again in a heartbeat."

"I know, Mas. Look after her, she is going to need you, and I'm here if you need me. Got it?"

"Got it, and thanks."

The days passed, and we made our statements to Kenzo's team of inspectors. They confirmed we were fine, and Sophie was clear in the shooting, a case of self-defense and protecting the client. Everything we had done was legal. Our weapons were returned to us.

Our friends and I would take care of Sophie.

Colleen was one call I did take, and we chatted for some time, making an appointment for a thorough sit down and going over everything we could without jeopardizing the DA's case.

Friends caught up with us, Fiend sent a bottle of champagne and an e-mail to thank me for keeping

Sophie safe. I'd never given him anything personal; I was pretty sure Sophie hadn't either, yet here he was, sending me a private e-mail, sneaky bastard. Father Benny called and congratulated us on stopping the violence. He closed the conversation by saying he would be praying for all those involved, which I took to mean the perps as well. Way to go, Father Benny. At least he was consistent with his faith.

Days turned into weeks. Life returned to kinda normal. Sophie went to counselling sessions. They seemed to help in resolving her actions that night. The first time she returned to the self-defense class, everyone applauded her as she entered. Which embarrassed her, and that was a first for "Miss I'm in control." She didn't tell me about that. Kenzo did via the instructor, who was *proud as hell of her.*

With Marie's help, we compiled everything we had done in detail and handed it off to Kenzo. It was a big file. He said it made for interesting reading, especially when the investigations took different avenues regarding the sex vs. religion threads.

We didn't care who was right as long as the four remaining perps went away for life. As I anticipated, Weymouth and his wife Mary, on examination, were found not competent to stand trial and permanently remanded to a secure psychiatric facility. The son Luther and his wife Sarah were found competent and would stand trial. It would be interesting to find out what their defense would be. I would put money on it being religion-based and end up using a temporary insanity plea based on his parents' situation and their influence on him.

Marie and Chung closed on Simon's house. On

closing day, they had a party in the empty house, but only after it had been inspected by a feng shui expert who had given it a clean bill of health, with only a few minor adjustments for when they moved in. He had been plied with gifts to smooth the inspection. I had to laugh at the mixture of traditional and modern attitudes and the cynical Marie going along with it. If it made her happy, go for it.

Sophie and I took a vacation. We drove down the coast, stopping wherever we wanted and staying in small hotels. We enjoyed the peace and the fantastic views of the Pacific Ocean. Turning around before we got to Los Angeles, did I mention I really, really don't like LA. Retracing our steps, we made our way back to San Francisco, which I love, and our home. 'Our home.' That sounded perfect to me.

A word about the author…

Richard Albion lives in Sarasota, Florida, with his wife (who is the pillar that supports him), two grown children out of the nest, and multiple rescued animals making the nest better.

He is a European melting pot, exceptional cook, clothing designer, artist, and writer of erotic thriller fiction. A graduate of both UK and US colleges, he is a retired sales professional now engaged in working on the artistic side of life. He enjoys travel, volunteering, and martial arts. He cannot live too far from the ocean—it's genetic.

Richards's novels are contemporary, Mystery/thrillers, erotic BDSM, and love stories. "Bodies in the Bay" is a mystery/thriller with erotic BDSM overtones. "Bodies on the Bridge" is a continuation of Mas and Sophie's adventures and soon-to-be-published "Bodies in the Park," the latest case for Mas and Sophie.

"Secrets Unveiled" is a mystery/thriller with romance and revenge set in London and Paris.

Also available. The Household series. "Maid to Serve," "Maid for Service," and "Maid in Service" track one man's journey into submission and finding physical and psychological satisfaction, but most of all, love. "The Mistress of O" is a gender flip; O is now male. "Waiting on Siren," one man's journey into submission.

https://albionwriter.wixsite.com/mysite

Thank you for purchasing
this publication of The Wild Rose Press, Inc.

For questions or more information
contact us at
info@thewildrosepress.com.

The Wild Rose Press, Inc.
www.thewildrosepress.com